A Little Piece
of *Me*

A Little Piece of Me

of

Me

Stephen A. Geller

authorHOUSE®

AuthorHouse™
1663 Liberty Drive
Bloomington, IN 47403
www.authorhouse.com
Phone: 1-800-839-8640

Published by AuthorHouse   01/21/2014

ISBN: 978-1-4817-6241-0 (sc)
ISBN: 978-1-4817-6232-8 (hc)
ISBN: 978-1-4817-6231-1 (e)

Library of Congress Control Number: 2013910419

Acknowledgments

To some degree a novel has contributions by everyone the author has ever known and all the writers he or she has ever read. To appropriately thank them all would require a memoir at least as long as this book.

Family encouragement, especially from my wife, Kate, was generous and unstinting. Her comments were especially useful in the early stages of developing the book. Jennifer Geller, our daughter, proved to be one of the most skilled, thoughtful and helpful of those who read this book; her editorial contributions were outstanding. David Geller, our son, provided excellent advice on the cover design. Irving Astrachan, my teacher at New York's Stuyvesant High School almost six decades ago, provided early inspiration for me to write. Latinee Gullattee gave further encouragement when I was a medical student but my pathology career kept me occupied for more than forty years. Pamela Freundl Kirst showed me ways to believe in myself as a writer. Claire Berman was one of the first to read the book and her suggestions were insightful. Others, including Aviva Layton, Nancy Hardin, Pamela Liflander and Erin Clermont provided useful editorial advice. Instructors in novel writing at the UCLA Extension Writers' Program, including Leslie Lehr and Susan Taylor Chehak, and at the University of Iowa Summer Writing Festival, especially John Griesemer, taught many skills which I hope have been faithfully and reliably adopted. The staff at *AuthorHouse* patiently awaited many rewrites. In particular, Richelle Keith and Sidney Cabading helped deliver a product of which I am proud.

My father, Sam Geller, taught me I could do anything if I worked hard enough. Lastly, and certainly not least, my mother, Alice Podberesky Geller, taught me to love reading—the most wondrous and valuable gift I ever received.

Stephen A. Geller

for

Kate, David, Cathia, Lila and Jennifer Lee

CHAPTER ONE

*M*arcia was uncommonly quiet as they drove to the mall. Then she suddenly burst into an almost laugh—a barely audible "ha" and then a snicker—stopping just as abruptly as she had begun. It sounded bitter, at least to Amy who was driving. She turned quickly to look at Marcia. "Something funny? What's up? Tell me." The toddlers, Marcia's Max and Amy's Julia in their car seats, also looked at Marcia, their mouths open, a little drool at the corner of Julia's mouth until Marcia reached back and dabbed at it with a tissue.

They had planned today's outing weeks before when they'd run into each other at Dan Fogel's office. Dan was their children's pediatrician and Marcia and Amy met in his office waiting room more than two and a half years ago at their first post-delivery check-up. Chatting while fussing with their newborns they learned their babies had been delivered within a day of each other, Julia on a Tuesday and Max the day after. It was the first child for each of them and they soon became the best of friends. Marcia once told Amy she was the closest friend she'd had since junior high school and it often seemed as if they had known each other their entire lives. In the months after their first encounter Marcia and Amy each met other women with children born almost the same dates as Max and Julia. They were all originally from different parts of the world— Marcia, from New York and Amy, from Hawaii, the only Americans— and, by the time the children were starting to sit up, they became a cadre of friends, informally calling themselves the "baby ex-pats" group. Over the years the group gathered fairly regularly at one or another of their homes for the children to play with each other and, less frequently, for shopping excursions. There were seven women all together. It was the biggest group of really good friends Marcia had ever had, although she remained closest to Amy and spent the most time with her.

Now, heading for the mall, Julia was chatting away, as usual, trying to get Max to pay attention to the pictures in her coloring book and her Barbie. Max was not as responsive as he generally was to her urgings, probably not so obvious to Amy and Julia but certainly clear to

1

Marcia. She had been a little concerned about him since yesterday, for a few days really, but he didn't have a fever and he was eating as well as usual. He looked up through the sunroof each time a plane started the descent to LAX and once when a helicopter was crossing overhead. Uncharacteristically, his stare would continue for a second or two after there was nothing to be seen, even until there was no longer a sound in the sky. The word that came to Marcia's mind was "sluggish." He wasn't at all cranky, but she was at least a little worried.

She discussed Max with Michael last night as they were turning off the den lights. "Maxie looks fine to me," he said. "Let's go to bed. You worry too much." And then, after checking the front-door lock again, he followed her up the stairs, walking closely behind her. "I have a big day tomorrow, and I was thinking we might get together . . ." He slid his hand between her legs, almost causing her to stumble at the top step. "What do you say?"

"Come on, Marsh. What's up?" Amy said, not giving up, and erasing Marcia's wandering thoughts.

Max looked at his mother to see if she would respond and then turned back to Julia as she offered him Barbie's Ken, dressed in a blue bathing suit.

"No, nothing to tell. Silly stuff. Really nothing," was all Marcia could say, and then they were at the mall looking for a parking space.

When Amy found one she put her hand on the rearview mirror as if to adjust it but mostly to again look over at Marcia, who was still staring ahead, deep in thought. The space between Amy's eyelids was ridged with concern, her brow wrinkled, her eyes half-shut for the moment, not quite sure what she should say. Marcia was Amy's dearest friend and she was positive that Marcia's laugh had not been a happy one. *Another tough morning with Michael?* Amy wondered.

* * *

A delicately pretty woman, with dark hair and even darker, almost impenetrable eyes, Marcia Kleinman was as slender as she had been before her marriage, before Max was born. Her belly was not quite as flat, more noticeable to her than Michael. He loved to put the palm of his hand on her belly and massage that extra little bit of flesh between his fingers, before reaching farther down to twist the slightly stiff pubic hairs, careful not to pull at them. "Pretty" was never quite enough to describe her. Her short dark hair framed a perfectly oval face dominated by full lips. There was a slight slant to her eyes and her upper lids were full without the usual folds—from her mother, Barbara, and Barbara's mother before her—those eyes adding a touch of distinctive and seductive mystery to her beauty. Every now and then someone who saw Amy and Marcia together would ask if they were sisters, although Amy's appearance was unequivocally Asian. Marcia had just a whisper of the Orient despite the fact that no one in the family could be traced any farther east than a *shtetl* fifty kilometers southwest of St. Petersburg. Slimmer than her mother and almost an inch shorter, she was unmistakably Barbara's daughter. The resemblance was even more noticeable when they glared at each other, which happened often.

In addition to her music and to her voracious reading, fiction and non-fiction, Marcia was athletic. She ran the New York City Marathon twice when they lived there "B.M."—before Max—and still jogged almost every day, at least ten miles a week, usually before Michael went to work and on weekends. She adjusted to Los Angeles almost as soon as the airplane's door opened. She loved living in a place where people played golf and tennis virtually every day of the year, even though she never tried golf and had given up tennis. Forbidden by Barbara to play most sports while she was growing up because of what might happen to the muscles of her hands, the flexibility of her fingers, she had learned to play tennis at college but never really enjoyed it with her mother's insistent warnings still inside her head, constantly exhorting her to "guard those precious hands." She earned a place on the junior varsity team but quit after two weeks when she scraped her knuckles on a metal fence while trying to return a low shot deep in the corner. A little betadine and a couple of band-aids took care of the injury but, as soon as she left the dispensary, she knew she would never play tennis again. She couldn't stop thinking about how easily it could have been to break her fingers or even her wrist and, for two days after the scrape, she kept feeling her wrist bones to make sure they were intact. She felt a grudging recognition that one day she might need her hands to be as perfect as possible.

Or maybe it was her mother overpowering her subconscious as it seemed her mother so often did.

When she started running again after Max was born it was no longer for marathon lengths. Running the New York marathon for the first time she was thrilled in the chaos and the vibrancy of the start, as the multitudes swarmed across the Verrazano Bridge, runners so close together they were mostly occupied with not tripping. She was exhilarated when her energy rebounded as she passed groups of cheering friends, particularly at that singular moment when Central Park first came into her view. Despite the excitement she was decidedly deflated when she learned her time didn't put her in the top half of finishers. She never thought of winning, but she hoped—expected even—that she would finish in the top quarter. When she ran the following year her time was a little better but still not good enough to even put her in the top half. By then she was able to laugh, saying, "Well, I'm older now, so this isn't so bad," and shrug it off. She knew then she wasn't going to run another marathon just to be another runner. She would miss the incomparable thrill, the pure rapture, the delirium she felt when crossing the finish line, but there was no hope of her ever winning so she stopped trying.

Music, not sports, ultimately defined her. Michael often told her she played the piano better than anyone he had ever heard. She also heard that from many professional pianists, including her mother. She had what she called her "happy music," which she either played on the piano or listened to on CDs, and her sad music. She only played her sad music when she was alone pondering something or feeling a little down, a little depressed. She always made a point of having her happy music on when Michael came home, usually after nine on weeknights. But lately, if she was upstairs or busy with Max and hadn't taken the time to change the CD, the sad music was on when he walked in. When he asked what she was sad about she would smile and hug him and say she just wished he'd come home earlier so they could spend more time together, always adding that she was happy now that he was home. He would remind her how busy he was and how he needed to work hard if he was going to eventually make partner at the firm. Eventually, he stopped asking about the music when he saw her after a long day and just got himself ready for dinner. She used to set the dining room table for dinner even if just for the two of them, but now they mostly ate in the kitchen and he would turn on CNN or worse, ESPN, and then they wouldn't hear the music at all.

*   *   *

The mall wasn't too crowded and the kids were free to run from store window to store window, laughing and cackling, screeching when they came to the Disney store—mostly behaving well, as they generally did. Julia attracted the usual admiring glances for her Hawaiian-Japanese mother's eyes crowned by a full head of curly, strawberry blond hair inherited from her father and his Russian-Jewish ancestors. Marcia sometimes wondered if Julia could have any idea how beautiful a woman she would almost certainly become. Julia could be quite coquettish when she attracted attention, which was often, and she loved to be photographed. Max's dark hair, Marcia's hair, was almost as curly and he was certainly a handsome, sweet-looking little boy. When he was in a carriage or a stroller strangers would often stop to admire him, but he always seemed disinterested. And he quickly learned to resist being photographed, just like his mother.

Usually there were more than Marcia and Amy on these sojourns. Generally at least three, sometimes four or more of the ex-pat group, besides the children. When that many of them went they had to take as many as three vehicles because of the bulky car seats. The women always looked forward to being out of the house with other adult women, enjoyed sharing the little landmarks of their children's growth and development, enjoyed meandering from store to store window-shopping, enjoyed especially finding a good bargain. Lunch together was great fun, at least while the children were still in carriages and easy to control. They all welcomed the intermittent opportunities that permitted them to talk about their husbands and get at least some understanding of their own version of what one of them called "the ongoing Venus-Mars wars." In the crafts store, the crystal department at Bloomie's or some other place with breakables, they held the children's hands tightly. One of them, the "designated watcher," would keep track of the little ones if the others wanted to concentrate on some serious shopping that might require particular thought or advice. When someone needed help in deciding if a dress fit well, or wanted an opinion about how a lamp would match the living room décor, or if the contemplated purchase was too expensive or not, the children were kept in tow.

However, today, neither Marcia nor Amy bought anything other than a gift Amy needed for a birthday party Julia would attend. During the ride home there was only a little superficial chatting. But when Marcia half-heartedly asked her in for tea, Amy decided to stay and give her friend a chance to talk.

After the children were settled in the den with a sliced apple to share, watching Max's favorite movie, *Finding Nemo*, Marcia and Amy sat opposite each other at the kitchen table.

"So, what's up?" Amy asked.

"Nothing important. Really." There were a few intermittent whistles from the teapot.

"Michael?"

"Nothing." This time a partly suppressed growl from deep in her throat and the slightest shake of her head. She hesitated and then poured the boiling water into their mugs and pushed the bowl of sweeteners to Amy.

Amy stirred her tea slowly and deliberately, waiting to respond, and then said, "What did he do now?"

Marcia blew at the steam rising from her cup, not yet sipping. "Does Brian dismiss the things you say? Does he ignore you when you're talking?" She raised her head to look directly at Amy. "No, no, he doesn't. Not the way Mikey does."

"Brian's an easygoing guy. It's hard to get him riled."

"I wish I could say the same about Michael." Her nostrils flared as she took a long, deep breath. "And I'm not sure I can take too many more of his damn 'things to take care of today' lists." She ran her finger around the rim of the cup expecting a sound, but there was none. "Today's yellow legal-pad communication was to remind me about the dry cleaning. I don't need those notes, but he just can't stop. He says he's trying to help and then he promises to stop, but after a few blissfully noteless days, there they are again. On the damn refrigerator. Under the damn ice-cream cone magnet. The size of the notes changes from full sheet to Post-its, as if that would make it different."

"So what was the laugh about?"

Marcia put her cup down on the table, inhaled slowly and with a forlorn smile said, "It's the same thing all over. The superiority, always sounding like the ultimate authority and making assumptions—making decisions—the same controlling crap." She held the cup between both hands, as if trying to warm up. "He always speaks *ex cathedra* or *ex judicia* or *ex* whatever. He always has to be in control. I don't think he really asks for my opinion except when he wants to buy something we don't really need. And then he won't listen to my answer." She cleared her throat. "And when he wants sex, of course. He listens then." *And the damn sex is usually pretty good.* "Sometimes I just get so weary." She took a long sip of tea.

"So, the laugh was . . ."

"The thing that made me laugh is that I just suddenly realized that I married my mother, but even worse. It's as if I'm still living with loving and controlling Barbara. But now there's also all that stupid male strutting attached." She snickered again, the same laugh she'd made in the car. "Isn't that worth a laugh?"

CHAPTER TWO

When Barbara Moss, Marcia's mother, was twenty-four, long before she married Alan Whitman, Princess Beatrix of the Netherlands came to hear her play at the Stadsgehoorzaal in Leiden. It was Barbara's first European tour, just seven months after earning a master's degree from Juilliard. Beatrix graduated law school in Leiden and was back visiting friends. Barbara had already played in Barcelona, Lyon, and Antwerp, receiving enthusiastic reviews. This concert in Leiden was sold out. After Barbara played—an all-Chopin recital—Beatrix came backstage and presented Barbara with a bouquet of flowers and, in almost perfect, delicate, English, patting Barbara's hand as they sat opposite each other in the cramped dressing room, said it was the best she had ever heard Chopin played. "I hope I may have the opportunity to hear you again someday," Beatrix purred.

The scrapbook photograph of Beatrix and Barbara, cut from the *Leidsch Dagblad,* Leiden's oldest newspaper, was one of Marcia's favorites. It was the one and only time Barbara was photographed with royalty and Marcia loved how youthful and excited and assured her mother looked. She and Beatrix looked like two old friends sharing recipes. Beatrix became queen just when Barbara's first stereo recording was released and Barbara sent the record to her as a gift. Three Beethoven sonatas, the *Waldstein,* the *Pathétique,* and the *Appassionata,* the record had already received some appreciative reviews. Beatrix' warm note of gratitude was on the scrapbook's facing page. When she was still a child Marcia liked to run her fingers over the raised royal seal on the stationery even through it was behind plastic and she couldn't feel it that much.

When Marcia began to walk, still mostly holding on to chairs and tables and people, she would unsteadily manage her way to the piano when her mother was practicing. Often, Barbara would sweep her up and sit her on the piano bench and put the little girl's finger on middle C, then C-sharp and then D. At first she was able to guide Marcia through a whole octave, note by note, but when she was not quite three, a little older than Max was right now, Marcia would sometimes pull her fingers away so she could slap at the keys without any help and then pound on them until she got bored. Often it took quite a while for her to reach that point and, although the sounds she made could be harsh and decidedly discordant, Marcia was generally quite content to let those cacophonous notes fill the room, her delicate baby face completely focused on her own music making. Despite the seemingly chaotic effort her soft small hands were deliberately directed. When she finally tired of it all she would scurry away from the keyboard and sit attentively, sometimes for as much as twenty or thirty minutes, while Barbara resumed practice.

Marcia would always return when Barbara paused to make some notes on the score. Barbara would sweep her up once again to let the process repeat. Except when Barbara was practicing for a performance. Then Barbara would tell Marcia that she didn't have time but would play with her when she returned from her trip. The first time she heard this Marcia cried until Barbara picked her up and handed her to Lorraine, the nanny, with the soon-to-be familiar instructions to "take her into her room and keep her happy." After a half-dozen times hearing this Marcia stopped trying to get on the piano bench and would sit in her chair in the practice room, pouting for a few minutes before she began humming loudly with the music. Barbara would call for Lorraine but that didn't stop Marcia who'd sing loud enough for her mother to hear, even after Lorraine took Marcia to her room and closed the door. When Marcia's father, Alan, suggested they get Marcia a child-sized piano Barbara objected, saying, "No, she needs to play a good piano. She needs to have the sounds of a good piano in her head. She'll eventually be able to handle the full keyboard." In good weather, the nanny would take Marcia across the street to Central Park while her mother practiced. On the weekends, whether or not Barbara was preparing for a concert, Alan would take Marcia and her older brother, Frank, to the park, the Natural History museum, a puppet show or a walk across the Brooklyn Bridge. At seven, four years older than Marcia, Frank was already taking violin lessons, somewhat reluctantly, and was content to stay out of Barbara's way.

But Marcia took every opportunity to try to play the piano. Despite ongoing encouragement, Barbara's intermittent critical comments made Marcia feel that her piano playing would never measure up to her mother's expectations. In spite of this, if Barbara wasn't at the piano practicing, Marcia would tiptoe into the room and just press a few keys, sometimes without making a sound, before breakfast or before she left the apartment for school. It was as if she needed the physical contact with the piano at least one or two times each day. After school she would throw her jacket or sweater and her schoolbooks on one of the refinished old church pews that hugged the wall in the foyer, often missing her target, and run to the piano, trying more and more notes, until Lorraine walked past and called her to pick up whatever was strewn on the entranceway floor. By the time she was four Marcia played short melodies of her own as well as the practice pieces Barbara had taught her.

On Marcia's fifth birthday, before cutting the cake, her mother handed her a package that was clumsy for a little girl and felt like an oversized magazine. When she tore off the ribbons and wrappings she saw that it was music. Ten new short practice pieces arranged for beginners and, in a separate large red ribbon, the complete score of Beethoven's *Moonlight* Sonata, whose name she had no trouble recognizing. Barbara liked to play that piece as a respite from whatever she was working on in preparation for a concert. Marcia loved to listen to the *Moonlight*, especially the last minutes. When she saw the brand-new score that was to be hers and hers alone Marcia jumped up and down, squealing with delight, and then put her arms around Barbara's neck and squeezed tight. "Oh, thank you, Mommy. Thank you. This is the best." Then Marcia tried to get Barbara out of her chair. "Let's play piano, let's play. Let's play." Dropping all the sheets to the floor except for the sonata, she pulled at her mother's hand. "Please," she jutted her jaw forward a little, her head nodding in encouragement, "please, let's play."

They all laughed as Marcia stood there, hurriedly bending her knees to a slight crouch over and over again, ready to dash away. Frank picked up one of the beginner sheets and handed it to Marcia. "Maybe you should start here."

"Yes, yes, okay, yes," she tugged at her mother's hand and, after half-heartedly saying, "What about the birthday cake?" Barbara allowed herself to be pulled to the piano. They sat next to each other, Marcia's hands folded into her lap the way she had seen her mother do when she was close to the date of a concert. Barbara smiled down at her and said, "Now that you are beginning to play so well we have to set up some rules, you know."

Marcia nodded in agreement and then said, a little louder than she intended, "Yes."

"In between our lessons you have to practice your scales. For as long as you play, even when you are very, very old, you have to practice your scales."

Marcia looked up at her mother, her head slightly turned to the side, determined to see both her mother and the keyboard in one glance. Then she said, very seriously, "I know that, Mother."

*   *   *

By the time she was six Marcia practiced at least one hour each day, usually more, without prodding. Sometimes on weekends she played the piano two or even three hours, often just scales. She was beyond the basic lessons within weeks and was soon playing children's versions of pieces by Mozart, Busoni, Haydn and Beethoven. Once, when in the middle of a Clementi piece she had recently mastered, she cried when her mother pushed her fingers aside and closed the piano. The family was waiting to go out.

At about the time Marcia was almost able to reach the piano pedals Barbara reduced her own concert schedule. When her agent could book a concert in or near London or Paris or Vienna she would usually agree to go, but mostly she played in the United States or Canada. She made several recordings but, despite good reviews, they didn't sell particularly well.

Barbara was fortunate in that she didn't need to earn a living. Her husband, Dr. Alan Whitman, did very well. He had a busy practice based in three hospitals which he gave up to accept the position as head of the new interventional radiology division at Mount Sinai in order to develop the first New York teaching program in his specialty.

Among the inducements for Alan to limit his practice and leave his other hospital affiliations was a beautiful, rent-stabilized, eight-room apartment on Fifth Avenue and 98th Street, overlooking Central Park, literally a half-block away from the hospital. The apartment was in a pre-war building with large rooms and high ceilings. Their place, on the eighth floor, had a front room just right for Barbara's piano.

When Marcia was seven Barbara was offered a teaching position at Juilliard. After considerable discussion with Alan and with her principal teacher, Nadia Olenko, she decided she did not want to teach full-time. She agreed to give a quarterly master class on the Beethoven sonatas, alternating with Nadia, and also began volunteering at two junior high schools in the neighborhood, one public and one parochial, teaching music appreciation. Later, when Marcia was in high school, Barbara offered a weekly class in music theory at the 92nd Street Y. She still practiced at least four hours a day as if she were preparing for a regular series of concerts but devoted increasing portions of the time learning late twentieth century music. Years later, when Frank was practicing law in London and Marcia had moved to Los Angeles, Barbara began studying twenty-first-century composers, such as Salonen and Vanessa Lan.

Within seven months of starting formal lessons with a teacher Barbara regarded very highly, Marcia could easily play well the full version of *Für Elise*. Marcia gave her first public performance of the *Moonlight* when she was eleven. When she was twelve Barbara arranged for her to play in a chamber group, with sixteen and seventeen-year-olds. At first Marcia went willingly because she had a crush on Seth Berman, the violist. When Seth asked her to accompany him in a recital she was thrilled but Barbara told her she didn't need to learn the skills of an accompanist and refused to let her do it. When that happened Marcia realized that the excitement wasn't really because of Seth—it was from being part of a group of talented musicians who needed to create music. She knew she didn't really want to make music with Seth alone, especially in a relatively passive role, no matter how cute and talented he was. By the time Marcia was sixteen she had an extensive repertoire. Barbara had encouraged her to learn at least a little ragtime and jazz, but Marcia was happiest with Beethoven, Brahms and Bach.

When Marcia started LaGuardia High School of the Performing Arts Barbara arranged for private lessons at Juilliard with Nadia and with Alexei Makhover, whose father was one of the greatest Russian pianists of his time. Both teachers were both fairly strict with Marcia but each of them privately told Barbara her daughter had that "special something" only the great pianists had.

Makhover once said, "You are knowing, Bar-ber-a, that mine own father was big man. Like Russian circus bear. She, your girl, she what weighs? Forty-kilo maybe? Mine father weight more than one hundred kilo. But she, your girl, when she wants, she make piano shake just the same as father. I close my eyes sometimes and I hear him play. And she, she also, she plays the *delicato* the way he play. Like angel come down." He leaned forward and half-whispered, "You are knowing, Bar-ber-a, she will play the Rachmaninoff opus 30 better than anybody." He paused and stared into her eyes. "Better than father. Better."

Nadia Olenko said, "She's got the talent, that's for sure. More than enough. And the brains. And the heart. And the music, she knows more about music than anyone her age. You've taught her well, although"— she shrugged— "I'm not sure she needs to be able to play Bob Marley." They were finishing lunch at a small Greek restaurant on Broadway and Olenko was lighting up a Gauloise despite the red and white no-smoking sign on the wall. Barbara, as usual, frowned in disapproval. "But I worry about her." Olenko continued, inhaling deeply and blowing the smoke from the corner of her mouth toward the sign. "She likes to practice too much. She would be willing to practice twenty-five hours a day if that were possible. Twenty-six." Then she reached over and put her hand over Barbara's. "You knew some like that when you were in school. The ones that like to practice too much sometimes don't like to give concerts."

Barbara didn't tell either of the teachers that Marcia didn't practice anymore when Barbara was in the apartment. Barbara couldn't help but offer advice about technique, about expressiveness, about the history of the piece. Marcia did not want to hear any of that. In general she was not a particularly rebellious teenager except when it concerned her piano playing and her mother's comments.

Once, when Marcia was learning a Chopin polonaise, the opus 53, which her mother loved, Barbara walked by and said, "That's not heavy metal, Marcia, that's Chopin." Marcia didn't practice for almost a week, even after her mother apologized twice, something she rarely did even once.

Sometime after her seventeenth birthday, a few months before going off to college, Marcia started listening to Barbara again. She wanted her advice now, not only about technique and intonation but also about the background of the piece, historical and musical events that influenced the composer, even the legends about the composer. She wanted to know every book Barbara had read about composers and music. Barbara arranged for her to go to the Steinway factory and see how pianos are built. Marcia had music playing all the time, either on the radio or the CD player, or she was playing the piano herself. She would read musical scores while she ate breakfast, while she walked to school, while she waited for a movie to start. Music had unequivocally captured her, even if she didn't think of it that way

CHAPTER THREE

*T*he first big fight between Marcia and Michael was a few days before their marriage and it was about a new kitchen trashcan.

Marcia had quietly accepted things Michael did that she did not like, reminding herself that they needed to get to know each other better. *Being married is not the same as living together, it's a different dynamic*, she told herself every now and then.

She liked when he sometimes helped clean up the kitchen after dinner, but she didn't like him rearranging the dishwasher contents. "You need to make sure the platters are next to platters, salad plates next to salad plates, et cetera, et cetera," he often said. She explained that they rarely had a completely packed dishwasher and it really didn't matter how they were arranged, but he persisted.

She definitely did not like the lists he prepared for her each day. With each redundant list she reminded him she had a terrific memory and almost never forgot anything. He inevitably would reply, "It's not a problem for me. Just reminding you as backup." Most times she let the issue pass and would throw the paper away as soon as he left. Once she asked, "Mikey, do you think the daily notes are maybe a sign of something? You know, some personality quirk. Maybe you could talk to someone about it." The television was on and he didn't respond at first. Then he lowered the sound and, looking very serious, nodded his head slowly and carefully replied, "You're probably right. I've thought of that. I know I'm a tight-assed, obsessive-compulsive pushy lawyer." He paused, "I really don't mean to be a pain. I'll stop. I don't need to talk to anyone. I'm really sorry." And he would stop. But after a particularly tough few days in the office or a hurried business trip, or for no discernible reason, he'd start up with the lists again.

In the months preceding their marriage there had been a number of little quarrels but they were usually resolved with Marcia acquiescing and

Michael providing a hug and a kiss. She quickly learned how forceful Michael could be, how determined he was to have things his way. The issues never seemed important enough for her to battle over, although her mother had told her, more times than she wanted to hear, that she had to set boundaries in their relationship. "Establish your domain," Barbara had said, or "Michael will just walk over you. He's a very controlling man." *You should know about controlling, you invented the word, Barbara.*

The battle of the trash can began when Michael and Marcia were moving into their new Brooklyn Heights apartment, bringing most of the furniture, small appliances, telephones, towels, sheets, kitchen and bathroom supplies from Michael's old place. There was very little, other than her clothes, her music, and her personal items that they wanted from Marcia's tiny one-room studio apartment on W. 84th Street.

His apartment had been relatively well outfitted but the plastic kitchen trashcan was small and scuffed, and the foot pedal didn't work. It was abandoned, with a few other items, in the disposal room after he locked his apartment door for the last time. They headed for the nearest store with wares for the kitchen and bath.

Michael added a set of two-dozen plastic food storage containers to their shopping basket. Marcia protested: "There's too many in that set, we'll never use that many, and I don't like those colors. It's easier to tell what's in the clear ones. Why don't we just get a smaller package and I'll supplement it when I need to?" And did they need that package of four patterned plastic cutting boards? "I know the wood cutting boards are supposed to harbor bacteria but neither of us ever seems to get sick from them. And I'll scrub it when we use it."

Then Michael wanted to buy the most expensive, largest, shiniest garbage can in the store. It was a 14-gallon stainless steel device that had sophisticated magic-eye technology that opened the lid whenever there was some movement within eight inches. It used special odor-containing "durable" garbage bags that had to be ordered from the manufacturer. With the power adapter it cost $130 before taxes.

"Mikey, this is ridiculous. Why do we need 'durable' bags, durable and *expensive* bags at that, if we're just going to throw them out?" As soon as she said it his hazel eyes looked more gray than brown. "Wolf eyes," she would later call them as she learned they usually meant he was annoyed or was about to get angry. Or was already angry.

"This is perfect, Marcia. You don't have to touch it or step on a pedal or anything."

"But our kitchen isn't that large and I'm afraid this gadget, this thing, will be popping open every time I'm in there."

"We'll put it somewhere so it doesn't," he barked.

"And we have to order those special bags."

"I'll take care of that."

"Don't you already have enough to do? You work long hours."

"We're buying it," his voice was rising and every word was separated by a distinct space.

"But I don't want it."

"Well, I do." He lifted the box containing the trashcan, ceremoniously put it in the cart and headed toward the checkout section.

Marcia followed. She had prevailed on the cutting board but the multicolored storage containers and the trashcan were still there. *Well, it'll be a conversation piece when we entertain.*

CHAPTER FOUR

*M*ichael didn't want to think about Max being sick. He'd had only one direct experience with illness and it had been bad, as cancer usually is.

The only child of Holocaust survivors, his life was relatively unblemished until his father developed colon cancer. His parents married late and were almost forty when Michael was born. His parents doted on him and provided him with every advantage they could. Sam, his father, was the son of a renowned mathematician and was himself a professor of physics at Columbia University. He expected Michael to follow in his footsteps and was clearly disappointed when Michael chose law as a career.

At Michael's graduation from Columbia, Sam, gaunt and weak, withering away from metastatic cancer, hugged his tall son and pulled Michael's head down so he could kiss him on the forehead. "So, you just didn't want to learn those times tables." They both remembered the only real fight they'd ever had, when Sam screamed at Michael because of a failing grade on a math exam. Now Sam patted his son's cheek, saying, "You didn't do so bad after all, even without multiplying."

Sam died three months later, five days before Michael was to start law school. He missed the first two days of class because Margit, his mother, insisted they observe the traditional mourning period and sit *shiva* for the full seven days.

*   *   *

Max's listlessness continued and Marcia told Michael, for more than a week, something wasn't quite right with their boy and that she had made an appointment with Dr. Fogel. Her friend Sanam came over for coffee after a play group session and remarked that Max seemed to be "off his feed." Michael had a small eruption when he heard that, saying, "What the hell does that mean? Max is not a damn horse." He told Marcia it was probably just a cold. He was handling three big drug liability cases and they were on his mind all the time. Todd Anderson, the managing partner, had emphasized more than once that the litigation concerning the major pharmaceutical company was really important for the firm and they were depending on him to put the cases together. When he allowed himself to think about Max his first thought was that he didn't have time for this. He wouldn't know what he would do if his little boy was really sick and required all of his attention. But he told himself, if that happened, he would make the time. "It's probably nothing," he said softly to himself, "Max probably needs some vitamins."

The northbound 405 traffic on Friday afternoon was at a pitiless crawl, inching toward Mulholland Drive. "This isn't an interstate it's a goddamn parking lot," Michael mumbled aloud. He held the steering wheel of his Saab lightly, almost carelessly, between his left thumb and middle finger. Every now and then he unconsciously ran the fingers of his right hand through his hair, hesitating at the forehead trying to determine whether it had receded any further since the last time he checked it minutes ago. It was the middle of August when, even in Los Angeles, everyone was supposedly away, but he didn't notice any reduction in the number of cars on the road.

Michael pressed the earpiece hard against his ear, willing his cell phone to come to life, but there was no changing the fact that the battery was dead. *Damn.* He had come home after ten last night, had worked until almost two and, uncharacteristically, forgot to put the phone in its cradle for recharging. He and Marcia had both gotten up when Max cried a little after three, and when the sun came up he was still weary and still rethinking aspects of his case. He hadn't given the phone another thought as he slipped it into his pocket. And his car charger was still in Marcia's minivan, where he had used it during the weekend.

He turned his cell phone off when he went into the deposition room. During the day he only made two phone calls and he used the office landline for both of them.

Why didn't I call Marsh from the court transcriber's office? Why did I wait until I was in the car? Too goddamn impatient, that's why. He briefly considered stopping at a store on Ventura Boulevard to buy a charger—or maybe a dozen chargers—but he knew the idea didn't make any sense. He had enough chargers. "I just have to fucking remember to put one in the goddamn car," he muttered between clenched teeth.

The morning's deposition had dragged on well after lunch into late afternoon, taking hours longer than he ever thought it would. Ed Weinstein, his client and a highly regarded obstetrician, was being sued for malpractice. Never sued before, Ed had done well, despite his nervousness. He had measured his responses carefully and mostly limited himself to just answering the questions, without volunteering any extra information, just as Michael had instructed. He even maintained his composure when Tom Hagedorn, the lawyer for the plaintiff, tried to provoke him. "Would a responsible physician have treated his patient the way you did?" Michael objected, but later Hagedorn persisted, "If you were to characterize a medical quack, how would that characterization differ from the way you took care of your patient?" Michael didn't need to object to that one. After a half-sneer, a well-practiced technique used just for depositions, Hagedorn added, "No, never mind. Withdraw."

Michael had taken off his watch and put it on the table beside his papers in order to keep an eye on the time. He needed to give his full attention to the medical details squeezed into every question and it was almost a surprise when Hagedorn concluded, "We're done. Thank you one and all." Michael was shocked when he saw that it was a few minutes before five. *Shit! A 3:30 appointment, so they should be out by now. Why didn't I ask for a longer break so I could call Marsh?*

Now, stuck in a coagulum of traffic, he was seething, angry at the mute phone, angry with Hagedorn, mostly angry with himself: *Why the hell didn't I go with them? I could have postponed the goddamn deposition. Family comes first, right?*

Michael and Marcia were at the Levy's home for dinner the week before when Amy commented that Max didn't seem to have as much energy as usual and suggested he might be anemic. Then Amy's husband Brian, a neurologist at UCLA, went into the den where Max and Julia were eating. When he returned he commented that the whites of Max's eyes seemed to have a yellowish cast and suggested their pediatrician should take a look at him. Seeing the expression on Marcia's face, Brian hurriedly added, "I can't be sure with these indoor lights. It's better to look for jaundice in daylight."

On the way home that night Michael and Marcia asked each other how they could have missed seeing the slight, but now suddenly obvious, lemony tinge to Max's eyes. Marcia bit her lip, trying to remember when Max had started to have less energy and wondering how she, how they, could have kept thinking it was just a cold and that it would go away with enough time. *What kind of mother am I? I should have paid closer attention.*

During the two days before the appointment with Fogel, Michael kept telling himself that it was probably some virus but, for no reason he could figure out, "leukemia" popped into his head more than a few times, especially when he was trying to sleep. "Max is okay," he said aloud in the car. "Max is fine." He flipped on the directional signal and tried to inch his way into the right lane. Maybe he could make better time on local streets. He raised himself up high to peer over the SUV in front of him, trying to see the next Sepulveda exit, but the multitude of SUVs seemed to have forged a conspiracy to block his view. Better to stay where he was and hope it cleared soon.

He never owned a car before moving to L.A., had never needed one, and he still wasn't comfortable driving. The 405 allowed him to travel an almost straight line to and from his Westwood office and in the evening he usually left so late that most of the traffic was gone. "Damn, damn, damn," he shouted and banged his fist seven or eight times on the console between the two seats.

*   *   *

Marcia's calm, her steadiness and her strength were his bedrock. They met at the Fairway Market on Broadway at the end of his last year of Columbia Law School and started living together about a year after he graduated. Before that they mostly stayed in his one-bedroom apartment on E. 76th Street but still spent an occasional night at her place, usually after a concert at Lincoln Center. She loved the Upper West Side, the polyglot neighborhood in which she lived, and reluctantly gave up her apartment when they decided to marry, calling it "my home base, my security blanket."

Six weeks before their marriage they found a comfortable and relatively affordable two-bedroom apartment on Hicks Street in Brooklyn Heights. During the first few weeks of settling in Marcia kept marveling at how she'd managed to survive for so long in her tiny studio apartment. She had been renting piano practice space in a studio across the street from Lincoln Center, but their new place was roomy enough for them to buy a used Baldwin upright. The second bedroom became her music room in the afternoons and his home office in the evenings. There was now more than enough room for all of their books and for her music. Except for that trashcan, she loved their apartment.

Michael was offered an exciting promotion at the law firm, jumping ahead of some of his contemporaries. After only a year in the Brooklyn apartment he and Marcia moved since the new job was in Los Angeles.

*   *   *

The house in Encino came complete with tennis court and swimming pool because Michael believed it important to purchase a house commensurate with the career he intended to have even if he hadn't yet reached it. Marcia's parents helped with the down payment. Soon after they settled into their new home Michael bought Marcia a rebuilt Steinway grand, similar to the one Marcia had grown up playing.

Marcia tried more than a dozen pianos in the showroom before deciding on the one they finally purchased, earning the obvious respect of the sales staff, even inspiring more than a few bursts of applause for her mastery of the Mozart, Rachmaninoff, and Ravel fragments she played. "I don't really need a big piano, Mikey, I'm not planning on giving concerts," she said when the salesman quoted the prices of the pianos, but Michael knew she really did, in fact, want a big piano. Right after the piano movers left the house Marcia played the first movement of the *Waldstein* and then "Summertime" from *Porgy and Bess*. Michael loved the sounds that filled the room, filled the house. Lifting her hands from the keyboard and placing them in her lap she sat quietly for a moment, then jumped up to hug and kiss him. "I love it. It's a wonderful piano. Thank you so much." He felt a wave of contentment reminiscent of when he easily won a potentially tough case, what he called "a no-sweat win."

*   *   *

Now, thinking back on those first carefree months after they moved to California, Michael cursed himself again for not recharging his phone. His inability to talk to Marcia, to hear her say Max was all right, was creating a block of ice in his chest and pushing it into the place where his heart should be.

He wanted—no, he needed—to hold Marcia and to hold Max, to make sure both of them were all right. Instead here he was, trapped by the unyielding hordes of cars in front of him and what seemed to be miles of cars behind him, their reflection completely filling his rearview mirror. He could hear the hum and rumble of their engines, even with the windows closed and the air conditioning on. He jerked the visor mirror down and stared at his hairline.

I need to start coming home earlier, when Max is still awake. I know damn well it would make Marcia happier. Once we figure out what's happening with Max, I need to change. I need to put them first.

As soon as Max is better.

And suddenly he was shivering all over. He wanted to be held and comforted himself, to be told everything would be all right.

He wanted that block of ice to thaw.

CHAPTER FIVE

*A*zaleas hid the wall on the side of their driveway leaving only a few patches of exposed and weather-pocked cement. Michael never noticed flowers when he lived in New York and the first week they lived in this house he was annoyed there wasn't some sweet and delicious azalea fragrance to accompany their dazzling vermilion color. He once sniffed the azaleas at a neighbor's house to make sure he had not, somehow, gotten defective plants. Marcia loved flowers. In contrast to Michael she always slowed to a crawl as she drove up the driveway, delighting in the dazzling brightness.

Today, Michael wasn't even aware of the azaleas as he drove straight in. The garage door was up, unresponsive to the remote control, as it had been for almost two weeks. *Why the hell haven't I fixed it by now?* He never left things in the car, especially case material. Now he bolted into the house, leaving his two briefcases and the two eight-inch-thick piles of deposition transcripts sitting on the backseat, his tennis racquet and sports bag on the floor.

"Marsh! Where are you? I'm home. Where are you?" *I know they're home, her car is in the garage.*

The kitchen, the den and the living room were empty and he ran up the stairs, two and three steps at a time, poking his head into each of the bedrooms. "Marsh?" Their Brooklyn rescue cat, Smedley, was resting in his favorite lookout spot at the top of the stairs. But for a few flicks of his whiskers the cat stayed still as he studied Michael's approach.

Their bedroom, Max's room next door, and the two extra bedrooms, one of which served as his home office and the other as Marcia's, felt more than just empty, more as if they had been evacuated. An image of the desolate and dusty San Francisco of *On the Beach* flashed through his mind and he shuddered. The CD player was on, a guitarist strumming some vaguely familiar melancholy melody that he remembered more for being on Marcia's sad music list than for what it actually was. The song was set for "repeat" and started up again.

Today was one of those awful hot and humid Valley days. Almost as soon as he got out of the car and started walking into the house he began to feel the moisture accumulating in his armpits and between his shoulder blades. His shirt was now stuck fast to his back and soon felt cold from the air conditioner which Marcia must have turned on when she came home. He walked slowly back down the stairs, each step steady and measured. "Marcia, where are you?" he called again when he reached the bottom.

The dining room was empty, the oak table bare. Marcia usually had a vase of Gerber daisies in the center, or mums when the Gerbers at the market wouldn't stand up straight. Today, no flowers.

And then he saw her through the glass door, out on the patio, in three-quarters profile, a study in gray shadows, completely still. She was staring toward the neatly clipped rhododendron bushes fronting the white brick wall that rimmed the far side of the swimming pool. Some green leaves had fallen into the pool and were clustered together in one corner, out of reach of the gentle pull of the filter.

Michael stopped and stared for a moment, remembering the way he'd found her only last Friday, sitting in almost the same position, after that appointment Max had with Dan Fogel. She was wearing a plain tailored dress then with low heels, her hair perfectly arranged, a pearl necklace and earrings. He commented how nice she looked for the visit to the pediatrician. She'd laughed and replied, "I guess you can't take New York out of the girl. I still feel I have to get dressed up when I go to a doctor." He bent over and pressed his lips to her forehead, "I guess you can't take the mother out of the daughter." She gave him a playful poke before telling him Dan hadn't found anything really wrong with Max, hadn't been too worried about his color. She continued, "But Max's eyes didn't look so yellow to me either. Dan did seem a little concerned when I told him Max was tired a lot and also when I told him Max's bowel movements were light brown for a few days. He said they'd take some blood tests to see if it's jaundice—actually, what he said was that he needed to do some tests to *confirm* that it was jaundice—and to figure out what kind it might be, and then we'll talk about it."

She paused again. "I didn't know there were different types, you know, of jaundice. He also said it can come and go. Maybe he just didn't want to tell me what he was thinking yet." They held hands for a while before turning to look over at Max, sitting quietly in his sandbox, engrossed in a new cloth alphabet book of animal pictures that Marcia bought on the way home. "Max was so brave, Mikey, you would have been proud of him."

Hearing how brave he'd been, Max, who they didn't think had been paying close attention to them, started crying. "The nurse hurt me, Daddy, she hurt me," he whimpered, pointing to the Lion King band-aid in the crook of his arm. Michael scooped Max up into his arms, saying, "Come here, young fella," and Marcia hugged them both, turning Max's tears into giggles, giggles that lifted her spirits.

Now, exactly a week later, her dark hair was not quite as neat as it had been then, stray strands fell about her ears and onto her forehead, almost in front of her eyes. She hadn't moved while he stood observing her. He thought she wasn't aware he was there.

He looked over at their little boy fast asleep on the cot they had set up under an awning so Max could take his afternoon nap while Marcia swam her laps. Michael glanced at the pool fence, as he always did, to check if the gate was closed. André, the pool man, had come this morning and the latch was unfastened. *Damn, how many times do I have to tell him? Of course Marcia probably never thinks to remind him.*

A lazy breeze stirred every now and then, nudging the leaves of the trees and bushes. The sun was still perfectly round, hanging low in a cloudless, hazy sky. A car pulled into their neighbor's driveway. Behind the hedges the engine raced once before becoming silent.

Michael shook his head to clear his thoughts and opened the glass door to step outside. "Marcia, didn't you hear me?" He knelt on the ground in front of her, eye level, resting his hands on her knees. Gently, he brushed the loose hairs from her face and tried to make them stay behind her ears. "Marcia?"

She looked directly at him and then pulled him into her arms and buried her face in his shoulder. There was no crying—Marcia did not cry easily—but her voice wavered as she slowly started speaking, leaving a space between each word. "I tried to call you. I am so afraid." The "so" and the "afraid" were prolonged and separated, almost a sound and its echo. She bit her lower lip as she tried to hold back the tears. "It's something with his liver. Jaundice. Bili something. I don't know. And he's not even three years old."

He said nothing, absorbing not so much her words as the way she said them.

"Not even three," she repeated softly.

Max turned onto his side, emitting, as he sometimes did when he was sleeping, what they called his little "piggy snort." Marcia pulled away so that she could look right into Michael's eyes, even past them. She whispered "piggy snort," and then started sobbing, the pent-up tears in an almost steady flow of water, her chest heaving as she gasped for air. He cradled her head on his shoulder, caressed her back, and whispered, "Sshh, it's going to be okay, hon, it's going to be okay."

"Mikey," she cried over and over again, "why is this happening? He's so little. Our Maxie's so little."

They kept their arms around each other for a while, the moist and cool back of his shirt tightly clenched in her right hand. She cried less forcefully now but continued making a small plaintive sound, almost mewing. He stroked the back of her head and her shoulders over and over again. They didn't speak for hour-long minutes and then at last the crying stopped. "Tell me everything that happened at Dan's office."

Marcia leaned back, looking from Michael to Max and back again, wiping the tears with the back of her hand as he handed her his handkerchief. "It was awful. I knew Max was sick, sicker than we thought. I just knew it. And I was so—" she looked up at the sky for a moment, searching for the word— "frightened. And he was taking so long to tell me." She reached out to touch Michael's cheek. "I know Dan is a good pediatrician and a good person, but, but . . ." She couldn't speak, as the tears returned, and he held her close until she caught her breath. Holding both his hands in hers, she said, "Mikey, it was taking so long for Dan to tell me that I wanted to strangle him. I, I . . . I really wanted to grab him and strangle him. He was reading his notes and I . . . I was afraid to hear what he was saying but desperately wanting to know. And it was taking so long and I was so angry, I didn't know what I was so angry about . . ." Her voice trailed off to a whisper. "I was afraid and angry and . . ." She struggled to keep from crying.

"Try to tell me exactly what he said."

She stroked his cheek again. "Oh, I am so sorry. Here I am torturing you the way Dan tortured me." She wiped her eyes again and took a deep breath. "That's it, no more. Crying doesn't do any good anyway."

Just then Max turned, stretched out his arms and legs and snorted his piggy snort again. Marcia and Michael hesitated and then laughed and hugged again, rocking together. She raked her fingers through Michael's hair, mussing it and then patting it back in place, giving a few extra pats to the right side where it was a little thinner. Then Michael gently asked, "Do you think you can tell me now?"

She nodded. Trying to not make noise he dragged a chair close to hers. He took her hand. No more delaying.

"Okay, then. Yes. The tests show something is wrong with Max's liver. Dan told me they don't really know what it is. But the lab tests show some sort of liver disease, that's why he hasn't been eating well and hasn't been gaining weight, that's why he's been so tired, that's why . . . that's why . . ." She stopped, collected herself, and continued. "His alkali something, some blood test, I don't know what it is, alkali something and bili something, I don't know. He said the tests tell about the bile ducts, Max's bile ducts." She paused as tears welled up again. She pulled a tissue from a box on the ground and blew her nose. "I wanted to take notes so I could tell you everything, so I could talk to Daddy, but when Dan said liver disease and then said it might be serious, all I wanted was to get out of there. I wanted to just run right out of there. And he took so long. I don't know—I didn't understand everything he said. I didn't even ask him what he meant by 'serious.'"

Michael started to reassure her but his words got caught in his throat. Max was waking, and they both went over to the cot.

"Hey, Max, how are you, buddy?" Michael reached down to pick him up. "Did you have a good nap, big guy?"

As Michael held Max, Marcia put her arms around them both. "Are you all rested now?" she asked. Max turned in his father's embrace, twisting to put his arms around his mother's neck. "Mommy, why you sad? I love you."

"Mommy's okay, sweetheart." She smiled and kissed his cheek.

Max kept looking at her, pursing his lips and then, turning back to his father while rubbing the sleep from his eyes, announcing, "Goopies."

"Yes, you have some really big goopies in your eyes. But you can wipe them out, can't you?"

Max nodded and kept rubbing his eyes with his two tightly closed little fists for another second or two before resting his head on Michael's shoulder.

Michael put Max down, waited for him to steady himself on his feet, and took his hand. "Let's go in the house. Daddy wants to call Dr. Dan."

"I talk to Dr. Dan?" Max loved talking on the phone, especially when the call was from Marcia's parents or Michael's mother, Grammy Margit. Sometimes when he was handed the phone, he would look all around the room, still not quite trusting where the sound was coming from.

"We'll see, Maxie. Daddy needs to talk to Dr. Dan first."

"'Kay."

In the kitchen the slanting rays of the setting sun fell softly on the butter yellow walls. The refrigerator door was covered with Max's crayon drawings, a small calendar, a clipping from the *New York Times* about new bistros in Paris, and Hollywood Bowl tickets for Tuesday evening. Michael, annoyed with the clutter, finally found Dan Fogel's cell phone number under the calendar, scrawled on a sticky note right next to the numbers for the police and the fire department.

Standing by the kitchen table, Michael pulled off his tie and punched the numbers in on the phone. Marcia brought Max a Tommy Tippee cup of milk and a chocolate chip cookie broken into four pieces. Max shoved some cookie into his mouth and chewed, the crumbs falling to his chin and dropping down onto his "Tigger" shirt.

Fogel answered the phone immediately. *That was too quick. One ring. Doctors don't usually get on the phone that quickly unless it's something serious, something bad.*

Dan Fogel's younger brother Bobby was Michael's roommate at Columbia. The Fogels grew up in Los Angeles, the sons of a physician. Bobby returned to L.A. after graduating to attend medical school at UCLA. Before Michael and Marcia moved to Los Angeles, Michael called Bobby with a host of questions. Bobby provided the necessary information about neighborhoods where they might want to live, gave them the names of two realtors, told them the best places to buy appliances and furniture, some of the ins and outs of the school systems, and about earthquakes, mudslides and where Santa Ana winds might fan raging fires. Bobby also told them about potential doctors, including his older brother, Dan, a pediatrician whose office coincidentally was less than two miles from the house they wound up buying.

"Dan, Michael Kleinman. Tell me about Max. What's going on? . . . Yes, you remember correctly, I do understand some medical terms. Yes."

Marcia put a glass of water in front of him, but he ignored it.

"Me talk," said Max. "Me talk."

Marcia sat down, wiping Max's mouth absently while watching Michael as he periodically nodded in response to whatever Dan was saying.

"Alkaline phosphatase, tell me again . . . is that high? . . . About twice the level it should be? What does that mean?"

As Max finished the last of the cookie, Marcia mouthed "What?" When Michael didn't respond, she mouthed it again.

"Yes, okay." Michael put up his hand to signal her to wait and continued talking. "I'm sure whoever you recommend will be fine." He looked over at Marcia. She nodded her head affirmatively and held out a piece of paper with some writing and a phone number on it. "Yes, she has the information . . . Yes, and the address. The appointment's on Monday, yes."

Max toddled over to pet Smedley who had sauntered over to his water dish in the corner of the kitchen, his tail straight up. But Smedley eluded his grasp and squeezed through the baby-gate and ran upstairs. Losing interest, Max headed for a pile of his toys.

"Of course, of course. We'll be there. We'll both be there. Of course . . . No, Dan, please don't. I don't know any more than you do if you should have made the diagnosis sooner or not. I don't care. I just want Max to get better, that's all . . . I don't think so. Hold on." He partially covered the mouthpiece and touched Marcia's arm to get her attention, which was now focused on Max navigating his way back to them, clutching a yellow and black Tonka dump truck. "Dan is asking if you or I have had liver disease, or if anyone in the family has."

"Dad-dee." Max was back at Michael's knee, reaching out for the phone, a few crumbs lingering in the creases of his palm. "Dad-dee," he said, a little louder and more insistently.

Marcia shook her head. "I already told him none in mine. I just wasn't sure about your family."

Michael took his hand away from the mouthpiece. "No, Dan, not that we know of . . . We'll be there, definitely. Yes, what's his name?"

Marcia was whispering, "I have it" but Michael, ignoring her, took a pen from his shirt pocket and started writing on the edge of a newspaper that he took from the chair.

"Oh, right, sorry, yes, *her* name. Yes, . . . Padilla? P-a-d-i-l-l-a? . . . Got it . . . Lena? L-e-n-a . . . Oh, okay, L-i-n-a, Lina Padilla. What? Are you sure?" After pausing for Dan's answer, Michael shook his head, his expression a little graver than it had been.

Marcia tugged at his sleeve, mouthing "What?"

"Yes, we'll be there . . . Yes, definitely. Thank you."

Michael hung up the phone and slumped down in a chair until Max tugged at his arm reproachfully. "I talk to Dr. Dan. You told me."

"Sorry, Maxie," Michael started to pat Max on the head but Marcia grabbed his arm. "Michael, what?"

His voice caught as he started to answer her. Clearing his throat, he said, "Max might need a liver biopsy. Dan thinks Max may have a liver condition but he isn't sure of the diagnosis yet. He's thinking, though, that Dr. Padilla might want to biopsy Max's liver."

CHAPTER SIX

*L*ina Padilla was about Marcia's height but somewhat stockier and, Marcia guessed, in her early fifties. "The best age for a doctor," her father often said, "with enough years of experience but not yet old enough to have lost some of the know-how or technical ability." Smartly dressed in navy slacks and a powder-blue sweater under her white coat, she was attractive but would not be considered a classic beauty. Her nose was slightly too large, her mouth wide and her frequent smile toothy. Her hair was cut short—very short, like a crew cut—and, for a fleeting moment, Michael wondered if she was gay. *I don't care what she is as long as she can help Max.*

As Michael and Marcia entered the examining room a few minutes after three the doctor smiled warmly at them while holding out her hand to shake Max's. Max hesitated and Marcia quickly explained, "I don't think he's used to the white coat."

Dr. Padilla bent to look Max in the eye. "Come now, you don't care all that much about my office coat, do you, Max?" He shook his head no, put his hand in hers and pumped it up and down. "Now, that's quite a handshake young man, quite a handshake."

"I know," Max shrugged and walked over to the examining table for a closer look at the cartoon characters that covered the steps in front of it.

"Do you think you can climb up those steps, Max, so I can talk to you while I feel your tummy?" The doctor turned to Michael and Marcia, still standing in the doorway while Max scrambled up past Scrooge McDuck. "Why don't you two come in and stand over here"—she gestured to the head of the examining table— "close to Max. Do either of you want a chair?" They shook their heads no.

"I'm going to pay attention to Max first and then we can sit and talk."

Max was on his knees on the table, looking at his parents. "Mommy said you 'zamine me."

"Yes, that is exactly what I want to do. First, you just turn around and sit facing me, so I can get a good look at you."

"'Kay. Dr. Dan 'zamine me too."

While he was lying on his back, to let Dr. Padilla feel his abdomen, Max craned his neck to look at his parents, checking to make sure they were still there. When the doctor pulled Max's shirt down at the end of the examination, then stood up to write some notes, Marcia leaned down, kissed Max on his nose, and whispered, "You are such a good boy, you are the best boy."

"I know."

After Max was settled on a floor mat to play, the three adults sat in the middle of the office on brightly colored yellow, green and red chairs. The examining room was more like a child's playroom than an office. There was no desk and Lina Padilla held a clipboard in her lap.

"Tell me when Max first got sick."

Marcia took a deep breath, looking over at Max. "The earliest I can remember that we first noticed he wasn't eating so well was four, maybe six weeks, maybe even two months ago. At this stage I'm just not sure anymore. He had some pain in his tummy that I didn't think much of." She looked at the pediatrician. "Sorry, abdomen."

"You can say 'tummy.'" Padilla said, with what seemed to Marcia to be one of the warmest and most comforting smiles she had ever seen. "I think I just did a few minutes ago."

They all smiled, and Marcia continued. "The pain lasted for a day, but then it went away. We didn't see Dr. Fogel but we spoke to him and he wanted us to watch him—watch Max—and see how things went." She paused. "Maybe we should have gone sooner," she said, a question barely veiled as a statement.

Michael started to say something, but settled for clearing his throat. He found himself staring at the doctor's black fountain pen as she wrote her notes and thought he could almost hear the ink flowing.

"The biggest thing we've noticed is that he doesn't have any energy," Marcia continued. "He's sleeping a little more than he used to and he's sometimes fretful. He's not always the same happy little boy he used to be. He doesn't have the same pep. But then sometimes he's the same Max he always was. Except for the energy."

"I'm surprised he's lasted so long today," added Michael, pointing to Max, who was lying on his back talking animatedly to a plastic orange kangaroo perched on his chest. "He didn't even nap on the way here."

"Dr. Padilla, should we have gone to see Dan sooner? Would it have made a difference?" Marcia asked tentatively.

"Lina, just call me Lina." She put her pen in the breast pocket of her coat and, crossing her arms, held the clipboard close to her chest. "You are both smart enough to know that guilt isn't always rational and that it doesn't help anything. However, I do want you to really listen." She hesitated and spoke more slowly. "You are here at the right time. Max is obviously not terribly sick, not in extremis, not declining before our eyes. So you're here at the exact right time." She looked first at Marcia and then shifted her eyes to Michael, as if to make sure they'd absorbed what she said. *She's good*, Michael thought, *she's really practiced, really good.* And then he told himself, *Don't be such a cynical bastard of a lawyer.*

Lina took out her pen again. "So, tell me again—when did Max first seem unusually tired?"

Marcia replied, "About two months ago. We thought maybe he'd caught a virus from someone in his play group."

"And his bowel movements? When did the color change?"

Marcia raised her eyebrows. "How did you know?"

"Dr. Fogel sent his records over to me and I spoke with him this morning." That warm smile again. "Go on."

"Yes, well, it was about three weeks ago, maybe four. A few days before the first visit with Dan. I didn't think anything of it until Dan asked me about it. We're just getting into potty training for the past few months now and, to tell you the truth, I help him wipe his bottom but I don't usually look to see what's there." Marcia held out her hands, as if pleading. "But I did notice they were really light brown, tan, for a few days . . ."

"I don't think most parents look that carefully at the color of their children's bowel movements once kiddies are on the potty. I think everyone's just relieved to get over the diapers. I know I was that way with my three."

"Thank you for saying that. I appreciate it." Marcia took another deep breath, exhaling slowly. "Anyway, it may have been about a month ago but, as I said, I'm not positive, and it mostly seems to be the usual color now."

"Dr. Fogel put Max on an antibiotic, didn't he?"

"Yes, we started it last Saturday," Marcia said. "Is that good?"

"And Max seems to have more energy," Michael added, "and he's a little less yellow, I think."

"Yes, that's fine. We'll just continue that for a while and see how it goes," Dr. Padilla murmured as she wrote some notes.

They went on to review family histories. Marcia now remembered one uncle had hepatitis years ago but, as far as she knew, was fine now. There was not much else that seemed relevant. Finally Lina set her clipboard on a side table and turned back to them. "Before you leave today I want to do an echo scan of his liver, and then we can go over other matters."

"What's an echo?" Marcia asked.

"It's nothing to worry about, Marsh," said Michael.

"Your husband's right. It's very simple and it won't hurt Max in the least. It's a lot like radar. We pass a kind of wand over his abdomen that releases a sound wave and then we measure its reflection. The device turns the reflection into an image that we can study."

"I see," Marcia nodded uncertainly.

"You probably had an echo when you were pregnant but they may have called it a sonogram."

"Yes," Marcia nodded again, some of the tension leaving her face. "Of course."

"But you should know that this echo may be—actually is—just the first step we take."

At that, both Marcia and Michael looked at each other with similar squints and wrinkled brows, similar concern on both their faces, and then back at the doctor.

"It may be necessary to put Max to sleep for some of the imaging studies. We'll see as we go along." Lina paused. "You know, one of the reasons I wore a white coat today is because Max will be seeing quite a few more people wearing white coats over the next few visits. I don't always wear a coat in the office but I thought this would be as good a time as any to start getting him used to it. You are aware that Max may need a liver biopsy?"

Marcia reached over and grabbed Michael's hand. "Yes, Dan told us. What exactly does that mean?"

"He'll get a little medicine intravenously, not full anesthesia, and he'll have a very nice sleep for the thirty or so minutes it takes to get set up and actually perform the biopsy. We'll likely schedule our imaging studies and the biopsy at the same time so we won't have to anesthetize him twice. I'll pass a special needle through his skin, right here." She put her finger to the right side of her body, a few inches above her waist. "We'll take out a core of liver tissue about an inch or two long and less than the width of the graphite part of a pencil. We'll have a pathologist who's expert in liver diseases look at it. I'll also look at it with the pathologist. At that point we should have a better idea of how to proceed.

"Max will sleep a little while after this whole business and then he'll be fine. He'll stay in the hospital for about four hours, just so we can watch him, and then he's home. He probably won't remember anything and probably won't have any pain. If he does have a little soreness we can give him some baby Tylenol. One or two doses usually does the trick."

Michael bit his lip. "Question?"

"Of course."

"How risky is it?"

"There's a risk to any medical procedure. I won't patronize you by listing the everyday things that are risky for us all, such as crossing the street, but I have been doing liver biopsies with children for more than twenty-five years and"—she smiled at them as she went over to the crib next to the examining table and tapped on a wooden strut— "touch wood, I've never had a problem. Not even one." She paused to make sure they were absorbing what she was saying. "We have to do a few more lab tests to make sure his blood clotting mechanism is okay, but I think Max will not have a problem with the biopsy."

The room was quiet, and then Marcia asked, "What was Dan talking about when he mentioned Max's alkaline . . . ?"

"That's alkaline phosphatase, an enzyme that indicates liver disease, particularly involving the ducts of the liver. Another enzyme that gives us similar information is also elevated in Max. Those things are helping us focus on the diagnosis."

"Which is? What do you think he has?" Michael couldn't hold back.

"I don't know yet. That's one of the reasons we need to do these tests. We'll start with the simple ones, like blood tests and the echo, and go to the slightly more complicated ones such as the liver biopsy. They can each tell us something."

"But don't you have any thoughts now?"

"My guess is that he has something wrong with his bile ducts, either outside the liver or inside the liver, but I'm not sure which and I'm not even absolutely sure I'm correct. I can also tell you that it's highly unlikely that he has a tumor, unlikely he has a cancer of any kind."

Michael started to speak but Marcia blurted, as her eyes widened, "Cancer? I didn't even think of that. I didn't think of anything, really, but I certainly didn't think of that. Are you sure? Don't we need to find out right away?"

Lina reached over and patted Marcia's hand. "I really do not think that is Max's problem. I am more than ninety-nine percent sure he does not have a tumor. The pictures and the biopsy will make it one hundred percent. I apologize for even bringing it up. But I do need to discuss something else with you before we decide how to proceed." She paused to see if either of them wanted to say anything, then went on. "Even without a biopsy, I don't think anything is going to happen too quickly to make Max worse, but I am going away at the end of next month. First I'll be giving lectures and then I am just going to relax and read. I'll be away for a little more than six weeks." She paused again and offered a half-smile. "I need it."

"Yes?" Marcia leaned forward and Michael scowled.

"Although I don't think it'll happen, it's possible, again depending on what we find, that Max could need something else done in the coming months and I won't be here to care for him."

"Yes?"

"What I'm saying is, after examining him and talking to both of you and looking at Dan's records, as sorry as I am to say it, I'm pretty sure Max has a significant liver disease that's going to get worse, so it might be easier for you to have another pediatric hepatologist around who can take care of Max from the beginning."

Michael looked at Marcia, to gauge her reaction, then back at Lina. "I have to tell you—we're really comfortable with you and, more important, Max seems comfortable with you."

"Yes, well, I would send you to a wonderful doctor, who would take very good care of Max and very good care of you two also. I'm sure you, and especially Max, would be comfortable with him. He's a wonderful person and an excellent physician, and—"

Marcia stood up quickly, almost losing her balance. "While you're away, what else might Max need?"

Lina held both of Marcia's hands in hers. "Most likely nothing for the time I'm away, but I can't be absolutely sure of that. Since we don't know exactly what's going on yet, we can't really predict the next stage." She waited for another question but, when none was forthcoming, she went on. "It's certainly too early to be sure, but it is conceivable that, at some time, he might need a new liver, Marcia. Max might need a liver transplantation. Again, we can't be sure of that yet. And certainly not right away, but I don't want you to be completely surprised if that is where we end up."

CHAPTER SEVEN

*A*fter hurrying out of Dr. Padilla's office they spent more than fifteen minutes in the Wilshire Boulevard traffic just going the one-mile to the 405 ramp.

"Michael, I don't think I can go to your retreat this year. Not with Max this way."

"What made you think of that right now? It's what—about six or eight weeks away?"

"I'm just trying to think about the next few months, trying to figure things out. I know how important it is to you but I can't go to some resort and lie there by the pool and pretend life is just fine. I can't." She sighed. The driver in the car behind them honked. The light was green but the traffic ahead had not moved. "I just don't think I can handle all the cheerfulness, all the having fun."

Each year, Caney, Wheeler & Mathewson held a retreat for their attorneys and paralegals at a family-oriented resort. Spouse and offspring attendance was not mandatory but strongly encouraged. The first West Coast branch retreat had come up only two months after they had moved to California. Marcia, seven months' pregnant at the time, was reluctant to accompany Michael, unhappy at the prospect of meeting his associates while feeling bloated and uncomfortable.

"Do we have to go? I'm as big as the *Titanic*," she pleaded.

"Yes, we do. I actually learn things at the meetings and I get to spend time with guys in the firm I don't get to see much of every day. And three days of tennis isn't all that bad either."

"For you maybe. Not for me," she pouted as she stood in front of the bathroom sink, rubbing moisturizer onto her face. She was wearing a pale pink support bra and white cotton panties sprinkled with daisies.

From under her protuberant abdomen the panties swooped down from one hip and up to the other. "I don't look exactly the way I used to in my bikini, you know." Her belly button, which had always been an innie, was now an outie. She stared dejectedly at her reflection as she continued massaging the cream into her skin.

Michael wrapped his arms around her, one hand on her breast and the other on the lower curve of her belly, a finger hooked under the elastic band to gently rub at the top of her pubic hair. "You make Demi Moore look like a boy," he said, sticking his tongue in her ear.

"Stop that." She twisted out of his arms. "You know I hate that, it tickles."

"Yes, I know how much you hate it and I also know how much you like it." He reached toward her again, but she sidestepped away from him.

"Never you mind about that. For your information I'm a proper pregnant lady."

He moved back behind her, sliding a finger under her bra and circling her nipple.

"Don't do that!" She gave him a disapproving look, her exaggerated frown soon relaxing into a smile. "At least not until I finish with my face."

"Yes, ma'am," he said, again sliding his hand down her belly and wiggling his fingers deeper.

"Michael!" She grabbed his wrist and pulled his hand out, placing it on the plateau of her upper abdomen. "Can't you wait until I finish?"

"Yes, proper pregnant lady," he said, but he moved his hand back and kept stroking.

"But really, listen to me. I don't want to go, not the way I look. All those leggy blonde California women in tennis shorts. You can just go without me."

"Okay." He again pushed his tongue into her ear and, before she could object, backed himself into the bedroom and flopped down on the bed. "Then I guess I'll go without you and bring my tennis racquet for company." He put his arms behind his head and grinned up at the ceiling. "Probably should bring a supply of condoms."

"You louse, you!" She threw the wet washcloth at him as she ran to the bed, climbed on top of him and straddled him. He pulled her down and kissed her, unclasping her bra as she pushed her hand between their bodies to untie his pajamas. "Okay, okay, I'll go," she barely managed to say before he silenced her with his tongue.

*   *   *

Marcia purchased three very stylish and, for her, expensive black maternity dresses to wear to the evening events scheduled at the retreat. Thursday evening would start with a cocktail party and she wanted to make a good impression in her West Coast debut social appearance before Michael's associates. She'd never forgotten an old late-night television movie she'd seen when she was a teenager in which Rex Harrison looked at his movie wife as they were dressing for a party and told her she looked "smashing!" For Marcia this remained the highest of compliments. She wanted to look smashing for the entire weekend. She especially wanted to look smashing at this cocktail party.

Growing up she had spent too many hours with her mother trying on clothes at discount shops to ever be completely comfortable buying anything that had not been marked down. This time she was willing to make an exception.

"Don't you dare ask how much I paid for these dresses!" she'd told Michael when she held them up in front of her for him to admire. "All you need to know is that even though they're not from Loehmann's I didn't get them on Rodeo Drive. *Close* to Rodeo Drive, but not *on* Rodeo Drive."

*　*　*

They travelled north with another couple, both attorneys at Caney, Wheeler. Judith Bellman worked with Michael in medical malpractice, "medi-mal." Her husband, Nicholas Drury, was in contracts and also handled divorces. They were flying to San Jose where they would rent a car and then drive the hour or two to Quail Lodge in Carmel. As they waited to board the plane Marcia brandished her copies of *Architectural Digest* and *House Beautiful* and proclaimed, "You guys can do all the office shop talk you want on the plane, but once we get in the car conversation is limited to movies you've seen, books you've read and the terrific new restaurants you've been to. Everything else is *verboten.*"

Judith hooked her arm through Marcia's as the call to board came over the loudspeaker. "Listen, what makes you think I'm sitting next to Nick? No way. I'm through with law talk until Monday unless someone notices me in the back row at one of the meetings and asks me a question. This trip is for girl talk. No kids and as little time with the husbands as possible." She playfully stuck her tongue out at Nick.

*　*　*

Before they left their room for the cocktail reception Marcia stopped in front of the full-length closet mirror and examined her reflection from head to toe and back again. *I look beautiful.* She surprised herself by thinking it. The black-on-black silk dress, the pearl necklace and earrings that her parents had given her when she graduated from Smith, and the splash of bright coral lipstick she'd chosen over her usual subtle shade were striking in combination. The dress was worth every penny since it elegantly cradled her bulging abdomen and accentuated the increased fullness of her breasts. She held her right hand at the side of her neck, turning slightly to admire the curves of her silhouette. Tonight she really did have that special glow pregnant women are supposed to have, something she had not felt before. *I really do feel beautiful.*

'God, you're beautiful!" Michael said, embarrassing her by echoing her own thoughts. He opened his arms to embrace her but she put up her hand to stave him off.

"Don't you dare mess up the display. Do you think it was easy transforming this beached whale into a reasonably presentable party girl?" she said, beaming. He went to his briefcase, pulled out his camera and grabbed her hand. He walked her out to the front of their bungalow, directing her into different poses before the lush greenery that almost obscured the windows. *He knows I don't like to take pictures, but I really am beautiful today, aren't I?* As he snapped away Marcia forced a broad smile to her face. *I am happy. I just need to get him to ease up and enjoy life a little more. He's so hard on himself. And on me. He's hard on me, too.*

The cocktails and dinner were at the conference center just past the tennis courts. As they walked by the consistent "whop-whop-whop-whop" of a couple's game was punctuated by the woman's half-suppressed shrieks every time she hit the ball. He was very handsome and she was strikingly beautiful and Michael and Marcia slowed to watch them play. The man was well into his fifties, or perhaps even older, with a full head of neatly trimmed hair, more salt than pepper, which stayed steadily in place despite the intensity of the game. The chiseled features of his lean and well-tanned face didn't change as he ran toward them to get a long, low shot in the corner of the court. But then, in the half-moment between when he hit the ball and before he turned back toward the net, he smiled and winked at them. Not visibly out of breath he ran back to the centerline, positioning himself where he thought his partner would send the next shot. The woman, perhaps in her late thirties, had long, well-tanned, tapered legs attractively accented by the contrast of her white shorts. She matched him stroke for stroke, her intensely focused gaze following the ball with the concentration of a falcon targeting a frantically scurrying field mouse.

As they walked away from the court Marcia said, "Well, so much for self-delusion. Did you see her legs? Those legs are precisely why I didn't want to come to this retreat." She looked over at him, frowning. "What a dumb question. Of course you saw her legs. And the rest of her, I'm sure.

Oh, well"—she put her arm in his— "come on, take Shamu to meet all your colleagues."

Michael abruptly turned her around and looked earnestly into her eyes. "Look, I just want to hold you and kiss you right now. I want to go back to the room and make love to you. You have to know there is no one here more beautiful than you are. You are spectacularly beautiful." He took her hands in his. "Spectacularly beautiful," and he let his glance sweep over her, head to toe. "Marsh, there isn't a man here who will not be jealous." The whop-whop-whop-whop of the tennis game stopped for the minute and he looked over Marcia's shoulder to see that the man had failed to reach another shot to the corner. He watched the woman as she ran to the net, hand outstretched to greet her vanquished partner. The man clasped his partner's hand and then pulled her close for what was clearly more than just a friendly over-the-net kiss. "Come on, let's go," Michael said, "I am one lucky guy. Don't you doubt it for a second."

A sweeping semicircular red brick path, its borders crowded with white and pink Lily-of-the-Valley, led down to the patio reception area. The air was sweet with the scent of the flowers as a staccato buzz of indecipherable conversations rose to greet them. A string quartet was seated in the far corner playing, "Hey Jude."

Approximately fifty people stood clustered in groups of five or six, balancing cocktail glasses and hors d'oeuvres. Some were seated at white wrought-iron tables. The servers were young men and women, mostly blond, dressed in white pants and crisp white polo shirts with the logo of the lodge. They unobtrusively offered more canapés and refreshed half-empty glasses.

Many in the crowd paused in their conversation to observe the newcomers as they approached. Michael, tall and straight, his light brown hair thinning just enough to lend a touch of maturity to his boyish face, appeared the confident up-and-coming young star he thought he was. Marcia, petite and dark, still slim except for the fullness of her belly, was stunning. Todd Anderson, the L.A. office's senior partner and Michael's boss, came over to greet them.

"Marcia, you certainly put a stop to whatever inconsequential chatter was going on." He smiled as he leaned over to kiss her on the cheek. "You look very lovely this evening."

His wife, Edie, arrived at his side, nodding in agreement. "Marcia, you really do. You make me want to sue my plastic surgeon or get pregnant again. Or both." She kissed Marcia on both cheeks and Marcia relaxed with the warm welcome. The four of them chatted for a few minutes before Todd said, "You'll have to excuse us. Edie and I need to work the crowd. You do, too." He grinned, giving Michael a playful jab and winking at Marcia.

Michael guided Marcia around the patio to introduce her to colleagues. A waiter offered a tray of fluted champagne glasses and tumblers of Perrier with lime slices. They both took the Perrier. The dinner featured wines from some of the local vineyards and Marcia allowed herself a few sips of the pinot blanc that everyone at their table was raving about, the resulting flush in her cheeks only adding to her glow. The evening she had so dreaded was turning into a complete success and she had to admit she was enjoying it. Periodically she felt the baby move. *This is perfect.*

One of Michael's colleagues, Angela Guardino, was at about the same stage of pregnancy as Marcia. A pretty woman, also dark-haired but with a slightly more olive complexion than Marcia, Angela was wearing a peach-colored maternity pants suit. Suspecting many of the guests were comparing them, Marcia felt a moment of sympathy for her. In contrast to Marcia, Angela looked too big and decidedly plain. *I should be ashamed of myself.* She could almost hear Bernstein's Maria trilling, "I feel pretty, oh, so pretty, I feel pretty and witty and bright." When Marcia learned this was Angela's fifth pregnancy she felt guilty, although she couldn't stop delighting in how beautiful she felt.

During dessert, Marcia noticed Michael abruptly stop eating, a forkful of baked Alaska poised in mid-air. He was staring at a table at the far corner of the room and she wondered what had caught his attention. Wiping his mouth with his napkin he stood up. "Excuse me, hon, I see an old friend from law school over there." Before she could respond he started to leave but then stopped himself and held out his hand to her.

"Come on, come with me. I want you to meet her. I've told you about her. Amanda. She's in the New York office now but she's in town for a case. She joined the firm just after we came out here."

Marcia hesitated. Michael had indeed told her about Amanda Martinez, the woman he dated for more than a year beginning in their second semester of law school. One of the things Marcia especially loved about Michael was his loyalty to, and affection for, his old friends, including some from as far back as elementary school. It was one of his best qualities. He would call them once or twice a year, just to say hello. To her own surprise, she sometimes felt a twinge of jealousy when the old friend turned out to be a woman, even if he had hardly seen her since the fifth grade. She knew it was absurd but, despite her ongoing annoyance with him, she could easily imagine that any woman who knew Michael would want him for her own.

"Marcia, it is *so* nice to meet you at last. I've heard so much about you from Michael." Marcia smiled as they shook hands, trying not to wonder about when Michael might have told her "so much."

A few inches taller than Marcia, Amanda was more than beautiful, she was professional-model gorgeous. Strong cheekbones framed by straight black hair that fell to the middle of her back, almond-shaped onyx-dark eyes, and a body that any man with a pulse would yearn to have. She wore an understated charcoal gray full-length brocade skirt and an eggshell-white silk blouse with a large, softly draped bow that accentuated her full breasts and narrow waist. A Gibson girl was Marcia's first thought—*does anyone still know what a Gibson girl is?*—and then, after that, not able to suppress the idea—*she must look fantastic stretched out on a bed.* She blushed at the thought and glanced at Michael to see if he had noticed, but he was still looking at Amanda. Marcia forced a smile to accompany her overly enthusiastic, "Yes, me too, yes, I've heard a lot about you also."

Amanda was decidedly not from the fifth-grade part of Michael's life.

People were table-hopping after dessert and Marcia sat down in one of the two empty chairs next to Amanda. As they talked, Marcia felt they could be friends. Amanda seemed to be making a genuine effort to put her at ease. They had a couple of acquaintances in common including someone Marcia had known in high school and they chatted about these shared friends for a while. After Michael got up to greet someone at another table, Amanda surprised Marcia by saying, "My biological clock is a few years ahead of yours and I'm very jealous. May I?" She held her hand just above Marcia's abdomen, not touching it until Marcia nodded her assent. "I'm actually considering artificial insemination or adoption or something like that. I don't seem to have much luck with men, what with long hours and always being occupied with cases."

Marcia briefly wondered if Amanda was thinking she might have been the one to have Michael's baby. Before they touched cheeks and said goodbye, they exchanged phone numbers and e-mail addresses, Amanda saying warmly, "I'll see you next year. With your baby. Or maybe sooner, since I probably will have to visit the L.A. office every now and then."

The times Michael mentioned that Amanda was in L.A. she apparently worked nonstop since Marcia never heard from her after their first meeting. She thought about pursuing a friendship with Amanda by reaching out but recognized her own ambivalence and didn't do it. She tried to imagine a cozy evening with the three of them dining together but it was never a comfortable thought and she let it drop.

*   *   *

Twenty minutes after leaving Lina Padilla's office Michael was still moving in and out of the two right-hand lanes, trying to stay a little ahead of the flow of traffic. At the crest of the hill, past the Mulholland exit, they started heading down into the valley. As Marcia turned and wiped the drool from Max's sleeping face, Michael touched her arm and asked, "Want to talk now?"

"Yes. We have to decide if we want to wait for Lina to come back from vacation or if we want to see the other specialist, whatever his name is."

Michael nodded, briefly looking over at her. "Yes, of course. I know that." He inhaled deeply. "There are obviously pros and cons to waiting for Lina. She was so highly recommended by Dan and we all liked her so much. But I still want to call a couple of the liver people I worked with in New York, even if they're adult hepatologists. I would guess that liver people know liver people. And then there's the radiologist who's a liver expert, the one your father set me up with when I had that liver case a while back. Remember? Maybe they can refer us to some people out here." He turned to her, but she didn't say anything.

Max piggy-snorted but this time they didn't laugh. After a while Michael continued, "It's time we talked to your parents. We need to tell them what's going on, don't you think?"

"And your mom. We need to tell Margit."

"Yes, of course." He always dreaded bringing bad news to his mother who, ever since his father had died, never regained her once optimistic and cheerful outlook on life. But it had to be done. "We'll just get the very best person we can, that's all. If we need to go somewhere else that's okay. We can go to Boston, Mayo, wherever. But let's decide now and get started with whomever. I don't like feeling undecided, unresolved . . ."

"I agree. I really liked Lina. She made me feel a little more secure. I wish the timing was better."

"But it's not. It is what it is. And, if you want, I'll skip the retreat this year. There are a few people from Chicago and New York I wanted to meet, but it doesn't matter that much. I can talk to them over the phone," Michael ran his fingers through his hair.

"No, I was being silly." She touched his hand. "We can go. I'll call Lina tomorrow and if she says Max is up to going, we'll go. And if she thinks he isn't, you'll go without me. Definitely. It's fine."

"No, screw the retreat. It doesn't matter."

"No, really, I mean it. We'll go. It might be a nice change. Max will enjoy it more this year. He was still too young to notice much of anything last year."

As Michael moved toward the exit ramp a red Mercedes sports car came up fast behind them and honked impatiently. "Fuck you," Michael snarled, turning to glare at the driver, a middle-aged black woman, silver hair carefully coiffed. Marcia shot a glance at him. It was as if an alien creature had just inhabited her husband's body. She hadn't seen him that angry in a long time and she felt a little fearful without knowing exactly why.

Michael drove down the off-ramp and waited for the light to change on Ventura Boulevard. "Fuck," he muttered at nothing and nobody, touching his hairline.

"Michael!"

"What?" The sharpness in his voice sliced the space between them. She was still staring at him. "What?"

"Why are you so angry?"

He closed his eyes for an instant, then shook his head and whispered, "Sorry, it just suddenly seemed as if there's too much happening. And Max . . ." He quickly glanced at her and then refocused his eyes on the road. "I just feel awful. Like a bucket of awful was poured on my head."

"I'm going to call Lina tomorrow to ask her about going to the retreat. But I don't want to wait until she comes back from vacation. I want Max to see the other doctor now. I want to get rid of the indecision as much as you."

"Yes, hon." He nodded, a weary smile on his face. "Yes, you're right. That's what we should do. Yes."

Michael didn't go back to the firm when they got home. He went directly upstairs to his home office while Marcia fed Max and prepared their dinner. *It's a rare weekday night when he's home for dinner. It's dreadful that it took something like this to make it happen.*

* * *

51

It was three months after Michael had started the new job in L.A. They were having an early Sunday dinner out on the patio.

"You know, I really thought they might be a little more laid-back here, but I guess lawyers are lawyers." He poked his index finger in the air as if to make a point. "I think we actually work even harder here. In New York a lot of lawyers have a martini or two with lunch and then after work everyone hits the bar. Half of my office used to end up at O'Neill's on Third. Or some other bar, some other dive. To tell the truth, one or two guys got wasted at lunchtime. Women too. I'm not sure they work as hard as they think."

It was the first time Michael had conceded that he worked long hours in Los Angeles. After too many overcooked, dried-out salmon steaks on the grill Marcia was not going to let it pass. "I thought you would try to come home earlier. The only time I really get to see you is on weekends. And even then you're working. I sometimes think I wouldn't see you at all if you didn't like sex."

"What are you talking about, Marsh? I'm really working hard. If I'm going to make it at Caney I need to put in the long hours. I'm doing this for us. You know that."

"You keep telling me how Todd and the other partners are there all the time also. Is this the kind of life we're going to have together? I'm not sure that's what I signed up for."

"Fine," he shoved the table, rattling the plates and the wine bottle before abruptly standing up and walking into the house. "Fine," he repeated as he went upstairs, knowing that Marcia probably couldn't hear him.

Marcia picked at her fish for a while, taking a forkful or two. After a sip of wine she took both of their plates into the kitchen and threw the dinner into the garbage.

After that, at least for a while, Michael did come home early enough to play with Max, and to sit with Marcia and talk before they were exhausted at day's end. They had sex a little more often, at least for some months. But slowly it was clear that the workload didn't go away, it just moved from the office to home.

*   *   *

As evening fell it cooled down considerably, reminding them, as it often did, that Los Angeles was basically a desert and nights are cold. After dinner, when Max was already fast asleep, they sat in front of the fireplace with their coffee and what remained of the dinner wine.

"I'll come along when you take Max to the new liver doc, Marsh."

"Yes, please. I'd really like that. I really would like you to be there."

Michael put his arm around Marcia and pulled her close. "Marsh, we're going to get through this. We'll be fine. Max will be just fine."

"Yes," she said, forcing a smile on her face but still only a heartbeat or two away from tears.

CHAPTER EIGHT

*M*arcia could immediately tell when her mother wanted to take charge. Since her marriage to Michael it was less frequent, perhaps because Barbara recognized Michael's need to be in control was more immediate.

During the three days since Lina Padilla had arranged for them to see a second pediatric hepatologist, Marcia spoke on the phone to her mother every day and a few times a week to her father. Barbara, as usual, wasted little time on solace in their early conversations. Alan, also as usual, was loving, comforting and supportive, but didn't help with the decision.

"Perhaps you should bring Max to New York," Barbara suggested.

"No, I don't think that would be so easy and, besides, we can't see any special advantages to going anywhere else. As far as we can tell—and Michael and I both spoke to Dad about it—we'll get good care here, as good as anywhere." Barbara was silent. "There's a lot of liver transplant experience here, if it comes to that."

There was still no sound. Marcia had called her mother's cell phone and she wondered if the connection had been broken. "Did I lose you?"

"No, I'm here."

"Where are you?"

"I'm in the extra room, Frank's old room. I was going to use the treadmill for a while. I just didn't realize we were talking about a transplant. Does your father know about this?"

"I'm sure we told him. But it's not definite, it's just a possibility. I shouldn't have mentioned it. We don't know for sure."

"That's pretty serious, don't you think? I suppose I didn't really understand that Max is that sick."

"*May* be that sick. *May*. We don't know yet. Not for sure." Sitting at the kitchen table Marcia traced her fingers lightly along a dish towel's floral pattern.

"And you said you were seeing another doctor somewhere else, is that what you said?"

"Yes, that's right. At Kates-Spencer Medical Center, in Beverly Hills. The doctor we saw at UCLA, Lina—the one who's going away—referred us to someone there."

"Well?"

"Well what?"

"What if he needs a transplant? Then you're not at UCLA."

"They do transplants at Kates too. Lina seemed fine with that. She assured us Maxie would be fine at either hospital. It's actually a bigger hospital than UCLA's, and they do a lot of transplants there. She said transplant patients go back and forth, I'm not sure why. I didn't ask for details. The doctor we're seeing worked with Lina for a number of years before going over to Kates to start up the pediatric transplant program. We're comfortable with this. Michael and I discussed it for a long time. Dan Fogel also emphasized this guy's great. Daddy spoke to somebody too, I think it was Dr. Schiffman or Shaffner or something like that, the big liver doctor at Sinai. We're okay with this. Really."

Barbara didn't respond, so Marcia nervously rushed on. "Lina actually said he was the one she would go to if one of her children had a liver disease."

"Okay, I understand. I do." A pause, then Barbara coughed and sighed. *Is she crying?* "Marcia," this time her mother's voice was quite raspy, "are you sure we shouldn't come out?"

"No, no, not yet."

"It's not a problem. If Dad can't come right now, I can fly out and help you."

"Not yet. We may need you—we *will* need you—before too long, but not quite yet."

A long silence and then, barely audible, "Okay."

Marcia now realized there was music playing in the background, a Chopin impromptu. "Is that one of your recordings?"

"Good God, no. I never listen to myself. That's Rubenstein. Chopin and Rubenstein."

"Quite a pair."

"Yes." Another pause, and then, "I could so easily just get on a plane . . ."

"No." Marcia raised her voice a little, rolling her eyes and looking up at the ceiling. The last thing she needed right now was Barbara taking charge, yet she was acutely aware that Barbara might get on a plane no matter her objections.

Marcia's mother faced life the same way she faced her music. When Marcia was about twelve she and her father had watched *Midway* on a movie channel and, for a long time afterward, she imagined her mother commanding those around her from the bridge of some great warship. Nimitz of the Steinway.

"Really, Mom. We need to find out more about what's going to happen with Max. I promise we'll call you for help when we need it."

"All right, Marcia, that's fine. Whatever you say, my darling girl." Barbara's voice was strong and forceful again.

When the conversation ended Marcia's neck muscles relaxed and she felt the tension ebb. She put the kettle on for tea. She loved Barbara and admired her more than her mother could possibly have guessed. Marcia took great pride in Barbara's accomplishments, envious that Barbara still had mastery of a fantastic repertoire that included not only Beethoven, Brahms, Chopin and Mozart, but also Bartok, Satie, Gershwin, even Scott Joplin, and so many others. She herself had never felt completely comfortable playing across the centuries, although she kept trying. She was most comfortable with the music of the nineteenth and early twentieth centuries. To Marcia it seemed Barbara could always push straight ahead into a score—any score—unswerving and confident, never giving up until she triumphed over it. Marcia had to forge a covenant with the music, with each and every note. She would do battle with the notes, the phrasing, the sound. Sometimes she would retreat, or every now and then even reluctantly surrender in what was, at least to her, defeat. But she always knew she would eventually return to the score that had vanquished her. Marcia didn't think about how close she might be to her mother in her own approach to life.

When Marcia was choosing a college Barbara urged her to go to her alma mater, pushing so hard that when Marcia received her letter of acceptance from Julliard she hid it for two days before even revealing that she had applied there. She had already decided, with her father's blessing, to go to Smith. She intended to major in music with a minor in art history before going on to get a master's in music theory and music ethnology at the Eastman School. Barbara reluctantly supported her choices.

Periodically she would play in public, both at Smith and at Eastman. Despite being praised for her performances she thought she was missing that feeling of excitement and exhilaration that was so obvious when Barbara performed. There was the constant feeling of not playing a piece as well as it should be played—as well as Barbara played it. Marcia wasn't convinced giving concerts was what she absolutely had to do with her life. After graduating from Eastman she was content to give piano lessons and to teach an introduction to music course at a junior college in New Jersey. She resumed her own lessons with Nadia Olenko at Juilliard, at first reluctantly and as an almost kneejerk reaction to her mother's steady nagging. Soon she realized how childish that was and how much she enjoyed working with Nadia.

If she was hesitant about performing she was the opposite about practicing. She still loved to practice for hours on end. Occasionally, begrudgingly, she would admit to herself she played very well, well enough to concertize if she wanted. Mostly she felt she'd reached the level of performance she was intended to reach, despite the high praise from both Nadia and, in her own way, Barbara.

Just before the California job came up for Michael she interviewed for a faculty position at Brooklyn College to teach music theory and music history, as well as piano. She thought she had a good chance of getting the appointment but when she became pregnant she decided to withdraw her application. Soon after it was out of the question when they agreed to move to Los Angeles. She told herself she would look for a teaching position and take lessons again in a couple of years when her baby was old enough for preschool.

The phone rang, startling Marcia from her reverie. She turned off the flame under the kettle and picked up the phone.

"Marcia, it's me again," Barbara said. "I'll be very quick. I just want you to know that your father is calling Andy Zeller, the head of liver transplant at Hopkins, and I'll talk to Libby Arthur, whose husband had a liver transplant in Pittsburgh. Also I want to stress that I won't push myself on you, I'll give you time, and we'll be there whenever you need us." For just a fleeting moment Barbara's voice caught. "And you'll be okay," silence for a second or two, and then, "and Max will be okay."

Marcia had to stifle an impulse to shout *Stop it, Barbara, stop taking charge!* But then she laughed and said, "I love you, Mom." She hung up the phone, wondering why she hadn't called her mother 'Barbara' this time.

When Michael called his mother the next day he did not tell her a transplant might be needed. He was in the living room and could hear Marcia preparing dinner, with Max's intermittent "Me help, me help."

Margit asked if Max was able to talk.

"Yes, Ma, he can talk just fine," Michael said, smiling. "Hang on a minute." Holding the phone away from his mouth he shouted, "Marsh, my mom wants to talk to Max."

Marcia opened the baby gate in the doorway. "Max, go in to Daddy. Grammy Margit wants to talk to you."

Max came running toward Michael, hands held out for the phone. "Grammy, Grammy!" Max grabbed for the phone.

"Yes, here, talk to Grammy." Michael handed him the phone which Max carefully studied from both ends before selecting the correct end to put up to his ear. He shouted, "Hello, Grammy! This is Max!"

Marcia came out of the kitchen and leaned against the door. "How is she?" she mouthed to Michael.

"Good," Michael whispered back, "she sounds good."

"Did you tell her?" Marcia walked over and sat next to him on the sofa. *Except for the slight yellow that's not always obvious, and the paleness, Max seems perfectly fine.*

"Yes, but I didn't go into any detail . . ." He stopped to listen to Max, whose tone of voice had become serious, even impatient.

"No, Grammy, Daddy *told* you before, they don't *do* that anymore. That was only *olden* days when Daddy was a little boy."

Michael and Marcia exchanged a smile, assuming Margit once again asked Max if the doctor had given him a lollipop. Marcia mouthed the word, "Lollypop."

"Yes, I do, I do." Max's answer to the "are-you-eating-your-vegetables?" question.

"Gotta go, Grammy."

Which is what usually followed the "are-you-eating-your-vegetables" question.

Max pushed the telephone back into Michael's hand and ran back into the kitchen. Marcia followed him and Michael heard the safety gate latch click.

"Ma?" Michael pushed his shoes off with his toes and put his feet on the coffee table. "Yes, he does. He sounds good. He's fine."

*   *   *

Michael glanced at his watch as he turned into the Kates-Spencer Medical Center parking lot. They were almost thirty minutes early for the scheduled time since he'd made sure to allow for heavy traffic. He looked over his shoulder at Max, asleep in his car seat, and then at Marcia. "Here we are," he said unnecessarily.

"Come on, sweetheart." Marcia kissed Max on his forehead as she lifted him into the stroller. "Here's Pooh, hold on to him." Max, fully awake now, hugged the stuffed bear close to his chest.

In the elevator a tall and frail old man almost fell over the stroller, his cane rapping wildly as he tried to regain his balance. Michael steadied the man, who murmured, "Sorry." Max looked around at all the people crowding them. He reached up to hold Michael's hand, his gaze fixed on a white-coated physician who, standing next to Marcia, was reading a medical journal called *Liver*. Marcia's eyes lit on the journal and she had to resist an impulse to put her hand on the man's arm and talk to him about Max.

The sign on the door at the end of the corridor said "Center for Solid Organ Transplantation, Liver Transplantation." To the left was a door marked with a long list of physicians' names, including Harvey Hirakawa, M.D.

As Michael put his hand on the doorknob Marcia pulled at his arm, leaned close to him and whispered in his ear, "Mikey, let's go home. We can come back. I really don't want to be here."

Michael looked at her and then down at Max. "Marsh, don't start. We need to be strong. You know that." He opened the door for her to push Max's stroller into the waiting room.

She sighed, feeling acutely uncomfortable, even desperate. She hadn't really meant that they should leave, she'd just wanted a little tenderness, a little encouragement. *I just need a hug. I'm scared.*

Harvey Hirakawa met them at the door to his office. He looked far more youthful than his almost fifty years. He was a slightly rotund man an inch or two shorter than Michael and his hair was cut short. His light-blue lab coat covered a lime green shirt set off by a yellow tie that was covered with assorted Disney figures. Donald Duck stood at the center of it, contentious as always, his almost-arms on his hips, one almost-hand clenched, his blue cap slightly askew.

Michael had read about Hirakawa in the *Directory of Medical Specialists* and was satisfied he was more than qualified. Born in 1954, he had done premed at UCLA and then gone on to Stanford Medical School. His residency in pediatrics was at Children's Hospital in Los Angeles. After that he completed a fellowship in pediatric hepatology at Boston Children's, returning to Los Angeles almost twenty years ago to work at UCLA before moving to Kates. His background put Michael at ease. When he showed photocopies of the information to Marcia she said, "Yes, that looks good. I was sure Lina would send us to somebody who was excellent."

The walls of Hirakawa's office displayed only a few diplomas and certificates but there were six awards for teaching. There was also a medal Hirakawa apparently won as a teenager while on the swim team at Beverly Hills High School. Mostly there were photographs of children of varying ages and races and, sadly, varying degrees of illness, accompanied by brightly colored cards: *Thank you, Dr. Harvey,* with a Crayola house and a stick-figure family; *Thank you, Dr. Harvey,* on orange construction paper with blue and green flowers; *Thanks you, Dr. Harbey,* painstakingly printed, each letter at a slightly different angle and in a different color; Muchas *gracias, el doctore Hirakawa,* with a stick-figure girl waving the barely recognizable flag of Mexico, purple where green belonged.

A colorful quilt partly covered with toys and books was on the floor in one corner of the room. Max briefly looked over at it as the three adults sat down together in front of the desk, arranging themselves in a half-circle. Max climbed onto Marcia's lap and began sucking his thumb, something he had stopped doing many months ago but sometimes reverted to when in an unfamiliar setting.

"Well, Max, I've heard a lot about you from Dr. Dan and from Dr. Lina." Dr. Hirakawa held out his hand for Max to shake. "It's good to meet you."

"Dr. Dan hurt me," Max pointed to his arm where blood had been drawn.

The liver specialist smiled at Max. "Well, young man, now I certainly know what we should not do."

"Yes," Max said solemnly, his mouth shutting tight as soon as the word was out, so earnest that Michael and Marcia laughed, causing Max to pout.

Hirakawa smiled even more widely. "I would be very happy if you would call me Dr. Harvey."

"Dr. Harbey." Max wrinkled his brow and thrust his lower lip forward as he contemplated what to do, and then he nodded and said, "'Kay."

They reviewed Max's history, Max seeming to follow every word before they went into the small examining room adjoining the office. This time the steps leading up to the examining table were just varnished wood— no cartoons—but Max didn't seem to notice and promptly scrambled up to sit in the middle of the examining table. *Already an old hand at this*, Marcia thought, knowing she could very well cry if she didn't watch herself. *I don't want crying to become a habit.*

After the examination, which mostly consisted of Hirakawa gently pushing his fingers into Max's abdomen just below the ribs on both sides, they went back into the office. Marcia walked Max over to the blanket of toys and gently urged him to sit down and play. She could tell he was tiring and she angled her chair so she could keep an eye on him while talking to the doctor.

Hirakawa eased himself into the maroon leather chair behind his desk. Max's chart, so far consisting of only a dozen or so pieces of paper, was lying in front of him. "I'm going to tell you what I want to do, why I want to do it, and when. I need you to ask questions. No matter how much I try to cover everything, I will inevitably forget something or say something in doctorese or think I've already explained something when I haven't."

He half-rose in his chair and looked down toward Max, smiling at Michael and Marcia, one by one, as he sat back down. "First thing we're going to do is repeat the tests. I don't doubt their accuracy. Dan Fogel uses a perfectly reliable laboratory and the lab at UCLA is also reliable but I don't want to go to step two until we have double-checked step one. Also, I want to order a couple of additional tests. Similarly, we're not going to go to step three until we've double-checked step two." Harvey pulled some forms from his top drawer and started filling them in. "He's going to need some x-rays, including one series that requires us to inject a special dye into his vein. Depending on what we find on those studies, but probably inevitable no matter what we find, he will need a liver biopsy. I know Lina already discussed this with you and we will discuss it more when we get to that step."

"Dr. Hirakawa?" Marcia leaned forward, brushing a strand of hair away from her face. Michael suddenly realized she was wearing the same blue dress, the same earrings, the same pearl necklace, no doubt even the same shoes she had worn for that first visit to Dan Fogel. He wondered if this was intentional or if she had pushed at least part of that first frightening time out of her mind and had just put on her "doctor visit" outfit.

"Just 'Harvey' is okay. We may be spending a lot of time together and unless you have some objection, I'm planning to call you by your first names."

"Okay, no, that's fine, Harvey," Marcia stammered, before asking, "Do you have any idea what Max might have at this stage?"

"Yes, sure. Everything I've seen from Dr. Fogel and Dr. Padilla, the tests they've already done, the alkaline phosphatase and the other tests, tells me Max has something wrong with his bile ducts, the structures that drain the bile from the liver into the intestines. Let me show you." From behind his desk Hirakawa pulled a laminated poster-sized anatomical drawing of a liver and the upper abdominal organs and pointed to the illustrations as he spoke. "This big brown thing is the liver. On the right side of the belly. The liver is one of the key organs in the body, controlling a lot of processes—a good part of metabolism as a matter of fact—and it also makes a lot of substances, including bile, some proteins, blood-clotting factors, other things. By and by we'll talk about some of the things the liver does but for now let's just concentrate on the bile ducts. Okay?" Again he waited for them to nod their assent before moving his hand to the right side of the chart. "This is the spleen. The size of the spleen tells us about the liver, so you'll hear us talk about that also."

Max left his toys and made his way over to Harvey's desk, curious about the diagram. "What that?" he inquired, leaning on Marcia's knee and pointing at the chart.

"That's a picture of what people look like on the inside," Michael replied. "Let's just listen to Dr. Harvey and hear what he has to say."

Hirakawa looked right at Max. "You can ask questions, Max. Why don't you sit up on your mother's lap? You can ask about anything you don't understand."

"What that?" Max pointed again at the picture.

Dr. Hirakawa tried a different approach. "This is a drawing that was made by an artist. You know what an artist is, don't you, Max?"

Max nodded vigorously, bumping his chin on his chest with each nod.

"That's good, Max. So this artist drew this nice picture of some of the things inside your body."

"I listen to Dr. Dan's specascope."

"Did you hear your heart beating with the stethoscope?" Max nodded even more vigorously. "I have the heart on a different picture. Do you want to see the heart picture?"

"That 'kay," and Max shrugged, got down from Marcia's lap and started back toward the toys.

"Max, hold on, I would like to do a few tests on you." Max looked at his father, who nodded, before he turned back to Hirakawa. "I will always tell you what is happening and I will always tell you if I think it might hurt."

At that, Max put his arms out to his mother and tears started to form. "But I don't think it will hurt you, Max." Max turned his head to Hirakawa, questioningly, but his arms were still in midair as he waited to be picked up. "I'm going to put some medicine on your arm that will not hurt at all. It might be cool, like cold water, but it won't hurt even a little. It will make your arm a little numb, and that won't hurt at all, and then, after about ten or fifteen minutes, I'm going to take a little blood from your arm and that won't hurt either." Hirakawa hesitated, watching the corners of Max's mouth turning down, and then said, "I promise, Max."

Hirakawa opened his desk top drawer and took out a tube of ointment. "Here, let's rub this on your arm and then, in just a few minutes, you won't feel a thing. That's not such a long time. You can go back and play with the toys while we wait for this to work. Is that okay?"

A tentative "kay" escaped from Max. When Hirakawa came over to him Max readily offered his arm for the ointment and then recoiled briefly as the chilled gel touched his skin.

"You can go back and play or you can stay here. Is that okay?" Max nodded affirmatively, but not as vigorously as before. "I'm going to mostly talk with Mommy and Daddy again." Max looked uncertainly at his parents and then at Hirakawa. "Or you can stay and listen." Max thought a moment longer then turned and went back to the toys.

Hirakawa resumed. "The bile gets into these green structures, they are not really as green as on the picture . . ."

Marcia could only focus on the occasional familiar word that resonated—bile, bile duct, intestine. After a while, Hirakawa interrupted his explanation to ask, "How are we doing?"

"So far, so good," Michael said. Marcia added, "You're explaining everything very well. I'm just not sure I can absorb it all." Her face was expressionless as her hands gripped the arms of her chair.

"That's fine. I can explain it again whenever you want. Don't worry about it just yet. Now," Hirakawa put the illustration down on the desktop and pulled out another one that reminded Marcia of an Escher drawing, "it gets a little more complicated." Michael and Marcia inched their chairs closer. Marcia kept her chair positioned so she could still see Max who was now lying on his back. His thumb was in his mouth as he pulled at the Velcro clasp on his sneakers with his other hand, that leg extended up in the air at an almost 90-degree angle.

"This picture shows what the liver looks like through the microscope. This part is usually a little harder for people to understand. It's kind of abstract so we can certainly go through this more than once if you'd like.'" Hirakawa swiveled his chair slightly and pointed to a projector sitting on one of the bookshelves. "I can give you a show on the slide projector but I think these diagrams do just as well."

"Thanks," and "Thank you," came simultaneously from Michael and Marcia. Marcia looked again over to Max whose eyes were now almost closed despite his obvious struggles to keep them open. She and Michael had always enjoyed watching him when he was trying to stay awake, willing his eyes to open wide when, again and again, his eyelids drooped downward. Now it only added to her sadness.

"These brown objects lined up one after the other are the liver cells. That's where all the liver products, including bile, get made." As Hirakawa droned on Marcia felt herself getting drowsy, her own lids getting weighty. "We okay?"

"Good, we're good." Michael reached over and held Marcia's hand but her stare remained glassy as she had stopped following Hirakawa some moments ago.

"I tend to sound like a not too exciting textbook and I suspect I might be putting you to sleep, as well as Max. Let's stop for now. We can do this part another time. Any questions?"

"Which part is Max's problem?" Michael pointed a finger in the general direction of the drawings. "The liver cells or one of the bile ducts?"

"Yes, well, from the test results it looks like it's the bile duct system. That's the alkaline phosphatase test." He looked at Marcia. "You've heard about that?"

She nodded. Her throat felt very dry but she didn't want to interrupt the discussion to ask for some water.

"That finding in the blood, the elevated alkaline phosphatase," Hirakawa pointed at the diagram again, "indicates bile duct injury. But we need to make sure."

Marcia cleared her throat and, her voice husky, said, "Lina Padilla said the ultrasound was normal. There were no changes in the bile ducts."

"Yes, that's true, but—say, would you like some water? I have some right here."

"No, no . . . well, yes, maybe. Thank you."

Harikawa filled a glass from a decanter on a sideboard behind his desk and gave it to her. She took a few gulps and then passed the glass to Michael who also drank.

"Where were we?" Hirakawa asked, filling another glass and handing it to Marcia.

"Ultrasound."

"Ah, yes. It's a good first step because it's so easy and so quick, even though it isn't sensitive enough to answer all the questions. I think this is a good time to draw some blood. If you'd like to wake Max up we can do it now and then talk some more."

When Max was fully awake and also had some water to drink, Hirakawa came from behind the desk and sat down next to him. Max was leaning almost nonchalantly on the arm of Marcia's chair but, at the doctor's approach, Max quickly climbed into her arms and hugged her tightly as tears threatened, then fell. Marcia wrapped her arms around him, tears welling in her eyes as well, and Michael knelt at his side. "Max, Dr. Harvey made it so it won't hurt. Don't you remember?"

"Max, won't you give me a chance?" Hirakawa added.

The tears stopped and, as he nodded affirmatively, Max hugged Marcia even more tightly. When Hirakawa inflated the blood pressure cuff and inserted the needle into a vein a few seconds later Max still did not cry. When Hirakawa said, "See, that wasn't so bad, was it, Max?" as the blood started to flow into the first tube, Max concentrated on keeping his arm as still as possible. He stared as one tube with a red stopper filled, and after that another tube with a purple stopper. As the blood pressure cuff deflated and Hirakawa removed the needle, pressing a gauze on the venipuncture site, Max resumed crying.

Applying a Donald Duck band-aid Hirakawa asked, "Did that hurt, Max?"

Max frowned and a few more tears escaped from the corners of his eyes, but he shook his head side-to-side and said, "No."

Marcia squeezed him in a tight hug. She laughed, as did Michael and Hirakawa and, before too long, Max.

When they finished, Hirakawa walked them to their stroller in the waiting room and put a band-aid on Pooh, just like the one on Max's arm. "I thought you might have an old friend waiting out here for you," he said gravely to Max, adding, "You are a very fine patient, Max, and very brave."

But Max wasn't paying any attention to him, putting all his weight and energy into pulling his mother toward the door.

"You should plan on coming back here next week at the same time," Hirakawa told them. "Is that good for you?"

Never would be good for me, but Marcia nodded yes and, her voice cracking, added, "Thank you so much," in unison with Michael's "Thank you."

*   *   *

After they put Max to bed and cleaned up the kitchen Marcia said, "I want to play the piano for a while before I come up. Do you mind?"

"Of course not, Marsh. You know I love to hear you play."

She hesitated, before telling him. "I'm going to learn the F minor, the opus 57. I'll be at the piano more than usual."

"Great. Which one is that?"

He was accustomed to Marcia—and, of course, Barbara—always referring to piano pieces, symphonies, chamber music, whatever, by the musical note and opus number, more often just the opus number. Marcia explained the system to him years ago, but he still thought it was a bit snobbish and inconsiderate when they used this terminology knowing most people, himself included, usually recognized classical pieces by the names they had been given or by the symphony or sonata number.

"A Beethoven sonata, the *Appassionata*. You've heard it, I'm sure. I started to learn it years ago, when I was in college, but just couldn't do it. I never got it quite right. I want to work on it now."

"So it's not one of the easier ones?"

Michael enjoyed classical music, but he was still relatively unfamiliar with most of it. He preferred jazz and Broadway show tunes but appreciated the music Marcia loved as she gradually introduced it to him. In New York they had gone to many concerts—both classical and jazz—and when they moved to L.A. one of the first things Marcia did was subscribe to a series of the L.A. Philharmonic concerts downtown. By now he could recognize widely known pieces such as Beethoven's Fifth or Tchaikowsky's first piano concerto, as well as less known pieces that were familiar to him because he had heard them in concert or when Marcia played the recordings at home.

"No," she responded, "it's definitely not one of the easier ones." She ran her fingers over imaginary keys in midair. "It's not the notes exactly, it's . . . it's . . . it's *capturing* it. Capturing the music. Do you understand?"

"I guess."

"The last few sonatas are tougher, some of them much more difficult technically, like opus 106—the Hammerklavier—also 111, others, but this one is harder to play." Her voice softened to a whisper. "At least for me it is. It's harder to get the depth of it, the heart of it." She closed her eyes searching for the right words. "The Beethoven of it."

"Yes, well, go for it. I'll see you later." At the bottom of the stairs, he picked up the folder of papers he had left on the fourth step.

"The last movement. That's the hardest for me, really difficult, really tough," she raised her voice slightly as he headed up. There was an urgency in her tone that caught his attention and made him stop and turn back to listen as she explained. "Really difficult. Barbara always said that it was one of the most difficult pieces of all for her, that it took her the longest to learn. She used to tell me she always felt Beethoven was standing over her when she played this piece in concert. That it was different from having butterflies, it was as if she was trespassing." She smiled, enjoying the memory. "And she said there was only one time, I think when she was playing in Bratislava or someplace else near Vienna, when she felt he may have approved a little." Her smile broadened to a grin as she added, "Not in Vienna, of course. She said she thought he wouldn't have liked the way she played it in Vienna. I remember so well when she told me that. I was still very young, maybe eight or nine, and I was just starting to prepare the *Moonlight* for a recital."

"So why are you so set on doing this one?" He paused on the steps. "Why not one of the other Beethoven sonatas? I really liked when you played the *Waldstein*. Why not that one, or maybe Chopin?"

"No, I want to play this one. It's . . . it's really important to me. I'm not sure I can explain why, but it is."

He waited, seeing that she was about to say more.

"Maybe I need something challenging, something to keep me from obsessing about Max all the time."

"So this was one that Barbara played a lot?"

She didn't answer at first, then very quietly said, "Yes." After closing her mouth and inhaling deeply through her nose, she added, "it was one of the pieces she played in concert. One of the pieces she recorded."

Michael thought about commenting on this, about telling her she probably wanted to play it because her mother played it, but he just said, "Okay, Marsh, give it a shot."

She walked over to him and he leaned forward to kiss her on the forehead. "I need to do some work."

"Don't wait up for me, Mikey. I'll be up later."

*   *   *

Michael could smell the morning coffee as soon as he came out of the bedroom. Sometimes he made it himself, when Max was still sleeping and Marcia wanted to stay in bed to watch the *Today Show*. This morning he had slept a little later than usual. A deposition scheduled for ten o'clock was at the opposing lawyer's offices in Century City and he was going there directly from home. When he came into the kitchen Max was at the table trying to fit brightly colored plastic objects—triangles, squares, stars—into the appropriate spaces in a sparkly tray that was almost the same buttery yellow as the kitchen walls. There were diced red grapes in a small plastic bowl and a half dozen on the floor around Max. "How's it going, big guy?" Max's Tommy Tippee cup was on the floor and Michael bent down to pick it up and put it on the kitchen counter. Marcia was at the piano and he heard a few notes, a trill that sounded brittle to him.

"Good morning, Max." He leaned down and Max turned to him, hugged his neck and said, "Morney, Daddy." Michael kissed him and slowly rose. Looking at Max's skin he tried to put an exact name to its hue.

He carried his cup of coffee into the living room. Marcia, at the piano, took the pencil she had clenched between her teeth and wrote something on a page of the music. She barely looked up as she said, "Hi."

"Hi to you." He sat down in one of the living room chairs, facing her. "How's it going?"

She put down the pencil. "This is one tough piece of music. I haven't gotten past the first twenty bars yet."

"Then why take it on if you don't need to? Don't make life harder for yourself."

"Mikey, I told you. I *do* need to." She turned toward him, speaking slowly, as if choosing her next words carefully. "This is going to be very hard for us, very hard for both of us. For all of us."

"Don't focus on what's going to happen, Marcia. We don't know enough yet. We still need to find out a whole lot more before we let ourselves get too down."

"Yes, you're right. But there's quite a lot we know already. We both know Max has something wrong and we both know he may need a liver transplant." She looked directly at him, directly into his eyes. "That's a lot to know."

"Well, I want to postpone thinking about it until we have to think about it. Maybe tomorrow, but not today. Not yet."

"And I don't want to ruin your day. I want you to have a good day. Today is the first Shechter deposition, isn't it?"

He nodded, closing his eyes for a moment. "Yes."

"That's important. That's what you need to concentrate on today. And truly, I want you to have a really good day. I don't want any of our days ruined, but you know as well as I do we're going to have some tough days ahead and . . . and we need to be strong for each other and we need . . . I guess I don't know what, I just, I just know we need to be strong."

"Yes, of course. And we will be. We'll take care of each other and we'll take care of Max." He got up to cradle her face in his hands and look into her eyes. "We'll come out of this."

She took his hands down but did not turn away from him. "I suppose I reacted when you just said, you were talking about the sonata, you said I shouldn't make life hard on myself." She paused. "What I need you to know is that I am going to play the F minor. I am. I am going to practice it whenever I can and I am going to learn it and learn to play it well. For the first time in my life I feel I need to play. I've always liked playing, but now I *need* to play." Another pause. Then, in a barely heard voice, "It's really important to me."

He held her close, not saying anything.

"I just need you to know that," she murmured. "I need you to be supportive. That's all."

Later that day, just as the seven o'clock news was starting, Harvey Hirakawa called. She didn't want any polite chitchat but she wasn't necessarily eager to hear what he had to say. "You're in the office late, aren't you?"

"No, I'm usually here at this time. I still have to make rounds in the hospital. How is Max?"

"He's good. No change. At least I can't see any change. He's still not eating much except for chocolate chip cookies and grapes and raisins, and not so much the grapes, but no big change."

"Good, good. I would have been surprised had there been. Is Michael home?"

"No, not yet. He had a deposition today and I'm sure he'll be in the office late. Why are you calling? Or do you always call the day after an office visit?"

"Well, I just got the lab tests back and I thought I would call you to discuss them."

"Oh." She was aware of the flatness of her voice and of the room seeming to darken, getting grayer. "I thought . . ." She closed her eyes. *Please God, let it all be a mistake.*

"There's no emergency, I hope you understand that. Nothing we didn't expect, but the tests helped rule out a lot of things and pinpoint others."

"And?"

"And I want to set up a time for Max to come in and get some more x-rays and a liver biopsy. We'll do them all at the same time. It'll be easier on everyone, especially Max. But on you two as well. And even though it's not an emergency situation, I think the sooner we do the additional tests the better off we'll be. We may have some planning ahead of us, so the more information we have the better we can plan."

"Yes, I understand," she said, forcing her voice to be firm, not to waver, but inside her head she was screaming. *I hate this, I hate this, I hate this!*

CHAPTER NINE

*H*arvey Hirakawa tore the surgical mask from around his neck and the blue tissue-paper cap off his head, pressing them into a ball in his hand. "Everything went well. Max is fine. I'm going in the back to look at the MRI. We'll have the biopsy results tomorrow morning."

The three of them were in a small, bare, waiting room in the radiology suite. Marcia had picked up a *National Geographic* from two years ago but hadn't been able to concentrate. Now she just held it open at a randomly selected page.

Hirakawa dropped his crumpled surgical hat and mask into the wastebasket in the corner of the room. "You can go in. He'll probably sleep another half hour or so, but he's good, he's just fine."

He's not fine! Why does everyone keep saying that? If he were fine, we wouldn't be here. Marcia's silent conversations increasingly bore no relation to the words that came out of her mouth, sometimes not even to her actions.

Max slept for almost two hours. Marcia and Michael sat at the side of his crib in the recovery area, Michael reading some legal documents and Marcia struggling to concentrate on the *Times* crossword puzzle. And then he woke, smiling. It was the same cheerful Max but with the slightest slur to his words.

Marcia helped Max half-sit and gave him a paper cup of apple juice which he eagerly slurped through the straw, making a loud sucking noise when he reached the bottom. The intravenous line attached to his left wrist slowly dripped a pale yellow fluid into his arm. Max didn't seem to notice. Bridget O'Rourke, the nurse on duty, handed Max his Pooh bear, saying, "Yer probably want to be talkin' to yer friend now, do yer not?" Max, silently and solemnly, nodded "yes." The nurse pulled the sheets tight at the corners and picked up the papers that Michael dropped on the floor when Max started to wake up. "Yer just a little lovey, now aren't yer?" she said when he handed her the empty cup.

"More?" he asked.

"Darlin', yer can have all the juice ye want. I'll be comin' right back."

Max said, "Mommy Dommy," the lingering effects of the sedative making a jumble of his words, then plopped back down on the mattress and started giggling. "Mommy Dommy, Mommy Dommy," he said, breaking into peals of laughter. Marcia started laughing with him, so hard she had to wipe tears away. Michael watched the two of them with a broad grin on his face.

Bridget returned with another cup of juice for which Max eagerly reached. "Well now, yer must be a little vacuum cleaner sucking up all that juice," she teased him.

Max looked confused at first and then started laughing again. As Harvey Hirakawa came in, Bridget said to Michael and Marcia, "Some o' the children come out of this sleep like little drunkards, y'know? Ready for a fight. This one, he's just a little lovey."

"Is it okay if he laughs as hard as that?" Michael asked, as Max kept breaking into bouts of renewed giggles.

"Oh, yes, he's fine now. He can laugh all he wants." Before she left the room, Bridget patted Max's cheek. "Yer just a little lovey, aintcha?"

Harvey didn't bother with chitchat. "Well, there's no tumor. That's good," he told them.

"I thought there wasn't any chance of a tumor!" Michael exclaimed. "What are you talking about?"

"We said it was highly unlikely." Hirakawa gestured to the chairs in the room but neither Michael nor Marcia moved. "I didn't think there was a tumor, there was nothing on the sonogram and he isn't behaving as if he has a tumor. We still needed to be absolutely sure. We need to get to the right diagnosis. There are some really rare tumors that are so diffuse you can't really see them on films but they're not usually seen in children. They only show up on the biopsy." Hirakawa shifted his glance from Marcia to Michael and then back again. "I'm sure that isn't Max's problem. I probably shouldn't have mentioned tumor first. I just wanted to get it out of the way."

Michael glared at him. Marcia said nothing.

"Hey, what's the matter, Michael? This is good news," Hirakawa said.

Michael's expression softened and he shrugged. "I'm sorry, Harvey. Maybe I was expecting you to say that everything is normal and Max is perfect and it's all been a mix-up and we should just pack up our bags and go home."

"I wish I could, Michael, but you both know"—he looked at Marcia, and then back at Michael— "that isn't going to happen. Max is sick, he's going to get sicker, and he needs all our help."

"Yes, of course . . ." Michael paused, as if searching for the right words, then settled for "Yes, we know. We know."

"We did learn some useful things from all those imaging studies. The bile ducts outside of his liver look pretty good. Whatever it is, it's in the liver itself. So we really need to wait for the biopsy results."

* * *

"Todd, I just want to keep you informed about Max," Michael said to the senior managing partner.

"Good. I appreciate that. What's happening?" Todd waved at a chair in front of his desk. "Have a seat."

Todd Anderson's corner office was spacious, its size befitting his position in a major law firm. However, in contrast to other offices for partners at his level, it was windowless, located at the center of the top floor of the fifty-five story building the firm occupied. He displayed the typical photographs that highlighted his relationships with celebrities and politicians. He also had a variety of objects from primitive societies he had visited. Masks and spears hung on the walls and a five-foot-tall ebony tribal drum loomed beyond the far end of the table.

"Well, Max had his liver biopsy." Michael flopped into one of the shiny leather chairs, noticing how weary he felt.

Todd came around from behind his desk and sat in the chair facing Michael. "You want something to drink? Some coffee? Water?"

"No, no thank you."

"Scotch?"

"Nothing. Thanks."

"How's Max doing? And how are you two holding up? How is Marcia?"

"We're doing okay." Michael leaned forward, his hands clasped before him. "But depending on what the biopsy shows . . . well, I just don't know."

Todd nodded sympathetically.

"We'll just have to see. We haven't discussed next steps because they don't have an absolute diagnosis yet."

"Why don't you take some time off? If we need you for something, we can always call you."

"No. Thanks. I appreciate the thought, but I'm really busy and can't get away just now."

"Michael, we're all expendable, especially for a short time. How much time do you think you'll need?"

The phone intercom buzzed and Todd yelled toward the door, "Hold the calls, Elaine."

"No really. I'm okay. I don't need time," Michael said again.

"Michael." Anderson waited for Michael to look up. "You could use a break. How much time?"

"I'm not sure, we just don't know enough yet. It all depends on what they find."

"Well, all right. We'll just wait and decide when we have to decide."

"It's just, well, you know I'm working on two big cases, and a bunch of others. The Lanzillin case is huge, but it's coming along and so is the Frable case. And Schechter. And, you know, others not quite at the starting line."

"Look, I know you've got a plate that's more than full. A couple of plates. And I can't give you free passes to just drop them completely, you understand that. But we both know they won't go up in flames if one lawyer has to let go for a while. Judy Bellman or Sonia can take some of the load, at least for those cases that will need some tending in the near future."

Michael looked up at him, moved by the expression of support, and cleared his throat twice. "Okay. Yes, thank you, I'll talk with both Judy and Sonia today." He started to get up and then sat down again. "Maybe just a few days while we get the biopsy results and figure out what we're doing next."

"Good. I'm sure that will be fine. We know where to find you if we need you."

"Just for a few days."

Anderson deliberately changed the subject. "Did the Schechter deposition go okay?"

"Yes, that went fine, no problem. The plaintiff's attorney, Robbins, he's one of these old, white-haired country-boy types. I kept expecting him to pull out a corncob pipe."

Todd smiled. "Yes, I know Bernie Robbins—very well. The silver fox."

"Yes, well, I could tell he was playing with me, seeing if I would fall under his spell."

"And?"

"Andy Sheffield read over the transcripts and he thinks it went well. He didn't see any landmines."

"Good. And I expect most of the other stuff can wait, right?"

"Yes, for a little while." Michael wanted to acknowledge his appreciation for his boss's understanding and support but the words stayed somewhere just beyond reach.

There was a single rap on the door and Todd's assistant, Elaine, came in without waiting for a response. "Sorry, I need to interrupt. Congressman Steinmetz needs to talk with you, on line one. He says it can't wait. And your father called, nothing urgent, but I told him you would call him back right after this meeting."

Todd got up and put his arm around Michael's shoulders. "Keep me posted," he said, as he walked with Michael to the door.

*　　*　　*

"He's got something a little unusual. We don't often see it in someone as young as Max." Hirakawa's hands were clasped in front of him as Marcia and Michael sat down in his office to discuss the biopsy findings and go over the lab reports.

Marcia responded, "My dad says you never want to be told that you have something 'interesting.' Is unusual better than interesting?"

81

"Sorry?" Dr. Hirakawa tilted his head. Marcia was beginning to recognize this quizzical gesture as an indication that Harvey didn't quite get her New York patter.

"My father, he's a radiologist, an interventional radiologist. In New York. He says you don't want to be an 'interesting' case because it probably means no one knows what's going on or what should be done."

Hirakawa laughed aloud. "Yes, that sounds about right."

"Is that what you meant then?" Michael asked. "Is Max that kind of an unusual case?"

"Well, yes, he is, at least in some sense. I think we know what he has in his liver. We just don't know exactly why he has it. Let me explain." He got up from behind the desk and sat down next to them. "The pathology shows that Max's liver is demonstrating the changes of what we call sclerosing cholangitis. It used to be called, primary sclerosing cholangitis, PSC, which is what you'll mostly see on the internet. It's what we thought we would find in the ducts outside the liver but instead it's presenting on the inside of the liver, in the ducts in the portal tracts. That is really uncommon in children Max's age, especially for someone who has otherwise been healthy."

Michael furrowed his brow, trying to remember something. "PSC?"

"Yes, you know it?"

"I had a case once where the plaintiff, the patient . . ." Michael closed his eyes. "Let me think for a minute. This was one of my first cases. The PSC had been misdiagnosed, as I recall. I think the plaintiff had ulcerative colitis or Crohn's disease, or something like that."

"Yes, exactly right. PSC usually develops in a patient with IBD." Hirakawa halted, seeing Marcia's puzzled expression. "Inflammatory bowel disease, IBD. Okay?" He waited for them to nod that they were following him. "The thought is that the inflammatory condition in the intestines—do you guys know about ulcerative colitis and Crohn's disease?"

"Yes, sort of. Marcia's cousin, he's about her age, he has ulcerative colitis."

"Okay, good. I mean, not good for him."

"Of course," Michael said.

"I mean it's good because it gives us another piece in the puzzle. These things run in families. So I guess you know that UC, ulcerative colitis, is an inflammatory disease of the large bowel, probably some peculiar immune reaction. In some people it appears the immune reaction that attacks the bowel can also attack the bile ducts."

"How sure is he?" Marcia asked.

"Who? The pathologist?"

"Yes."

"He's pretty sure. He said it was a textbook picture. He said he would take a photo of it as a classic example. He's going to e-mail it to me."

"But Max doesn't have inflammatory whatever," Marcia said, a questioning look on her face. "He doesn't have anything like what my cousin has. I don't think Max has had diarrhea since he was an infant."

"Yes, well, sometimes, in some people, the PSC comes first. Before the UC. And sometimes the UC never develops at all. Sometimes the bile ducts are the only affected part and—"

"Can anything else look like this?" Michael asked before Hirakawa finished his sentence. "Should we get another pathologist to look at it? I know some people in New York."

"Yes, of course, we can do that. Our pathologist is pretty experienced. He just does liver cases. He's a well respected guy in the liver world but we can certainly get someone else to look at it, if that makes you more comfortable. It's not a problem for pathology to send it to someone else, but don't get your hopes up. He doesn't miss things very often—my impression is he never misses things—and he was quite clear about Max's biopsy. I looked at it with him in his office."

"I might still like us to get another opinion. He won't mind, will he?" Marcia said.

"What else looks like this?" Michael repeated.

"Well, you can get this picture from a few other conditions, but we ruled them out with the ultrasound and the MRI."

"Oh?"

"We're going to need to get an MRCP now."

"What's that?"

"It's like an MRI but it concentrates on the bile ducts and the pancreatic duct. It's a little more sensitive than the routine MRI."

"Why the pancreas?" Michael asked at the same time Marcia said, "What's wrong with his pancreas?"

"Nothing. Nothing. There's nothing wrong with his pancreas as far as we can tell, although these changes sometimes, uncommonly, affect the pancreatic duct also. The duct to the pancreas and the bile ducts are right next to each other. They get studied together. That's the *P* in MRCP."

Michael thought about asking what the *C* was, but didn't, and wondered why they hadn't done this while Max was asleep for the last procedure.

"We'll use that same sedative again to knock him out for a few minutes, just as we did for the MRI and the biopsy. It will help solidify the diagnosis."

"I thought he was sure, the pathologist. I thought you said he was sure."

"He is, but we need to do this for two reasons. One, the principal focus of this disease, this condition, is almost always in the bigger bile ducts, not the ones within the liver. The liver usually gets affected as a secondary response. We want to make double sure the big ducts are fine. Understand?" They nodded. "And we also need to know what those big ducts outside the liver look like so the surgeon is prepared."

Silence slammed down for a few moments and then Marcia and Michael spoke the same word at the same time. "Surgeon?" Except the word got caught in Marcia's throat so it was barely audible.

Hirakawa leaned forward, his arms resting on his knees, looking, Marcia thought uneasily, as if he would rather be somewhere else. "Transplant surgeon. I should have said that. We're going to be able to treat Max for a while. Antibiotics, other things. He'll probably feel better and will be less tired." He paused. "However, the pathologist thinks Max will eventually need a transplant, a liver transplant. That's my opinion also. Eventually." Hirakawa leaned forward. "It could be relatively soon or could be five or ten years."

Marcia took a deep breath that was almost a gasp, noisily forcing the air out of her nose. Knowing a transplant was a possibility hadn't prepared her for hearing it stated as fact.

"Marcia," Hirakawa reached out for her hand, "we talked about this."

She said nothing at first and then blurted out, "Can I look at the biopsy? I'd like to see it also. Do you think we can do that?"

He patted the back of her wrist, saying, "Yes, I'll set it up."

* * *

Amy was in Marcia's kitchen, glancing at the Arts section of the *New York Times*. "What an amazing city," she said, turning another page. "It must have been great living there. Look at all the concerts. And theater. Amazing."

Marcia closed the dishwasher door and stood staring into the backyard. "Yes," she said, distractedly. She picked up the dishcloth and wiped her hands, then folded it in half and then in half again before laying it on the counter.

"You want to talk about it or you want me to keep my peace?" Amy leaned forward, her chin propped on her hands. Her reading glasses—half-glasses—were perched on the end of her nose and her gaze was directed at Marcia.

"Amy, sometimes I feel like screaming," Marcia said, clenching and unclenching her fists. "I am so afraid. I understand all the words they tell me yet I have no idea what's happening. I know Max is sick but he doesn't seem all that sick. I'm just so confused."

"Brian says it's not that uncommon a disease in adults but it's really rare in children."

Marcia frowned, then sighed deeply. "That doesn't really help all that much, does it? I've heard that a few times, from the doctors and from the nurses. But what am I supposed to do with that piece of information? Is it so rare in children that he doesn't really have it? I'm not sure I understand why the level of 'rare' should matter."

"I'm sorry. I don't know why I said that. That is absolutely about the least helpful thing I could possibly have said."

Marcia came around the end of the counter and touched Amy's shoulder. "Listen, I didn't mean anything. I know you just want to help. You're my best friend."

Amy stood up and put her arms around Marcia and hugged her. They had never hugged each other before and Marcia felt a little uncomfortable. *Amy's not a hugger, is she?* But then she hugged Amy even tighter. *I guess I'm not usually a hugger either.* They stood there, not saying anything, the intermittent peals of laughter from the children in the next room floating to them, and then they separated. Marcia went back to the sink, picked up the folded dishtowel and started wiping the already spotless counter again. Catching herself, she abruptly tossed the towel onto the butcher block and turned to face Amy. "I'm sorry. I guess I've been a little irritable lately."

"Marcia, really now. I sometimes wonder if you even know how to spell irritable." Amy sat back down at the kitchen table and picked up one of the children's cookies. "I wish you *would* get a little irritable. I don't think I've ever heard you say an angry word. If it were me, I would be cursing a blue streak and throwing dishes."

"Well, I can tell you that I am pretty angry right now. I feel angry all the time and Michael's no help. He stayed home for a day and a half when we got the biopsy results, mostly working in his office, and now he's back to his old routine. He's almost never home, and when he's here, he'll listen to me for a little while and then he'll go back to his transcripts or depositions or whatever, sometimes while I'm still talking. Or he's constantly checking his email and texting on his phone."

Amy nodded, encouraging Marcia to continue.

"I guess most of the time it's really Michael I'm angry at, and that doesn't seem fair. But it makes me furious that he's so hard to reach. We used to be able to talk about . . . things, you know." She looked at Amy. "Do you know what I mean?"

"Maybe hiding from you—and even from Max—is his way of dealing with all this," Amy suggested. "Not that it makes things any easier for you, though."

"I know you're right, but how can I know what's going on with him if he won't talk to me about it? And . . ." she struggled to find the right words, ". . . and I expect more from him. I need more from him."

Julia called out to Amy for a glass of milk. "No, no more milk, Julia. We really should go home, Marcia. She's going to get cranky any minute now and I need to get dinner ready." Amy took a few steps toward the den and then turned back. "Hell, I can take Julia home and come right back as soon as Brian comes home. He can feed her and himself just fine when he gets home."

"Thanks, but I'm okay. Really." Marcia touched Amy's arm. "Just, thanks for being such a good listener."

CHAPTER TEN

The first meeting with the transplant team took place a week later in the surgical suite down the corridor from Hirakawa's office.

A half-dozen people, patients and family, were in the open and airy waiting room when they arrived. Michael went up to the desk and signed in as Marcia sat in a straight-backed chair and checked to make sure her cell phone was on in case Mrs. Brogan, the babysitter, needed to reach her. A door opened and a young woman, tall, blond and tan, came toward them. She wore a white lab coat over a beige pants suit and carried a yellow folder labeled "Kleinman, Max."

"Mr. and Mrs. Kleinman?" She extended her hand as they both rose. "I'm Valerie Cooper. Val. I'm one of the nurse coordinators. I'll be working with you." She gestured for them to sit down. "I want to talk to you for a few minutes before we go into the conference room, so you know what's happening." There was a slight singsong inflection in her voice and Marcia smiled. *A Valley girl named Val?*

Val turned to acknowledge several of the other people in the room. "Aldo, how're you doing? You look great. Edwin, you're looking a lot stronger this visit. Sylvia, how are you?" She waited for each of them to respond, then turned back to Michael and Marcia.

"First, this is the secret folder." She smiled broadly as she held it up. "But it will never be secret for you. I'm not even sure why we call it the 'secret folder.' It may fill up quite a bit and you can ask to read it any time you want. I don't have to be here and none of the doctors have to be here. You can just come into the office and ask either Patty or Claire for it." She indicated the two receptionists. "We are going to be throwing a lot of information at you today but we'll be going over all this stuff again later, and more than once. The easy parts, the hard parts, the scary parts, you will hear it all again and again."

"Okay," Michael leaned back in his chair and loosened his tie, "that's fine. What are we going to do when we go into the conference room?"

"Well," Val stood up, picking up the folder, "we'll be giving you a list of everybody's phone numbers, some things you should know about the hospital . . ." As she guided them through the door at the front of the reception area she turned and made an unhappy face. "And, of course, the inevitable paperwork and insurance forms will have to be dealt with."

Halfway down a corridor crowded with medical equipment and people rushing here and there, she led them into a small conference room and seated herself at the head of a long cherry-wood table. Michael and Marcia sat side by side at her right. Behind them, on a formica-covered table, were coffee, tea, soft drinks and bottled water.

"Even though Max is not ready for it, conceivably might not need a transplant, we want to prepare for it anyway. There's a lot of information and we should talk about it all."

Michael shifted in his chair. He looked at his watch and then up at the clock on the wall. He crossed one leg over the other and then adjusted that, reversing leg positions, twice. Now both feet were on the ground and he was silently tapping his toes. Marcia recognized the signs and knew he would soon start touching his hairline. "I thought we were going to meet the surgeons," he said.

"You will, you will. They're going to come in here in just a minute or two."

"Why don't we talk about all this stuff after we meet them?" Michael persisted.

Val looked at them and Marcia thought about apologizing to Val. *He's going to be tough to deal with.* Val leaned toward them. "Look, I know you want to move through this as fast as possible, believe me when I tell you everyone does. You just want it to disappear, to go away—"

Marcia nodded.

"And there will be times you want to scream at us, at me, because of the way we're doing things or not doing things or because of what seems to be the impossibly slow progress we're making, or really just because of . . ." She hesitated, searching for the right wording, settling for repeating, "the way we're doing things." Val waited for a response but there was none. "And there will be times, especially if Max does have a transplant, when you'll be mad at all of us, sometimes just one of you and sometimes both of you, and there may be times when we get upset with you. But in the end, we all want to make Max better. We'll always try to work together in a coordinated manner and hopefully we'll be happy with each other most of the time."

Marcia sighed. Michael started to say something but Val continued. "You'll see that we can be pretty flexible about a lot of things, but pretty rigid about others. We like to follow the same set of procedures because we've done them over and over and they're successful. For us. For our patients."

Michael put his hands together on the table, fingertips touching as if in prayer. "You know, if we seem a little antsy, it's . . . it's not—"

"Mr. Kleinman—okay if I call you 'Michael'?" He nodded. "You seem antsy because you *are* antsy. You *should* be antsy. I know that and it's okay. Really." She smiled for a moment, waiting for a responsive grin from Michael and, when none was forthcoming, she resumed in earnest. "I'm sorry we can't make all this move faster. Or better yet, make it go away, which I know is what you really want." She laughed. "I think I said that a little while ago."

Val stood up and went to the side table. "I need some water. Anything for you?" They both shook their heads 'no' so she sat down, unscrewed the cap and poured some water into a plastic cup. "What I want to talk about with you today is the way donor livers are obtained, the way the national organ allocation system works, and the possibilities for Max, if and when he needs a liver."

It took almost twenty minutes for Val to brief them about the transplant procedure and all the preparation that would take place beforehand. She told them approximately how long Max might be in the hospital and what to expect when he was discharged. She discussed the possibility of blood transfusions and urged them to arrange for blood donors. She reviewed the medications Max would likely have to take after the procedure. She told them they would hear all this again and again. Just as Val was finishing, others began trickling into the room to sit around the table, with Val introducing them by name and role. Harvey Hirakawa came in first and sat on Marcia and Michael's side of the table. Three surgeons followed, surgical caps still on their heads, one wearing his long white coat. Then another nurse coordinator, a nutritionist, a psychologist, a pharmacologist and someone they called the "patient representative," whose exact role Marcia was not sure she understood since they already had Val.

The head of the transplant surgery team, Milton Spellman, the one in the white coat, re-introduced himself by walking around the table to shake their hands. Then he re-introduced the two other surgeons at the table and mentioned they were missing one member of the team who was still in the operating room. Dr. Spellman had skin the color of coffee with more than a touch of milk, perfectly placed wavy gray hair, and a precisely trimmed mustache. He was soft-spoken and somehow elegant even in his rumpled teal surgical scrubs and starched white lab coat. Slowly and clearly, in a rumbling *basso profundo,* he began to review the options.

"Well, technically, it is easiest to use a whole liver from another child about the same size as Max. But those are hard to come by, especially at Max's age, and Max will have to be a lot sicker than he is now to qualify. And the donor blood type has to be the same as Max's. Another choice is what we call a 'split liver.' That's where we divide a single donor liver, almost always from an adult, into two, using it for two adults or an adult and a child. There are some technical issues with that and we will discuss them if and when we consider that option. Again, Max will have to be sicker than he is now to qualify." He stopped, looking at each of them as he stroked his mustache. "Finally, we can use a living related donor. Also some technical concerns with this. The donor could be either of you, or someone else in your family, or even a friend, as long as that person is healthy, has a normal liver, and, as I said before, has the same blood type as Max.

"Let's assume it's you, Michael. We take a portion of your liver, just a small part of it, the smaller left lobe, and put it in Max after we remove his liver. The reason I mentioned technical issues is not because the surgeons have to work harder." The corners of his mouth curled up for a moment in an almost-smile. Then he was completely serious again, leaning forward as if to compensate for his attempt at humor. "It's because there's more potential for post-operative complications than when we can put in a whole liver. We can talk about those complications in more detail another time, but first let's discuss why we would even consider a living related donor." He stopped and looked at them. "And you can interrupt me any time with questions."

"What about the risk to the donor?" Michael asked. "There have been some bad experiences, haven't there?"

"You bet. This is big-time surgery for both Max and any living donor. There is risk here. That's the tough part for you both. You have to weigh everything involved, then make a decision and never look back. There's nothing easy about a liver transplant."

Marcia glanced at Michael, and then asked, "What does that mean, Dr. Spellman? What do you mean, 'never look back'?"

"I mean we will help you understand as much as possible about what is happening, and what can happen, before we start on this journey together." He stopped and looked at both of them before saying, "And this will definitely be a journey." He leaned across the table to Marcia, one hand palm up and open. She didn't respond until he moved his fingers a little closer and then she put her hand into his, feeling uncomfortable as she did it, as if they were actors in some kind of performance. "We will be a part of your family. But there are things we may not always tell you. Not deliberately—there won't be any secrets— but because of the urgency of the moment or just because you're not here when we think of them or because we just forget. We will need to make some key decisions. We will do most of the driving on this journey but some of the hardest choices will fall on you. We can help you and try to support you, but your shoulders are going to bear the heaviest weight. Your shoulders and Max's. When we boil it down to the most important, the most elemental, to the bottom-line fact, it is only you two and Max who go on this journey." He paused and patted his coat pockets, looking for something, and shook his head slightly as he realized there was nothing there.

"So what I mean by not looking back is that you will have lives that will go on after the transplant. Until then you will have to deal with lots of things you can't even imagine. And it will be a lot easier for you, for us, for Max, if we don't spend time questioning and doubting the decisions we've already made."

"We won't look back," Marcia's voice was a little louder than she planned as she eased her hand from Spellman's. "What do we do now, though?"

"Well, the big advantage of using a living donor, as I am sure you understand, is that it is elective. We pick the optimal time. We don't have to wait for a cadaveric liver to come on the scene." He paused to look at them before resuming. "If living donor is an option for you, and it may not be, it may not be what either of you want to do, but if it is an option we should start testing any and all potential donors now, we should start as soon as possible short of emergency speed. We need time to find a blood type match and a healthy donor. And get a liver biopsy from the donor, if appropriate."

"It's an option," Marcia said quickly but almost inaudibly. She cleared her throat and said again, louder this time, "It's an option."

Michael nodded and concurred. "Yes, it is definitely an option. Just tell me what I have to do." Marcia forced herself to keep from turning to look at him. *It's not you, it's us.*

"Okay," Spellman resumed, looking from Michael to Marcia, "let me tell you a little about it. And remember, you or any other donor can change your mind right up to the day, the minute, of surgery. It won't be as if we have a contract that must be met, no matter what."

They both nodded. A beeper sounded and one of the other surgeons got up from the table and left the room. The door clicked and Marcia was acutely aware of how many people were sitting here, listening to Spellman. Almost as soon as the door closed Harvey Hirakawa's beeper also went off, but he just wrote something down on an index card he pulled from his pocket and returned his attention to Spellman.

"And I might note," Spellman continued, "that we are all a team here. We all—and that includes you two—we all will know what's going on as much as possible." He waited and then asked, "Any questions at this time?" Marcia shook her head "no" but Michael didn't react at all. "As I said, with a living donor," he went on, "we pick the time of transplant. With a whole liver donor, we don't. Another big advantage of having a living donor is that we can put the new liver in before the patient gets very sick, before the native liver, the sick liver, fails completely. The disadvantage is that we have to subject two people to surgery and each of them, the recipient and the donor, can have complications."

One of the receptionists came in and crooked her finger at Val who then got up and left the room. She held the door as it shut so there was no sound.

"What about the cost?" Michael asked.

Marcia turned to look at him. "Michael, I thought that wasn't an issue for us." Michael turned his head to her and said, "It's not. I just like to know." He faced Dr. Spellman again. "We're fortunate that we're well insured and, whatever it costs, we can handle it." He momentarily gnawed on his lower lip. "Mostly I'm curious about the living donor part," he resumed. "On the internet it says that sometimes insurers won't pay for the living donor. Like Medicare won't pay."

Dr. Spellman gave him a puzzled look, tilting his head to the side. "You know Medicare won't be part of the equation. You're both too young." He cleared his throat. "And Medicaid doesn't come into it at all. You're too affluent, I would assume."

"No, no, I was just using it as an example. Some insurers apparently won't pay either. Not just Medicare."

"That's actually correct. We have a financial coordinator, Maureen Nettles. She'll work with you on that."

"Yes, but how much could it be?"

"Well, I really can't tell you exactly. Each case is different. Not because of us, but because of the insurer. We have various contracts with the insurance providers. Maureen will review your policy and make an evaluation. If I could take a guess, without being held to it, I would say, depending on your policy, there could be out-of-pocket charges to you of a few thousand dollars to as much as seventy or eighty or more. At this stage I can't be more exact than that. But Maureen will figure it all out. Unless you have a distinctly unusual policy you probably won't have to worry about finances."

Marcia pursed her lips and looked at Michael, who shrugged as if to indicate that whatever it was they would manage to deal with it.

"So I guess what I'm hearing from you is that we should begin testing the two of you, and anyone else you tell us about, and then see where we go from there. If some folks are in other cities Val can speak to their physicians about what needs to be done." Spellman abruptly stood up.

"What does the testing involve?" Michael asked. They were all standing now.

"Blood tests, chest x-rays, some scans of the abdomen and liver and, as I mentioned, sometimes we have to do a liver biopsy. Anyone we consider will have to be perfectly healthy, with perfectly normal blood tests. We sometimes need a biopsy when the blood tests are not completely conclusive to make sure the liver is normal, or even when there is something unresolved in the medical history. Not every program does living donor biopsies, but we have found it useful. We tend to be overly cautious."

Michael shook hands with the doctors while Marcia waited by the door, anxious to leave as soon as possible. *Max is not yet ready for a transplant, they said. We can try to put it off as long as possible with antibiotics and other medicines. We want to be prepared. We need to start thinking about it. Just in case. To be prepared for the worst. Val told us this, more than once.*

They decided not to go out for dinner. Neither of them was hungry. On the way home Marcia took Michael's cell phone and called her mother. "Barbara, I think I'd like you to come out here, if that works for you." A pause, and then, "There's no big rush. Whatever's convenient. Yes. Just let me know. I'll pick you up at the airport . . . Yes . . . Thank you. Really, thank you. I'll talk to you later." But she didn't hang up right away. Instead she said softly and a little slowly, suddenly realizing how vulnerable she felt, how she wanted someone to take care of her, "Mom, this is more for me than for Max."

CHAPTER ELEVEN

*M*arcia often sat back while working at her desk and marveled at the breadth of information she was able to find on her computer. She loved the idea that all the great books might eventually be available online. She found more music scores than she ever imagined, including all the Beethoven sonatas, piano concertos, chamber music and more. Mozart, Brahms, Bach. Other composers work also. She wished someone would also add copies of all the original scores of the great pieces of music. The piano sonatas were well done and easily printable but they didn't show the notations Beethoven scratched on those first sheets in his chilly rooms. *How wonderful, how glorious, to be able to study the original scores of all the great composers without having to travel to Vienna or Paris or St. Petersburg.*

She usually visited the online sites of the *New York Times* and the *Los Angeles Times,* even though both newspapers were delivered to her front door daily. She searched the Web for dinner recipes, concert tickets, movie times, travel directions, and book reviews. She considered creating her own Web page devoted to the history of music but never got around to developing it. Three or four times a year she scrolled down the list of extension courses offered at the local universities even though she had yet to sign up for one. After Tower Records went out of business she easily shifted to buying recordings from iTunes and Amazon.

Since Max became sick her Web searches changed radically. Now she spent hours tracking down everything even vaguely related to sclerosing cholangitis. About the condition itself. About the treatment. About other bile duct disorders. About transplantation. About liver biopsies. About whatever else she could think of that could possibly relate to Max's liver. *To Max.*

When the email pictures of Max's liver biopsy came a few days later—*Harvey is so good about following up on things*—Marcia sat in front of the computer screen for a while before clicking on the first view. Rubenstein's version of opus 57 was playing on her computer's CD player, blocking the contemporary music playing in the living room. The onscreen images were preceded by a short paragraph from the pathologist, Arthur Warner, offering to discuss them by phone or in person. She read his message twice before clicking on the first icon.

Against a bright white background a gently curving pale red band crossed horizontally, filling the central third of the picture. There were some tiny clear areas in the band, along with two larger pale pink oval areas sprinkled with blue, which, without understanding why, she identified as the enemy. *That's my Maxie's liver? That's what's making my little boy so sick? Those oval areas are killing my son?* The thought of "killing" made her burst into tears, her chest heaving with the sobs. She stared at her right hand, still clutching the mouse, as it shook. The fingers and the hand seemed to belong to someone else, acting on their own. She moved her left hand to cover her right, as if comforting a stranger. She remained that way until the tears stopped, and then she steadied both hands by placing them flat on her desk. She turned her attention back to the screen.

What is that curve? A sine curve? No, not really. It looks like a meandering pink river. How do I read this, this symbol of . . . of what? Pain? Sadness? It's a hieroglyph. It must be saying something to me. Every image reveals something about its painter, its creator. But who is the artist here? Is it Max? What is Max's liver saying to me? Or do I really want to know? I don't know if I want to understand what those areas are, those pink boxes, that clear space. Are those the ones that are hurting Max? I don't even know if I want all the answers.

The house was peaceful. Michael was at work and Max was taking his mid-morning nap. The Rubinstein recording finished playing. Now she could hear the stereo in the living room. The same Roberta Flack CD was playing over and over again, "The First Time Ever I Saw Your Face." She often sang this song along with the record when Max was an infant, marveling at every bit of fuzz on his head, his bright blue eyes, his little upturned nose, those chubby, ruddy cheeks and the magically curving folds of his ears. "Killing Me Softly," the Flack song she loved most, the one she often put on when she was feeling sad, would be the next track.

But she didn't want to hear it. She didn't want the word "killing" to ever sound in her home, however beautiful the song was.

The following Monday Val telephoned and asked Marcia and Michael to come in. "We need to discuss donor issues," was all she would say. Before hanging up Val said, "Nothing to worry about. Really."

The lawn sprinkler started up, its rhythmic *ka-chung, ka-chung, ka-chung* nudging itself into her concentration. She went downstairs, turned off the CD player, picked up the phone and called Arthur Warner's assistant, Gloria, to make an appointment.

"Dr. Warner is out of town for two weeks. Can I arrange for one of the other pathologists to help you?" was not what Marcia wanted to hear. She hadn't prepared herself for that and her tears started flowing. *It's not fair.*

At first the line was very quiet. When there was no response Gloria said, "Are you all right? Maybe there's some other way I can help you."

"It's just," Marcia stopped crying, breathed deeply and coughed once. "Excuse me, I'm sorry. It's just that somehow I thought he would be here. It didn't occur to me that he might be away."

"Not a problem. Let's see if I can help you."

Marcia told the assistant her name and Max's name and how Dr. Warner had encouraged her to call and come in to see him. "How soon can I get an appointment?"

"I can schedule you for the day he gets back, but perhaps one of the other pathologists can meet with you in the meantime."

"No, thank you. No. I'll wait. I need to discuss my little boy's liver biopsy with him"

I need to discuss Max with him. I need someone to help me understand all of this.

CHAPTER TWELVE

"*M*ichael, you and Max have different blood types," Val began. "You won't be able to be the donor."

Michael's confusion immediately gave way to anger. "I don't understand. How can that be? I'm his father, aren't I? Just look at him."

"Of course you're his father." They were in Val's office, the half-folded laboratory report on the desk in front of them. "Your children don't always have the same blood type as you do. In the same way your hair color can be different." She turned her head to look at him. "You know that, don't you?"

As Marcia reached over to hold his hand Michael inhaled deeply and sat back, letting all the air out in a rush. "Yes. Of course." He ran his fingers through his hair. "I never understood it all that well but I do know it."

"You're type AB. Marcia is type B and Max is type B. Not a common type. I gather you have other possible donors being tested on the East Coast, is that right?"

"Yes," Marcia answered, "my parents—well, my mother's here getting tested, but my father and my brother will do it in New York and London. They have the information sheets you gave us. Also some cousins, but they both have small children and I probably wouldn't consider them unless as a last resort."

"That's fine."

"But it doesn't matter. I'll be the donor. You said I match so I'll be the donor." She looked at Michael, breathing deeply, her voice tremulous. "We've discussed all the possibilities."

"Wait a minute, Marsh," Michael leaned forward, "we still need to talk about this. There are lots of things to consider."

"What do you mean? What things?"

"Look Marcia, all I'm saying is we need to talk about this."

"I don't understand." Marcia looked from Michael to Val and back again. "What do you mean?" She looked as if she were in pain, half-squinting, her breathing labored.

"I'm not sure I want you to be the donor. I'm not sure I'm going to let you be the donor, that's all."

Marcia stared at him. "*Let* me? What do you mean, *let* me?" She stared at Val. "What does he mean? Why can't I be the donor?"

"Whoa, you two," Val's tone was soothing as she continued, "we're not there yet. We still have more testing to do. Marcia, we'll need x-rays and blood tests to see if your liver is normal. We still have to decide if Max even needs a transplant for sure and, if so, what the best kind would be for him. So we're really not there yet."

Valerie continued to try to mollify them until the end of their appointment, her calm and steadiness evidence she had witnessed many similar exchanges over the years.

Marcia and Michael walked in silence to the garage. When they reached the car Marcia glared at him. "What was that about? Just what was that all about?"

Instead of answering, Michael moved toward the passenger side door to help her into the car but she yanked at the door and climbed into the seat, ignoring him. He walked around the back of the car and got in behind the wheel, started the engine, backed out of the space and headed for home. Gripping the wheel with both hands, he looked straight ahead. After a while he pushed the radio button for NPR. Someone was talking about the housing market and a rash of foreclosures in the Midwest. He turned the volume down so they could just barely hear the commentators jabbering. Michael headed toward Benedict Canyon, avoiding the 405.

Marcia waited until they passed Santa Monica Boulevard. "Michael?"

"What?" His voice was sharp and he kept looking straight ahead.

"Michael?" Marcia brushed her hand over his fingers, still clenched firmly around the wheel. His jaw was tight and his eyes had that "wolf eyes" look and she felt as if the whole world had turned gray. She was sad for herself and sad for him. "Mikey," she whispered, "please talk to me."

They approached Will Rogers Memorial Park at Sunset and Cañon, a one-block long triangular oasis of lush green and shaded benches. Michael pulled into an empty parking space on the street. His foot remained on the brake until Marcia reached over, pushed the gear into "Park" and turned the ignition key off.

A family posed for pictures up on a little grassy knoll just to the right. Laughing and joking with one another in Spanish, two parents and their four children, all tanned with coal-black hair. Marcia was fleetingly cheered by them, but envious of their carefree happiness.

She turned to Michael and said again, more urgently, "Talk to me, please." *He looks so tired. He looks as tired as I feel.*

"Marsh," he began, but his voice was so hoarse Marcia turned and reached into the backseat for a half-empty bottle of water. She offered it to him but he didn't move to take it, his gaze still searching for infinity.

"Marsh."

She moved closer to him, reaching over the center console of the car to put her arms awkwardly around him, hugging him as tightly as she could. His hands stayed gripped to the wheel, but he turned his head slightly to kiss her forehead and then they both started crying. Marcia half-laughed, between tears, as she said, "I'm really getting good at this crying business, but you haven't practiced at all."

At that Michael let go of the wheel and put his arms around her, enveloping her until she was breathless. She gently freed herself and held both of his hands in hers. "Tell me what's going on."

He took a tissue from his jacket pocket, wiped her eyes and then his own, and then patted both of her cheeks until they were dry. "Marsh, I . . . I . . ." The tears came again but he kept talking, "I'm scared. I'm not sure I could manage this thing with Max if you weren't here to help. And . . ." He paused, his face seemed poised for more tears, then he breathed deeply half a dozen or more times. "And . . . I'm scared I might lose you." Now he took his handkerchief out to blow his nose. "I know I'm not easy and I don't always make time for you and . . ."

She put two fingers on his lips and said, "Sshh. Not now. That doesn't matter now."

"It's just . . . there was that case in New York a couple of years ago. The donor . . . they lost the donor and . . ." He stared ahead again and then abruptly shifted in his seat to face her directly. "I don't want to lose you, Marsh. I can't bear the thought of losing you. What if there's a complication? What if? You heard Spellman say donors can have complications. I've talked to people. It wasn't only that one case in New York. You heard about that one, didn't you?" The apprehension, the fear, in Michael's voice filled the air.

"Oh," she said it loudly, suddenly realizing what he was feeling, what he was thinking. She leaned toward him and rested her head on his shoulder. "Oh Mikey, you won't lose me," her voice barely audible. "I promise. They're just going to take a little piece of me," and then a little more forcefully, "just a little piece. That's all."

CHAPTER THIRTEEN

$\mathcal{B}$arbara covered the mouthpiece and held out the phone for Marcia, whispering, "It's Valerie. Should I take a message?"

Although the call interrupted Marcia's practice, she welcomed the break. She was on the verge of yelling at her piano, frustrated because she wasn't making the pedal respond the way she knew it should. Before going into the kitchen to answer the phone Barbara had been standing in the arched doorway listening to Marcia practice. Barbara hadn't said anything but Marcia knew all too well that, although she was getting the notes right, she wasn't getting the sound of the piece, the ever elusive *Beethoven* of the piece.

She reached out and took the phone from her mother who had been holding it to her chest. *What does Val want?* Almost three months had passed since their last meeting and Max was doing well. She knew he was still far from eligible for a cadaver donor. Marcia had been in and out of the medical center for various tests, most recently three days earlier for a scan of her liver, but she hadn't seen Val for almost a month.

"Yes Val, how are you?" She held the phone away from her ear, for Barbara to listen, but Barbara didn't move closer.

"Great, I'm great." Marcia tilted her head, listening to Val's responses. "We're fine. Max doesn't seem to have changed much since I saw you. Not that much better and not that much worse. Some days perhaps a little less tired. Harvey says his chemistries are a little worse but not significantly, whatever that means." Marcia walked over to the window and looked out at the pool. It was one of Los Angeles' rare rainy days and each drop seemed to float down very slowly, very deliberately, as if wanting to hit the surface of the pool on its own, to make a tiny solo splash.

"Good, that's good." *Get to it, Val.* "You want me to come in and see Dr. Spellman? Sure, of course. What's up?" Marcia faced her mother and shrugged her shoulders and repeatedly opened and closed the hand not holding the phone, exercising her fingers. Then, still listening, she frowned. "Something showed up in my liver in one of the films?" She looked at her mother as she repeated Val's words for Barbara's benefit.

Barbara leaned her head back against the wall and closed her eyes. She remained motionless except for the shallow heaving of her chest and the tears slipping down her cheeks. She made no sound. She didn't move to stop the tears, didn't try to wipe them away.

"It's benign?" Marcia asked Val, her voice suddenly hoarse. "You can tell by looking at the MRI?" Marcia shivered as she looked again at Barbara, her rock, standing frozen in front of her, a Gibralter shedding tears. The sight astounded Marcia. Her mother, her powerful mother, her incredibly controlled and incredibly controlling mother was no longer in control of anything.

"Yes, of course I'll come in to go over it." Marcia's voice caught in mid-sentence.

Marcia was confused. It was as if an earthquake had started but she didn't know where to hide.

There was no doorjamb to stand under to feel safe.

*   *   *

In the months after they moved to Encino Marcia occasionally felt small tremors, sometimes when she was sitting in the backyard reading. But they were never strong enough for concern and certainly not strong enough to make the evening news.

Michael was different. The first time he felt an earthquake was when it awakened him at about three in the morning. Max was almost four months old and was just learning to turn over.

"What was that?" Michael jumped out of bed, jolting Marcia from a deep sleep that the shaking hadn't penetrated. "We're having an earthquake!" he said anxiously, just as a second gentle wave passed through their house.

"Yes," Marcia yawned, "I think you're right." She turned over and pulled the covers up to her neck.

"Marsh"—Michael leaned over and shook her shoulder— "Marsh, I think we're supposed to get up and stand in the doorway."

Marcia yawned again. "Oh, Mikey."

"What? Wasn't that an earthquake?"

She reached over her bedside table and turned on the light, then sat up. "Mikey, they happen all the time, these little ones."

"Well, not to me they don't. Shouldn't we just check to make sure everything's okay?"

She eased the covers aside and stood up, yawning one more time, then rubbed her eyes with one hand and held the other out to him, smiling. "Okay, okay, come on. Let's check on Max."

Max was fast asleep, his bottom up in the air, his pacifier—his binky—resting between his chin and his hand. The covers were pushed through the rails of the crib. Marcia let the side of the crib down and felt his diaper to make sure it was dry. She then settled the cover over him and kissed his cheek. As she carefully pulled up the side of the crib Max snorted and rubbed his nose against the sheet. She looked over her shoulder and smiled at Michael, standing with his hand on the light switch. She walked over and put her arms around his waist as he turned off the light, leaned over and kissed her.

They stood in the doorway of Max's room kissing for a few seconds until Michael took an embarrassed half-step back and mumbled, "Morning mouth." She smothered the words with kisses. At first they were short pecking kisses and then deeper kisses, their tongues urgently pushing into each other's mouth. Her hand slipped into his pajama pants and she felt his penis quickly swelling as he slipped his hands under her nightgown and started caressing her nipples. They sidestepped awkwardly toward their bedroom, still kissing, holding each other. He let go of her only long enough to pull her nightgown over her head and drop it to the floor. With one hand around his now full erection, she untied his pajamas with her other hand and he stepped out of them. They sank together onto the bed. As she lay back she pulled him on top of her and guided him inside of her, their mouths still pressed together.

It was their most passionate lovemaking since Max had been born. When it was over they lay together, panting softly, their short breaths in rhythm. The light sheen of perspiration on their bodies cooled them as it evaporated.

When they both caught their breath, Michael said, "Now that's really feeling the ground moving." Marcia kissed him and laughed. "I knew you would say that sooner or later." He kissed her back and they made love once again, and it was almost as good as the first time.

That was also the last time they made love twice in the same night.

*   *   *

Marcia remembered that night, and Val's call, as she sat at the piano before starting her evening practice. *This is very much a different kind of earthquake we're having now. The ground feels so much shakier.*

Michael was upstairs preparing for tomorrow's work. He had the bedroom television on and she could hear some familiar theme music but couldn't remember the show to which it belonged. She briefly tried picking it out on the piano to see if that helped her recognize it and, failing, refocused her attention on the opus 57.

The fingers of her left hand moved slowly across the white keys, up and over and down into the spaces between the black keys, while her right hand slowly turned the pages of score. Back and forth, from middle C to the lower keyboard, she touched every key without striking a sound, her thoughts bouncing between the music and Max. Then she moved her right hand to her abdomen, to the space under her ribs. She pressed slightly at first and then harder, until it hurt. She wanted to feel whatever was there, whatever had shown up on the MRI. She wanted to grab it and squeeze it until it was completely gone. But all she felt was her self-inflicted pain. With her left hand she slowly pressed down on six black keys simultaneously, creating a harsh, ugly discordant noise.

I don't care what's on my liver as long as there's a little piece for Max. They said that's all he needs. Just a little piece.

CHAPTER FOURTEEN

"Now, I don't want you to get discouraged. This is just a temporary setback." Milton Spellman was in his surgical scrubs, the teal green almost iridescent against the metallic-blue leather of his chair. He had a large unlit cigar in one hand. Marcia sniffed once but there was no odor. "This is a relatively small, benign growth. You can still be a donor if everything else works out. Harvey Hirakawa tells me Max is still pretty stable and there doesn't seem to be any urgency." He waved his cigar. "Some transplant programs would disqualify you with this lesion, but I don't think that's necessary."

"How did I get it? What is it?"

"Well, it's called focal nodular hyperplasia. We don't know how you got it. It sometimes occurs in women who have used contraceptive pills for a number of years, but it also occurs in men and may not be directly related to the pill at all. We might never have known about it if we hadn't done the MRI."

"How common is it?" Marcia asked.

He waved the cigar again, this time pointing it at her. "This okay with you? I don't smoke anymore, between my wife and all the rules it just isn't worth it. But I do like to hold them between my teeth. Some people say even the smell of an unlit cigar bothers them."

She tried to say, "I don't mind" but couldn't find her voice, so just fluttered her hand affirmatively toward him.

"Well, good." He leaned forward. "Anyway, FNH—that's for focal nodular hyperplasia—is one of the most common benign liver tumors affecting women, but it's still pretty unusual."

"How do you know that's what it is? That it's benign?"

"Well, most of them have a characteristic imaging pattern."

"Imaging?"

"Well, yes, the MRIs showed the tumor pretty clearly with the typical central scar."

"Scar? Why does it have a scar?"

"Well . . ." *I wish he would stop saying 'well' so much. Professor Blue at Smith used to bellow 'well is an intellectual burp' and the word has irked me ever since. It's so annoying.* ". . . FNH probably develops because of some change in the blood vessels," Spellman continued, "some interruption of flow, which also causes the center to scar."

She looked at him for a moment, aware of the ticking of his desk clock: *Clocks don't tick anymore, do they?* Then she reached down into her bag and pulled out a notepad. "I'm not sure I was concentrating enough on that. Can you tell me again? I'd like to take some notes."

He moved a glass paperweight filled with tiny red, yellow and blue flowers from the front of his desk to the back for no obvious reason. "Of course. I was just saying there probably is some change in the blood vessels . . ."

There was a sharp knock at the door and Spellman's assistant looked in. "Your four o'clock is here."

Marcia put away her notepad and started to stand up, but quickly sat back down again and leaned forward. "I still need to ask you some things."

"Marcia, you take as long as you want. It's just the hospital administrator here for a regular meeting. He is probably going to tell me something I don't want to hear." He put the cigar into a large mahogany ashtray carved with an elephant head on one side. "You don't have to rush. If I'm really lucky, he'll go away."

Spellman answered all of her questions, looking directly at her while he spoke. "No, we're not going to biopsy it, we'll just remove it . . . Well, no, we wouldn't want to wait until we do the transplant. We prefer to take it out and let you heal up and then do the transplant . . . We might not want to do the transplant for many months in any event." He glanced at the clock and she started to stand, but he again waved her down. "Just checking the time. Sorry. Didn't intend to rush you. You finish your questions."

"How long will I be in the hospital?"

"Well, the surgery won't be that difficult. The tumor looks as if it is on a pedicle, a bit of a stalk, and we may be able to snip it off pretty easily, taking only the smallest rim of normal liver tissue. Probably just a couple, three days."

"Will I have a big scar?"

"No, I don't think so. We're not necessarily going to have to open you up since we'll be using laparoscopy, a small tube. Your tumor is a little larger than we usually take out by laparoscopy but we'll still try to get it that way. We might need a slightly longer incision than usual. Maybe a couple of band-aids instead of just one. I won't know for sure until we're there. Two or three days later you won't even know it happened." He continued with considerable more detail and Marcia bit at the inside of her cheek when her eyelids felt a little heavy. "You know, we wouldn't do this surgery if we weren't considering a transplant. FNH usually regresses if you leave it alone. I just want it gone before we resect your left lobe."

"Yes, I understand. I want it out also." She tugged at the hem of her skirt and looked directly at him. "Any effect on childbearing?"

"No, I can't imagine any of this will affect your ability to have more children. You will need to talk to your OB/GYN about whether you should ever use the pill again."

Marcia stood up and reached out to shake his hand. "Thank you, Dr. Spellman . . . Milt."

He stood up and walked around the side of his desk and put his hand in hers. "This is a disheartening setback for you, I know that. But don't get discouraged. We should schedule this for sometime soon. One of the nurse coordinators—who are you working with? Val?"

"Yes."

"Well, Val will call you and set things up."

She nodded and smiled. Then she looked at her watch and frowned. "It's almost twenty after. I hope you didn't miss your appointment."

"I hope I did, but I suspect he's still out there. It's awfully hard to discourage an administrator. They take courses in persistence. I guess they have to," he groped in the ashtray for his cigar, "since they deal with us doctors." He rested his hand on her shoulder. "Marcia, you can call me anytime. Anyone on the team. You know that, right?"

He walked her down the corridor to the reception area. An anxious-appearing, short, pale middle-aged man, with close-cropped thinning hair, carrying the jacket of his light gray suit over his arm, stood up from a waiting room chair. Spellman waved to him and said, "Be right with you."

As she left Marcia heard Spellman say, with credible sincerity, "Well, Marv, sorry to keep you waiting. What bad news do you have for me today?"

CHAPTER FIFTEEN

*M*arcia was browsing in the hospital gift shop until her appointment with the pathologist but she had trouble keeping her mind on the things she was seeing. She kept thinking about what Milt Spellman had said about contraceptive pills being the possible cause of her tumor. She had stopped taking them four years ago, when she and Michael had decided they wanted to have a baby. After Max was born they tried an intrauterine device but it gave her cramps so she was back on the pill again now for over a year. Her father always worried about the pill and told her she shouldn't be on it for too many years. Michael was adamant about not having another baby until he made junior partner although he once asked, a month or two before Max got sick, when she would like to have the next baby.

She started taking the pill regularly about two weeks after Michael proposed. Before that they relied on condoms although every now and then they forgot to use one.

*   *   *

They strolled back to her studio apartment from Il Pomodoro on Columbus Avenue with a half-finished bottle of Montepulciano. The night air was chilly and Michael settled his jacket over her shoulders. They picked up the Sunday *Times* at the newsstand on West 79th Street and, once they were cozily in bed, read until after midnight, finishing the wine at about the same time they tired of reading. Marcia swung her feet over the side of the bed to get up and wash the newspaper ink from her fingers. As she started to stand Michael pulled her back down on the bed and tugged at the middle of her flowered yellow nightshirt. She raised her hips helpfully, grinning over her shoulder, and he lifted it over her head, throwing it on the floor. She twisted around into his arms and kissed him, pushing him back and straddling him, her hips moving back and forth as she enveloped him.

After it was over, while he was still inside her and while they were still breathless, he slowly pushed her backwards as far back as he could without separating from her. He then let go and, as she fell back, her head hanging over the foot of the bed, he kneeled over her and thrust himself deeply into her again, both of them taking abrupt, shallow breaths that got quicker and quicker until they climaxed, gasping for air.

The last thing she said to him before drifting into her usual deep sleep was, "Don't go to tennis tomorrow. Stay here and play with me." She woke up very briefly during the night. *Did Michael forget to use a condom?* But she was fast asleep almost instantaneously.

In the morning the sharp click of the lock as Michael closed the door behind him woke her, as it usually did. She rolled over onto her belly, wanting to savor the last moments of the night. She felt the delicious soreness, happy it was still there. *No, 'sore' isn't exactly the right word.* She smiled into the pillow, trying to think of a better word. Her eyelids were getting heavy again when she was jerked awake by the radio unexpectedly blaring forth a Sunday morning Bach organ piece. "Damn," she said aloud, "who set the alarm?" *Is that the "Dorian"? I can never tell one toccata from another. It's Sunday. Damn.*

Rubbing her eyes Marcia wished there was some fresh-squeezed orange juice in her refrigerator. Now, fully awake, she stared at the scattered serpentine cracks in the white-painted tin ceiling, the plain squares decades old and without the fancy patterns that made tin ceilings popular again. She reached over to the side table and pressed the radio's "Off" button, slicing a rumbling churchly chord in half. Then she picked up the phone from its cradle on the floor, also grabbing some of the newspaper nearby and tossing it near her feet. Falling back on the pillow, she held the receiver in her right hand, moving her left forefinger toward the black and white numbers but never quite touching any of them. *This is ridiculous. I should call them. I know they're already awake. If Frank was here, I'd call him first.* But her brother was studying international maritime law in The Hague. She would call him later, when she was sure he'd be in his flat. *Why couldn't Michael have skipped his damn tennis game just this one Sunday morning?*

She grabbed the TV remote and pushed "4". "Meet the Press" was on. Tim Russert was talking, his chin jutting forward, his cheeks flushed, earnestly questioning Madeleine Albright, a map of the Mideast in the background. Marcia poked the Mute button and fixed them into grim-faced pantomime. Tim leaned even closer, almost ready to pounce, his jaw seemingly more than halfway across the table. The Secretary of State Cheshire-cat-smiled, her eyes shining, the warm pink of her round cheeks borrowed from Renoir, the pearls at her neck from Sargent.

Marcia jabbed the number into the phone, slowly, precisely. After the first three rings her mother answered.

"Barbara, did I wake you? . . . I want to tell you something." Marcia cleared her throat. "You and Daddy. Can you ask him to pick up the extension? . . . Oh, all right. I can talk to him later." She paused and absent-mindedly looked out the window.

"Michael asked me to marry him," she said, sitting cross-legged on the bed. "We're getting married . . . we haven't decided yet. Probably in June, when the school year ends."

She waited, listening. "Yes, Barbara, yes, I'm planning to keep on teaching," she said, a bit sharply, "You know that I like teaching, right?" She straightened her legs and slipped down on the bed, stuffing two pillows behind her back and pushing the sports section from the edge of the bed with her foot. "Sorry, I didn't mean to be sarcastic. Really."

Outside, a car horn beeped twice and the wail of a siren came close before fading away. She reached for her mug and took a long, slow swallow of the three remaining drops of last night's wine and again thought about orange juice.

"June just seems right to us." *Why can't anything be simple and easy with her?* "I know it's almost March and I know we may have trouble finding a place in Manhattan. That's not such a big problem. We might look in Brooklyn Heights or even Park Slope. Prospect Park. Bronx Zoo. Whatever. But Michael says now's the time, that we should get married in June. We're not having a big wedding. And I guess I'm ready."

She closed her eyes. *Damn! Wrong words again.* "No, I didn't mean anything by that. And I'm not guessing about this '*also*,' or whatever you mean by 'also.'" She held the phone away from her, then put it back to her ear and spoke, interrupting her mother. "Look, I just wanted to call you and Daddy and tell you first thing." *Or almost first thing,* acknowledging to herself she could have called even earlier. She waited, took two deep breaths, and then said, "And Michael wanted to know if you'd like to get together later for brunch."

Just past her window an adolescent voice, cracking in mid-phrase, yelled "Hey, Richie, gimme the ball, gimme the ball, gimme the goddamn ball."

Marcia waited for her mother to answer, fingering Michael's Grateful Dead T-shirt she was wearing. During the night she felt a chill. Naked, she had gotten up but, in the dark, couldn't see where Michael had thrown her nightshirt. She grabbed his crumpled shirt and a pair of plaid boxer shorts from the floor where he dropped them during their lovemaking. Michael would have been disgusted that she had put on something that wasn't completely clean but she was sure he didn't notice as he hurried off to tennis.

She picked up the magazine section. They hadn't done the crossword puzzle together in a couple of months, ever since Michael realized Marcia could usually finish it in an hour or so working on it alone. Together it often took two hours or more. *Maybe I'll give it a try this morning.* Anything to get over the mood she was in after talking with her mother. *After not saying the right thing the right way again.*

"Whatever time you say. How about twelve-thirty? We'll come over to the East Side."

On the television screen, Albright was replaced by Orrin Hatch, who, still muted, was laughing about something. But Hatch's eyes were narrowed, not fully sharing in the joke, ready for the next probing question. Marcia clicked off the television, opened the magazine section to the crossword puzzle and started filling in the boxes. In the corner of the page she scribbled, "call doc monday—pill."

*   *   *

Arthur Warner's office was long and narrow. His desk was at the far end, to the right. Bookcases covered the wall to the left. Some sort of complicated apparatus—Marcia recognized a microscope as part of it— was on a table in front of the bookcases. Stacks of medical journals were on the floor and the chair at the side of the desk was piled with books and papers and stuffed manila envelopes.

The room was so crowded she was momentarily disoriented. Her glance focused on the middle shelf of the bookcases directly ahead of her where there was a stereo amplifier and a CD player and two speakers, one at each corner. A Bach violin partita filled the air, lending a calming element to the disorder.

Warner stood up and, turning the volume of the sound system down a little, stepped out from behind the overflow of his desk to greet her. He wore frameless glasses and she stared into his light blue eyes, struck by how pale they were and by their sparkle. There was something vaguely familiar about him.

She wondered how he could work amidst all this clutter. She watched him shuffle through a stack of cardboard trays with microscope slides on them, suddenly pulling one out and waving it at her with a warm, slightly shy, smile. She realized he saw order in the shambles, that he was one of those people who sees beyond chaos.

"So you looked at the pictures I sent? Of your son's biopsy?" She nodded. He gestured for her to sit down on a small chair that had been squeezed into the narrow space between the bookshelves and the table. "That's terrific. I hope you could figure them out a little." He sat down across from her. "This paraphernalia looks a lot more complicated than it really is." He gestured at two turrets of the microscope apparatus on the table. There were two separate viewing units, with two sets of eyepieces attached to the microscope, one in front and one in back.

Marcia had the impression he was in his sixties or even older. He was nearly bald in front, his white beard and mustache short-trimmed. On the lapel of his white coat was a small anti-gun pin, a revolver covered by a red X. She had never seen one like it before and wondered where he'd gotten it.

"Let's get to work." He flipped a switch on the side of the microscope and the eyepieces in front of her filled with light. "I'll focus first and then you can adjust the focus on your side. Stop me if something doesn't make sense to you."

He moved a lever that activated a green arrow in the microscope field to point out what he was discussing, occasionally rotating the cluster of lenses, which he called "the objectives," to change the magnification and demonstrate one point or another. They spent most of the time looking at the pale pink, blue-dotted areas she remembered from the images he had emailed to her. Now he explained the circular pattern that he called "concentric laminar fibrosis," as his arrow moved in a circle and then pointed to the bile duct. "It's a form of scarring, with a special pattern. It's definitely abnormal but overall not very advanced." He moved the slide slightly so he could read the slide label. "Max." She nodded her head in confirmation. "Max doesn't have cirrhosis yet." He moved the arrow. "See how the bile duct is infiltrated by lymphocytes—those small blue things without any visible pink cytoplasm."

"What does cirrhosis look like?"

"Let me show you." He stood, reaching behind her to pull out one of the more than fifty flat rectangular black boxes on the shelves. The box was labeled "primary sclerosing cholangitis" at one end and was filled with glass microscopy slides in individual slots. He pulled a slide out, put it on the microscope platform and patiently pointed out feature after feature, going back and forth from Max's slide to the slide of cirrhosis.

When she finally told him she had absorbed all she could, at least for now, he pushed the table to the side so they could look directly at each other instead of over and through the microscope.

119

"Did this help?" *What wonderful eyes this man has, so blue, so calm. I need calm.* "Yes," she said, "I think so. I really do think so." She hesitated. "I really appreciate your spending the time with me."

"No, not an issue. Don't mention it." He gestured to a more comfortable leather chair near a floor-to-ceiling window. The windowsill was stacked with journals. "Why don't you sit over here? You must still have a lot of questions."

The music stopped and he stood up, his hand poised at the CD player. "Is the music interfering? I should have asked before."

"No, not at all. I love the Bach partitas. Is that Perlman?"

"No, Nathan Milstein." He pushed a button.

"Aha," she said, as the music started up again.

"You know Milstein?" He peered over the top rim of his glasses. "A little before your time."

"Milstein is one of my father's favorites."

"Mine, also."

"And I'm a musician. My mother was a concert pianist. Barbara Morse."

He wrinkled his brow. "Sorry, I'm not sure I know of her."

"Yes, well. I guess that doesn't matter. Can we get back? To Max's liver?"

"Yes, of course. I apologize."

"It's just that I need to know a few more things."

"Yes. Tell me."

"What does this all mean? Is it permanent? How sick will he be? How long will this go on? Can he get better?"

"You must understand that I don't know everything about the clinical aspects of liver disease. I don't see patients themselves, just their livers."

"Yes, I understand."

"What we see with the microscope doesn't always correlate precisely with how the patient behaves. And the liver can look a lot better in some areas and maybe even worse in others. We just have a tiny core of it." He waited, giving her time to say something if she wanted to, and then went on. "But these changes in Max's liver are real. And they're not going away. Eventually, and I can't tell you when that will be, he's going to have more bile duct damage, more fibrosis and probably cirrhosis."

She stared at a pile of medical journals on the floor to her right. The top one, maroon and blue and titled *Liver* in a crisp white italic font. She looked back at Warner.

"You know, I think we saw you once, Max and I," she said.

He smiled quizzically at her. "Yes? Where?"

"Do you ever go to the building across the bridge? The medical office building?'

"Yes, definitely. My dentist is over there. The bank, also."

"I think we saw you in the elevator some weeks ago." She gestured at the journals on the floor. "I noticed you because you were carrying that magazine."

"Could be. I was probably on my way to my dentist and thinking about how I was a few minutes late, as usual. I always take a journal with me, in case I have to wait. He's never late, so it's a useless gesture, but I still do it."

"It was probably you." She hesitated. "You know, I never heard of anyone seeing a pathologist. I know pathologists because of my dad, but I didn't think pathologists saw people." She smiled. "Saw patients is what I mean. Do people often come to your office to look at slides?"

He smiled back at her. "No, not that often, but more in recent years. I wish more patients would. I think it helps them understand their diagnosis. Looking at their own slides helps, helps them with their overall understanding of their problem. Even when it's a bad diagnosis, they seem a little more at ease with it after they come to see me and we talk."

"Yes, I can believe that." She started to stand and then sat back down. "One more question. About treatment. Is there anything that will help?"

"Again, Dr. Hirakawa can tell you more about therapy than I can. I do know they can often control some of the symptoms. I'm not sure they significantly slow down the disease progression. I know Hirakawa doesn't hesitate to use antibiotics if they're needed. I think he believes that he does prolong the course by avoiding infections." Warner held his hands before him and shrugged his shoulders. "He may be right, I'm not sure." He took a deep breath before continuing. "The liver people who take care of adults will use steroids, but I think Harvey does this very sparingly because steroids can affect a child's growth."

"But do you think he will need a transplant eventually?"

"I think so. I really do." He cleared his throat and then said, a little louder than before, "but I could be wrong on this. You need to discuss this with Harvey, of course."

"Any guess as to how long?"

"I can't tell you that either. Remember, this slide is only a tiny part of the liver. As I said, it could look better in other areas or it could look worse and he could be much sicker in a couple of months. Some kids seem to go a really long time, however. My best guess, from the degree of fibrosis I see here, it would be no more than two or three years until it progresses, depending a little on the medicines and on his response to them."

She again started to get up, then sat back down. "I said that I was only going to ask you one more thing, but I promise this is the last." He shrugged and nodded for her to continue. "Can you tell me about FNH? Apparently I have one. They want to take it out before they'll consider me as a donor."

"Really?" He leaned back slightly in his chair and clasped his hands together at his chin, index fingers extended straight up in front of his nose, his lips slightly pursed. "Not exactly easy for you, is it?" Marcia didn't say anything. "No, I'm sure none of this is easy." Now he moved forward in the chair again, his elbows on his knees. "But it's benign. I hope someone has told you that already."

"Yes, they have."

"How was yours found?"

"One of the x-ray studies checking me as a donor. Or imaging, I guess they call it, not x-ray. Does that sound right?"

"Yes, the imaging can be very characteristic because these tumors have a typical central scar."

"Can it become cancer? I read that on the internet."

"Listen, if you do a search on the internet you may come up with some obscure writings that say liver cancer develops in these, but I'm not convinced that's correct. I've never seen it and I really doubt it happens. But if it does, it's exceedingly rare and it's so unlikely you shouldn't even think about it." His emphasis on "rare" and "unlikely" comforted Marcia.

"They want to cut it out. Dr. Spellman wants to cut it out."

He nodded, closing his eyes for a moment. "He's very good, you know. Spellman, White, Kurtz, the whole team. I wouldn't hesitate to let any one of them operate on me if I needed it."

"Will you look at it when it comes out?"

"Yes, I will. I have no more trips planned for the coming months."

"I'm glad." She stood up and extended her hand. "You've been very kind. I'm very grateful."

He walked her to the door, his hand lightly holding her elbow. "You can call me anytime and you can come in and see me anytime. I'm sure this isn't going to be so simple for you or your family. I'll do whatever I can to help."

"Will your assistant send me a bill? She didn't ask for my insurance information or anything. Or should I give you a check right now?" Marcia started to open her handbag.

"There's no charge. I'm happy to help."

"No, really. You've spent a lot of time with me. Please."

"No. I mean it. There's no charge."

"I don't mind, really." She turned to face him again. "Please let me pay you."

He laughed and patted her shoulder. "I wouldn't even know how to bill this. I would have to find the right code and spend time with the billing company telling them how to account for this and then it would probably be rejected anyway. It's not worth it. I'm happy to help. Honestly."

They were at the elevator now and he pushed the button. "Remember, you can come again and we can even look at your FNH whenever you want."

CHAPTER SIXTEEN

*M*ax had already finished his dinner by the time Michael came home, but Marcia let Max remain in his chair next to them as she and Michael ate. Marcia and Michael didn't talk much during dinner, content to listen to Max's happy chatter—about going to the playground, about his friend Antonio, about his new shoes. Marcia wanted to tell Michael she expected him to take more than just a day or two off when something unusual was happening, such as Max's biopsy and her upcoming surgery, but she wasn't sure she knew what that would accomplish. Anyway, she would wait for later. While Marcia cleared the table, Michael put Max to bed.

Marcia was physically tired but not sleepy. Still, she went up to bed early to read. Michael had to do some work at his desk but also came into bed earlier than usual, bringing some legal papers to read. Marcia turned off the television and then the light on her side of the bed. It was almost eleven and she didn't feel like staying up to watch the news. She curled up against Michael, her head on his chest. He moved his arm under her to hold her close, keeping her from rolling onto her back even if she'd wanted to. His half-frame glasses were still perched on the end of his nose as he let the document he'd been reading slip to the floor. Then, very slowly so he didn't disturb Marcia very much, he lifted the glasses from his nose and put them on the night table.

"Marsh, I still don't understand what exactly is going on. You need to tell me again. There's no chance the tumor you have will become malignant?"

"That's what they said. Or I guess that's what Dr. Warner said." She moved to prop herself up on one arm so she could see his face in the half-light. "Milt Spellman said this type of tumor can develop in women who take the pill a long time. But then Dr. Warner said he didn't think the pill really caused this kind of benign tumor—they called it FNH— and also that it won't become malignant. He said the pill association was much stronger for an adenoma. I think that's the gist of it." She sighed deeply and wrinkled her brow, scouring her mind for the important parts of what she had learned. "So malignant change is rare in adenoma and probably doesn't exist for FNH." She shifted a little to make herself more comfortable. "Adenoma is a benign liver tumor and FNH is even more benign." She waited to see if Michael wanted to say something. "I'm not completely sure, but that's what I think he said."

"Okay."

"I asked them both that, specifically."

"Yes."

"Yes, what?"

He eased his arm out from under her and sat up straight, propping his pillow vertically behind his back. "Yes, I'm listening. Keep going."

"That's it. I have a tumor." She sat up, facing him. "It's benign and it needs to come out. I don't know anything more than when I called you."

"You weren't on the pill for that long before we decided to have Max."

"But I took it from the time we got engaged until I was pregnant with Max. Besides, that's not the point. They said they might not even remove the tumor if they weren't going to do the surgery. And they didn't really have a good reason for that, for removing it, they just think it's best. Something about regeneration of my liver after surgery that I didn't really understand. Milt said it was like the Prometheus story, but I didn't remember what that was and didn't ask so I googled it. Prometheus is the gold statue at the Rockefeller Center skating rink. He stole fire from the gods, from Zeus, and gave it to humans and then Zeus punished him by chaining him to a rock where an eagle ate his liver every day and then each night the liver grew back and was eaten again, over and over."

"I'm not sure how Prometheus fits in."

"It's just a metaphor for what happens." She waited, staring blankly ahead. "Let me think about it so I get it right."

"Is Prometheus that important?"

"Well, it shows how the liver can repair itself. Taking out the tumor will not affect me in any way. The same thing when I give a piece of liver to Max. The liver will grow back to its original size."

Michael wrapped his arms around his legs and stared into the mirror above the dresser. There was no sound in the house, no sound outside. He turned to look at her. "What if you stop taking the pill? The tumor might regress, if it's at all related. Don't they think that's possible?"

"Well, yes, I could get the IUD again, although I didn't like it. Even if the pill did affect the tumor it could take a while, maybe a long while, for it to go away. Also you can never be sure it's all gone so they wouldn't consider me as a donor for Max."

"So, except for wanting to be a donor, there's no real reason to take it out. Is that right?"

"Umm, yes. I guess that's right." And then, after considering it some more, her head nodding slightly, "Yes" again, with stronger emphasis.

Michael didn't say anything more. Marcia couldn't tell if he was worried or annoyed or something else. *Do I still worry about what Michael feels?*

"But I don't think I would be happy knowing I had a tumor in me, no matter how benign it is. I would still want it out." She turned and reached over to get a tissue from her bedside table. "Milt said a lot of people are like that."

"There's still more to discuss, you know. There are other choices for Max. Donors do come up, even for his age group. We don't have to rush into anything. Even Harvey said he's doing fairly well." She started to respond but Michael kept talking. "We may not have to deal with the transplant issue for a long time and the FNH can shrink. I'm not sure

I like the way this is playing out and I'm not sure it's necessary and I'm not sure I'm going to let it happen. There are other paths we can follow. We can watch and wait for a while."

"Even if Max didn't need my liver, I would want this . . . this growth, removed. And I want it removed as soon as possible."

"What's the harm in waiting a while?"

"Why? Why should I wait?"

He didn't answer, still looking straight ahead. Knowing she couldn't out-talk him, couldn't 'out-lawyer' him, Marcia closed her eyes a few minutes later and pretended to fall asleep,.

*   *   *

Marcia stood next to Barbara at the kitchen window and stared out at the backyard and the pool, watching the shadows steadily recede with the ascent of the morning sun. Michael came into the kitchen, kissed Max on the top of his head and said "See you later, guy." He turned to kiss Marcia but missed, so all she felt was his breath on her cheek. Max waved good-bye with his cereal spoon.

"I'll try not to be so late, Marsh." Michael took a quick sip of her coffee, forced a smile at Barbara, and left.

"Marcia, he's having a really hard time with this." Barbara sat down at the kitchen table and wiped some milk from Max's mouth. "He's hardly said anything in the last few days," Barbara whispered, as if to keep Max from hearing. Max was now banging his spoon for more Cheerios and Marcia poured some from the box into his bowl as Barbara continued, "Come, sit down here, sit down with us. Rest a while."

"I don't need to rest, Mom. I'm not tired. I can rest after it's over. We'll be fine."

The garage door scraped open as Michael started up the car and then it scraped shut again as he drove down the driveway. As Max ate his hand drooped and the spoon hit the edge of the bowl every now and then, making a soft click. The television on the countertop was on but the sound was turned down. Al Roker, with his usual big smile, was talking to someone in the crowd in front of the *Today Show* studio. A young redheaded woman was furiously waving a pink sign with blue lettering, "Happy Birthday, Don!!!" at the camera. Marcia wanted to look away, to do something, anything, but couldn't.

"I know you'll be fine but meanwhile it might be good to discuss things. It's less than two weeks before your surgery, Marcia."

"I don't know what you want to discuss."

"Mommy." Max banged his spoon on the high chair tray three times.

"Yes, sweetheart," Marcia used the corner of his Eeyore bib to wipe bits of cereal from his mouth.

"For a start, why don't you tell me why you and Michael are hardly talking to each other? I can feel the chill."

"Watch *Big Bird* with me, Mommy. Put *Big Bird* on."

Marcia leaned over and kissed him on the nose, handing him an alphabet book. "A little later, sweet boy. He's not on now. We'll watch it a little later." She went over to the sink and started loading dishes into the dishwasher.

"There's nothing to talk about. We just can't agree on some things. There's nothing wrong with that, is there? We don't always have to agree on everything."

Barbara aimed the remote at the television and clicked it off.

"Come on," she insisted. "Talk to me."

Max stopped eating and looked at his grandmother and then at his mother, milk running down from one corner of his mouth, his eyes a little wider than they had been. Marcia picked up the cereal box and took it into the pantry.

"Marcia," Barbara's voice was softer now, almost pleading, "maybe I can help."

Marcia picked up the remote and clicked the television back on. Max looked at Barbara for a moment, as if waiting for a reaction, and then fixed his attention on the screen again. "Mom, you know you're not really good at helping. You're more of a doer than a helper."

"Why don't you give me a chance?"

"I need to clean up the kitchen and—"

"I can clean up the kitchen and it doesn't even have to be done now."

Marcia shrugged and walked over to Max, easing his chair away from the table and lifting him down. A few Cheerios clung to his pajama top, along with spots of orange juice and milk. "Come on, Maxie, let's go for a walk."

Max looked up at her and then over at Barbara.

"Let's go," Marcia said, putting her hand out for his, "we'll talk to Grandma a little later." She gave Barbara a look. "Grandma and I will talk after our walk, while you're taking your nap. Let's go upstairs and put on some clothes. Is that okay?"

Max put his hand into hers as they walked out of the kitchen. "Yes, 'kay."

"'That's okay.' Max, say 'that's okay.' You know how to do that."

He looked up at her, tilting his head to one side, the corners of his mouth pulled down, pouting. "That oh-kay. That oh-kay."

Marcia sat down on the floor and pulled him into her arms, hugging him tightly.

As they headed down the driveway Marcia felt her mother watching them from the window. She looked back at her. *I could have asked her to come with us.*

It was a crisp January morning. The sun and the dense, white clouds were slow dancing with each other, creating gliding shadows on the empty streets and neatly manicured lawns. Max asked if he could take his new tricycle. Marcia, thinking it might be too strenuous for him and also knowing it would be more effort than she could manage right now, said they were just going for a short walk. She offered to wheel him in his stroller instead but he didn't want that.

"No, that oh-kay," and he put his hand into hers and tugged her along the sidewalk. When the sun fell behind the clouds she made sure Max's denim jacket was buttoned all the way up. She then tightened the scarf around her own neck. There was a chilling breeze as the clouds periodically masked the sun. An ominous gray cloud hung somewhere to the west over the ocean and Marcia wondered if it was going to rain inland later on.

As usual there was no one else out walking in their neighborhood except for Dina, who was across the street pulling her cart and delivering the mail. Marcia waved to her and then Max waved to her and cried out "Mail me, Dina?"

"I'll get to you in a little while, Max," Dina called as she turned into a driveway, leaving her cart near the curb.

"Mommy, we get a dog?"

They stopped at a corner. Before they crossed the road Marcia made a show of looking both ways. Reminding him to do the same she suppressed a smile as he rapidly turned his head to the right and the left five or six times in quick succession.

"I did look, Mommy. We get a dog?" he repeated as they walked across.

"*May* we get a dog?" She said, emphasizing the first word. "What made you think of that?"

"Antonio has a dog. I want a dog."

"Antonio has two older brothers to take care of the dog."

"I take care. And Daddy. And Grammy."

Marcia smiled at the prospect of Barbara taking care of a dog, even if it was for Max. When Marcia and Frank were growing up they never had a pet. When Frank was in the sixth grade he prepared a detailed schedule for walking the dog he wanted, a brown-and-white basset hound in the window of a neighborhood pet shop. Frank was convinced the dog looked so sad specifically because their family wasn't buying him and bringing him home. Frank's list included "dog chore" assignments for himself and Marcia, but Barbara was unyielding. Marcia thought ruefully about the image of Max playing with a puppy as she said gently, "Now is probably not a very good time for us to get a dog, sweetie. Maybe next year when you're a little older."

"Why?"

She knelt down to his level, gently grasping each of his arms just below his shoulders. "Well, for one thing, Mommy needs to go in the hospital for a few days and have a little surgery, a little operation."

Max frowned but didn't speak. Marcia stood up and took his hand in hers. They walked five blocks. At the corner she asked, "Should we turn around, Maxie?"

"Oh-kay."

The back of his jacket had ridden up and she knelt again to pull it straight, pretending to also adjust Pooh's tan felt hat. "We need to make sure you fellows are nice and warm, don't we?"

"Yes, we do." The frown was still there.

Still kneeling, she brushed his hair from where it had fallen over his forehead.

"Mommy?"

"Yes, Max?"

"I go to hospital. Not Mommy."

"Well, yes, that may be. We're going to see Dr. Harvey next week and he'll examine you and maybe we'll know more after that. But Mommy has a little bump on her liver that needs to be taken off." Marcia put one hand down on the sidewalk to steady herself.

"Mommy," now Max's brow was even more deeply furrowed, "my libber, not Mommy's libber."

Max looked so serious she had to restrain herself from hugging him close, from letting even the smallest of smiles appear. She wanted to grab him and hold him and never let go, just stay there. The two of them. In this moment. For as long as possible.

The wind picked up and another dark gray cloud appeared, its front flowing toward the mountains behind them. All the clouds seemed to be moving quickly now, getting wispy at their edges. She looked up and inhaled deeply, as if trying to smell if it was going to rain. The lawn next to them looked dry in one area, the blades of grass brown, and she suddenly remembered a favorite poem from high school and college. The words filled her head: *A child said, What is the grass? fetching it to me with full hands; How could I answer the child? . . . I do not know what it is any more than he.* She vividly recalled Thornton Overton, her poetry professor at Smith, seated on the lush campus lawn, reading Walt Whitman's *Leaves of Grass* aloud to the class. He insisted they read Whitman—Overton called him the American Blake—outdoors, on the grass itself.

She turned her attention back to Max. She didn't want them to get rained on, didn't want Max to get soaked, but she had to finish this conversation. A car alarm went off somewhere down the street and she waited the half minute or so until it stopped.

"Yes, you're absolutely right. We are going to take care of your liver but we need to take care of Mommy's liver first. That way, after Mommy's liver is perfect again she can give you a piece of it if you need it."

She paused, still distracted by her memories of the poem. *Or I guess it is the handkerchief of the Lord, A scented gift and remembrancer designedly dropped, Bearing the owner's name someway in the corners, that we may see and remark, and say Whose?*

She first read the poem in eleventh grade as part of an assignment that required her to memorize at least twenty-five lines of a poem, any poem, to be recited in front of her class. That is when she discovered Whitman, his last name the same as hers. She immediately loved the energy—the muscle—in his poetry. After studying the poem and reading about the poet she asked her father if they could visit Whitman's grave in New Jersey. She had read about it in the encyclopedia. They went the next weekend. She could still picture the simple stone mausoleum flanked by two arching maple trees. The tomb reminded her of pictures she'd seen of Stonehenge, but with a triangular stone resting on top, bearing only Whitman's chiseled name. A few feet in front was a plaque set on a low stone pedestal between two American flags. "Interesting coincidence," her father commented after reading what was written there, "Whitman died on March 26, just as Beethoven did. Two of your favorite people died the same date." Marcia cried, not completely understanding why.

Marcia recalled the whole of stanza six perfectly when she studied it again at Smith. Professor Overton had asked the class to write a poem of their own based on one they selected from the literature. Although she couldn't recall her own poem, she was surprised, amazed really, and pleased, to find she could still remember Whitman's.

Max was quiet, lost in his own thoughts. He put his arms around her neck and rested his head against her chest as she knelt at his side. He whispered, "I love you, Mommy."

"I love you too, my sweet boy."

CHAPTER SEVENTEEN

*M*arcia could feel her arm moving, rising ever so slightly, but it seemed separate from the rest of her. She heard muffled sounds, almost like F-minor chords. She recognized the sounds as voices, but they were still only an unintelligible rumbling. She heard a soft, steady, solemn drumbeat. *Poco ritardando.* It was getting softer. *Dimuendo.* She was somewhere new, but wondered where that somewhere was. Then her arm was falling, falling, falling. And then it wasn't moving anymore, but somehow it still seemed as if it was falling. She heard, "Pressure's good," and then there was space, a white space, and the squeezing on her arm that started quickly, faded. And then more space, with that same endless drumbeat, even softer. And white, she mostly saw white. *Dimuendo.*

And then just space.

*   *   *

The blood pressure cuff on her arm was inflating. At the periphery of her vision a nurse was standing beside the bed adjusting the intravenous flow. Marcia didn't feel any pain, just a dull discomfort on her right side. There was some sort of alternating pressure device on both of her legs, rhythmically inflating and deflating, and something with a red light at one end gently squeezing her left forefinger. Cool air—*it must be oxygen*—gently flowed into her nostrils although she wasn't sure she could feel a rubber tube there. A steady beeping behind her competed with the fluctuating low hum of voices outside of her room.

"Well, awake then, are yer?" Marcia recognized the Irish lilt and remembered Max's nurse when he woke after the liver biopsy had also been Irish. This one had frizzy light brown hair and a lot of freckles unlike the porcelain skinned black haired Bridget. *Are all the nurses at this hospital Irish?* She shook her head as if to clear it, feeling the tape of the intravenous plastic tubing on her arm tug slightly with her movements. She ran her tongue over her cracked and dry lips and tried to ask "May I have some water, please?" but all that came out was a croaked, "Water."

"Yes, well, I know yer thirsty." The nurse adjusted the pillow under her head and then pushed a button, raising the top of the bed to an almost thirty degree angle. "We can't have a drink just yet, but I can give yer a few ice chips and something to make yer mouth feel a little better." She put a flat object that tasted of plastic into Marcia's mouth. "Let's get yer temp'rature now, shall we? And then we can let yer family visit with yer in just a few minutes."

"Thank you," Marcia mouthed but there was only a gravelly "unnh."

"There, that's just fine." The nurse removed the thermometer and eased a Styrofoam lollypop into Marcia's mouth. Marcia could taste mint. "This here will help with the dry feelin'. That's a good girl. Yer doin' just fine. My name is Susan and here's my magic wand." She walked to the other side of the bed and put the call button in Marcia's hand. "I'll clip it right here, near yer hand, and yer can push the button anytime yer need somethin'." She patted Marcia's wrist. "Yer doin' just fine, dearie."

* * *

Michael, Barbara, and Alan stood up almost simultaneously as Milton Spellman strode into the waiting area, tearing off his surgical mask but still wearing the cap tied at the back. He stopped at the coffeepot and poured himself a half-cup, then came over to them.

"She's fine." He took a quick sip. "They just brought her into the recovery room. As soon as they get her settled you can see her, but she's going to be pretty groggy for a few hours. It was a good-sized tumor, just as we saw on the films, about five to six centimeters across, maybe a bit more than that. It'll go down to pathology and they'll give us a report in a couple of days, but it looks like a textbook FNH."

Only then did the family smile in relief, murmuring overlapping "Thank heavens" and "Great news."

*   *   *

"How long will Marcia be in the hospital?"

Todd Anderson was at the door of Michael's office, leaning against the jamb. He was, as usual, smartly dressed. He and Edie had recently returned from a snorkeling trip to the Caribbean and he had a deep tan.

Michael lifted his glasses from the end of his nose and set them down on the papers heaped at the rear corner of his desk. The bookshelf behind Michael's desk had framed pictures of Marcia and Max together, and one of Max at Disneyland, taken when Max was not quite eighteen months old. In the photo Max was looking fearfully up at a towering Goofy, his chubby little fingers swallowed up in Goofy's white-gloved, oversized hand.

"When is she coming home?"

"Probably just one day more. Her doctors say she's doing very well, no problems at all." He waved for Todd to sit down. "Coffee?"

"No, no. I've had more than my share today."

"They have her walking up and down the halls. As usual, she tried to do more than they asked. She was ready to check out as soon as she had her first sip of water."

Todd sat down on the beige sofa against the wall. "I'm glad to hear that. Edie will be, too. This has been one crazy roller-coaster ride for you."

"Yes, roller coaster is the right word for it."

"For you both."

"Definitely. No argument about that."

Anderson crossed one foot in front of the other. "Look, I was talking to Tommy Mitchell in the New York office."

"Oh?"

"He's going to call you. Some case you worked on is coming to trial and he'd like you to fly back and spend some time with the team preparing it."

"How soon does he need me?"

"No sooner than the week after next."

"Shouldn't be a problem. Marsh seems fine. She'll be home and walking around long before then."

"Great." Todd rubbed his chin. He started to say more, stopped and cleared his throat, and then added, "There's something else."

"Something else? What's up, Todd?"

"Tommy wants you to come back to the New York office when Gil Loceri retires."

"Is that so?" Michael started to say more and then stopped, his head tilting slightly to the left.

"Gil is taking early retirement. Apparently he wants to sculpt."

"Sculpt?"

"Gil wants to get out soon. He says he's burned out. Tommy wants you to head up the medi-mal section. You would be stepping in ahead of a couple of other people but Tommy says it's yours for the taking. Partnership is a part of the deal, of course. It would be a big jump for you."

"Yes," Michael's voice was low, and he rhythmically tapped the eraser end of a pencil against his desk. "I'm not sure what to say."

"He's happy to wait until Marcia is out of the hospital and back up to snuff before you talk seriously about it."

"Hmm." Michael's mouth and lips suddenly felt dry. He went over to the mini-fridge discreetly hidden in the bookcase unit. "Pellegrino?"

"No. I'm good." Todd hesitated. "He thinks you'd be an excellent fit in their office. As the head of medi-mal this time," he emphasized, not sure Michael had heard that part.

"Have to tell you Todd, although I've certainly thought about being back in New York at some time I haven't even raised the possibility with Marcia. I figured, if it was going to happen, it was at least a few years in the future." Michael drained the bottle of water in one long swallow. "It's not just Marcia, you know. It's also what's going on with Max."

"Well, just keep an open mind. You'll certainly discuss it with Tommy when you're in New York sometime this month." He leaned forward on the edge of the couch. "Understand, I don't want you to go. I really like working with you. You have a great career ahead of you." He shook his head, a rueful smile spreading across his face. "In fact, the only bad thing I can say about you has to do with that forehand slice of yours."

"Right." Michael put the empty bottle down on a coaster. "Which is why I never seem to be able to beat you."

"Is that so? I hadn't noticed." Todd grinned. "I suppose we do learn a few tricks over the years."

"Seriously, Todd, what do you think I should do?"

The older man hesitated and then said, "I think it's a great opportunity. One that you should consider very, very seriously."

*   *   *

Marcia phoned Max and assured him she would be home in a day or two. She and Michael didn't want Max to get upset and didn't bring him to the hospital to visit Marcia.

"Is he eating well, Barbara?"

"Well, if Cheerios and chocolate chip cookies are the measure, with an occasional raisin, he's eating just fine. If broccoli is the measure he could be doing a little better."

"He's never had much broccoli except as a puree."

"It's good for him. You and your brother ate broccoli at his age."

"And don't forget all that wheat germ and yogurt you made us eat. Maybe that's why Frank won't ever touch broccoli to this day." *Barbara always manages to bring out my mean streak.* But her mother didn't react.

The hospital room was full of flowers—aromatic roses and chrysanthemums—and Gerber daisies that didn't smell at all but looked fresh and cheerful. Her cousin Linda had brought a two-pound box of dark chocolate truffles. "My pusher," Marcia told her gratefully, "you know what I really want."

Arthur Warner came to see her the day after her surgery. When he came into her room Marcia assumed he was just another in a parade of doctors and it took a moment or two to recognize him as he held out his hand to shake hers, re-introducing himself, "You came to my office to look at your son's biopsy. I'm the pathologist."

"Yes, of course." The intravenous line in her right arm constricted her movement and she gestured awkwardly for him to sit in the single chair. "I'm sorry. Of course, I know who you are. I guess I didn't expect you to be here."

He drew the chair up close to her bed.

"Well, was it an FNH or not?"

"Yes, it was. Very typical. I can email you a picture of it, if you'd like."

"Yes, please. So it wasn't one of those really rare FNH's with malignant change, I trust?"

He laughed out loud and patted the back of her hand. "No, decidedly not. Just a run-of-the-mill FNH. We won't be able to write up the case for some journal."

Milton Spellman was out of town but John White, one of the other surgeons on the liver team, came to see her on the morning she was to be discharged. He examined the incision and changed the bandage, replacing it with a strip of gauze. He then sat in the chair at the side of the bed, the window at his back.

"Keep this on for another three or four days, until we see you next week. You can sponge-bathe now if you keep the wound and the bandage perfectly dry. You can go back to showers after you see us next week when we take the bandage off. The incision is healing very well and that redness will disappear before too long. We've given you some medicine for pain but you really won't need it that much. No driving for the next two months. Do you tend to get constipated?" She shook her head "no" but her response didn't seem to slow him down. "We're also going to give you a prescription for a stool softener and you should take it for the next two weeks. No sex for about the same period of time—two months, not two weeks. No tennis," he peered over at her now, "for about three months. You do play tennis, right?" She shook her head "no" again. "All righty then," he continued, "other than that, not too many restrictions. If you have any problems at all just give us a call but we want to see you early next week no matter what. Val or one of the other nurses will make the appointment."

Marcia wasn't sure he had taken a breath during his rote recitation. He certainly hadn't shown any emotion. She hesitated and then, with a small stammer, asked, "Dr. White?"

Tapping some notes on his BlackBerry, he didn't look up.

"Max. When can I give him my liver? When can I give Max my liver?"

White put the BlackBerry down and looked at Marcia. She thought she could feel icy fluid flowing into the vein in her arm, even though the intravenous had been discontinued earlier that morning. She was sure she could feel the creases in the sheets under her back and she was aware that she was holding her breath. He leaned back in his chair, less rigid than before but not quite relaxed. "We're going to want to wait a while. Maybe six months or so."

Marcia raised herself up on one elbow. "What if Max needs it before then?"

"I don't think he will. Hirakawa says he seems to be doing well. You know he could even go for a couple of years the way he is."

"Then is it possible he won't need a transplant at all?"

"I don't think so. I'm afraid it isn't likely. With the medicine he feels good and looks good, but his numbers haven't changed that much and every now and then, as you know, are slightly worse. I haven't examined him recently and we haven't had any films for a while but Hirakawa says his spleen is getting a little bigger. That means more liver fibrosis. But his platelets are still okay, so he's probably not cirrhotic yet."

Marcia didn't understand the implications of most of that, but the "not cirrhotic yet" part reassured her.

She watched him finish his BlackBerry tapping. After a minute or two he put it in his pocket and, for the first time, smiled at her. "You're doing really well."

*   *   *

In Marcia's dream Amy was pregnant, jumping up and down, deliriously happy. Her belly looked bigger than Amy herself, an ant carrying a watermelon. Marcia stared at the protruding belly button, imagining the veins coursing down toward the pubis, the abdominal skin taut and shiny and threatening to split apart and spray the entire room with amniotic fluid. But she could not focus on the belly button since it was moving up and down so fast. In the dream Marcia thought she was jumping also, wanting to share the joy, and then it became even harder to see Amy's belly button. Soon she was leaping up and down so fast she couldn't see Amy at all anymore. And then, suddenly, there was the baby. But this baby didn't look at all like Amy or her husband, Brian. It had bright, shiny hazel eyes, just like Michael's. Eyes that took in everything, eyes that delighted in what they saw. It was a girl. Marcia didn't know how or why she knew that, but she did. It was a girl—with eyes that were jubilant. The word *jubilant* sang in her ears. What a funny word. And then she was laughing at the word, repeating it over and over again as she resumed jumping. Jubilant, jubilant, jubilant.

She woke up feeling warm and happy and loved. That baby, those eyes, that dream. They left her feeling joyous. *Jubilant.*

Stretching her arms, back home in her own bed, Marcia turned on her side to steal another few delicious moments of sleep before Max woke up. She curled into a fetal position and pulled the comforter up to her neck, then up to her ears, her knees almost touching her breasts. She thought of Amy's baby of that dream and of those luminescent eyes, and she envisioned herself as contented and protected and safe.

*   *   *

Marcia didn't like looking at the incision. When they changed the bandage on the second day after the surgery she was alarmed. Her skin was bright red and puckered on both sides of the almost imperceptible incision line. After the resident and the nurse left her alone she had put her hand over the bandage, wanting the tears to flow, but they didn't. *I'm okay, I'm okay.* The incision was a wrinkled, slightly raised, bumpy line when Marcia went back to the office for a checkup. It was taking longer to heal than she had expected although Dr. Asherban, the liver transplant resident who was helping with her case, told her it was healing in less time than usual for an abdominal operation. "It looks real good." They had hoped, he said, they would be able to excise the tumor with an incision the size of three band-aids, removing it through the laparoscope, but they couldn't. The FNH had been a few inches more to the back of the liver than they anticipated and they weren't able to see the base without making the incision an inch or two longer than planned.

Michael saw the scar when she took her first shower. He silently watched her as she dried herself, even reaching out to steady her when it looked as if she might lose her balance. She knew when he was disappointed about something and she felt that now. He always liked to rub her belly and she supposed he was thinking about that, but when she turned to him and asked if everything was all right he only said, "Sure. Why not?" It occurred to her at that moment that she also didn't necessarily have logical thoughts about the surgical line. She imagined the scar somehow representing her getting older, a sign of her vulnerability. Perhaps her concerns about the scar were actually about Max's illness, about the likely transplant, about Michael and his stresses. *Maybe it's not all that complicated. Maybe I'm wrong about Michael's reaction.* She continued toweling herself dry and got dressed.

She didn't say anything to Michael, wanting to sort out her own thoughts before she discussed anything with him. A month later the scar wasn't quite as colorful or as prominent so she didn't think about it anymore.

CHAPTER EIGHTEEN

*I*t was almost five months since her surgery and Marcia felt completely well. An MRI a month ago showed her liver returned to normal. But she was positive Max was getting weaker. Although he couldn't play for very long and he needed more naps than ever, Harvey Hirakawa kept reassuring her he hadn't changed much. She watched Max as he slept. True, he was still a happy little boy most of the time and he didn't look sick. Somehow Barbara had gotten him to eat broccoli, and then cauliflower, but there were days when his appetite was too poor even for chocolate chip cookies. Harvey started treating him with steroids, warning her the medication might make him seem healthier than he actually was. The plan was to only use steroids for a short time to see if there was any change in Max's condition. When there wasn't a positive laboratory test result response the steroids were discontinued.

Peter, Paul and Mary were singing. The CD player was on to help Max sleep. When Marcia was five her father took her to an antiwar concert in Central Park, soon after it became known American forces had invaded Cambodia. That was her first introduction to live folk music. She was entranced by the trio, fascinated by how they could make her feel sad and then joyful, even if she didn't understand the deeper meaning of the words that well. Over the next few years she often heard their recordings while sitting in her father's lap in front of the fireplace as he read to her. If it was a Dylan recording, or Joan Baez, or Peter, Paul and Mary, Alan would sometimes stop reading and have her listen to the words. As "Where Have All the Flowers Gone?" played he would hold her closer than usual. As she got a little older, too old to be read to, she understood that her father was thinking about his youngest brother who had been in Vietnam and was one of the last to die, just a few weeks before the Saigon retreat. Since then she loved folk music, particularly those terribly painful songs from the Vietnam years.

It was getting darker outside and the rain tap-tap-tapped at the windows. As "Where Have All the Flowers Gone?" started playing tears welled at the corners of Marcia's eyes. Especially during the "Where have all the graveyards gone?" stanza. But then the first notes of the next track on the album, "Puff the Magic Dragon," lifted her gloom.

Two weeks earlier she finally struggled through all of the *Appassionata*. She forced herself to ignore scattered misplayed notes and unpredictable finger stiffness that plagued her every once in a while. To her ears the first few bars were really sloppy until she got to *poco ritar* and then, suddenly, unexpectedly, each hand seemed to know what the other was doing and she played through until the very last quarter note of the second movement. The finale still filled her with anxiety because of its inherent complexity but even more because of the mixture of soft whispers and dark roars that charged forward to end in what Barbara called Beethoven's final crash of despair.

As soon as she finished playing the opus 57 she immediately started with the opus 79, the 'cuckoo' sonata, which she first learned when she was thirteen. A relatively short piece, full of fun, seemingly easier to play than it really was, it quickly restored her cheerfulness.

During Barbara's most recent visit she spent considerable time at the piano with Marcia, helping her with pedaling, with accents, with interpretation. Marcia always knew that her mother was an "intellectual pianist," as a critic once labeled her, but until now she hadn't fully appreciated the depth of her mother's knowledge about the piano itself and how vital being a pianist was for Barbara. Her mother's grasp of musical history, and of Beethoven in particular, seemed encyclopedic. *No*, she corrected herself, *it is encyclopedic.* Barbara's passion for the music, her intrinsic need for it, inspired and nourished Marcia.

"Marcia, keep in mind that Beethoven changed the meter of the first movement, the *allegro assai*, from 4/4 to 12/8 to make it more exciting, to heighten the drama. Remember as you play, remember he was reaching for that drama. And realize how that drama works without slipping into excess like some not-so-smart actor who knows his lines but doesn't really understand them. That's the hard part. Beethoven wants you to understand him. He didn't put those trills into the first movement as decoration. They add to the uncertainty of that section.

Too many pianists, even the really good ones, don't seem to realize it needs tension there. And then he soothes the music." Barbara jabbed at the score. "See here, see how he wants *pianissimo,* but very fast. These upper keys weren't available on pianos when he first started. Play them as if they are still the new tool, a new invention, as they were two hundred years ago. Keep remembering he composed opus 57 not long after he had finally accepted his deafness. He's opening his chest and plucking at his insides—no, more than that, he's yanking his heart out and laying it on the table, beating wildly for everyone to see. That's his heart in this sonata. You have to make that aspect of it heard by anyone listening to it. It needs to have that feeling, that fortitude, that resolve. This is a piece about bravery, about Beethoven's daring, his audacity, his spirit, about his lion heart." She paused, to emphasize the point. "You need to show that to whoever is listening, and to yourself. His lion heart."

After one of these discourses, Marcia would feel a mixture of exhaustion and euphoria, with some trepidation about the next section she had to master. But on the day Barbara tilted her head, nodded and whispered, "Yes" as Marcia finished the first movement, she felt complete exhilaration. If she had a football she would have triumphantly spiked it into the carpet.

Michael was still struggling with Marcia's determination to put herself through this exercise. When recently he plaintively asked once again, "Why this piece? Why even Beethoven, if he's so challenging? I just don't get it," she thought a while before responding, determined to try to make him understand. "My first real music teacher, other than Barbara—his name was Mr. Letanche. He was Italian, with a French name, from Alsace. He spoke German. I thought he was ancient, but I guess he was about sixty then. '*Liebchen,'* he would say, 'Bach, he speaks *for* God, adding his own *beschonigung,* his own version, and Mozart, Mozart speaks *of* God, and how *phantastich,* how *wunderbar,* is that to write of God when you're Mozart. But Beethoven,'" Marcia paused, just as Letanche had decades ago, "and he would always stop here, he must have told me this a half-dozen times in the many months I studied with him, 'Ah, *liebchen,* Beethoven speaks *with* God. He is directly speaking with God, arguing with him, yelling at him, begging him, and, in the end, praising him and damning him. We are hearing only a little of what he is saying. You will see that someday, *Liebchen,* you will see that.'"

She wasn't sure the story made her resolve any clearer to Michael but he did stop asking her why she was struggling over this particular piece of music.

After the fifteenth try at the final twenty bars Marcia's fingers finally lifted smoothly, lightly, from the keys, and she whispered to herself, "This is good." She picked up a pencil to make some notes on the score. *It still needs a tremendous amount of work.* Suddenly she realized she had accomplished something important, something that came from deep within her, and that the playing was somehow healing her—calming her fear.

Over a three day period she listened to different recordings of the sonata, following each note on her copy of the score, occasionally adding a comment for herself. On the third day she listened to Barbara's *Appassionata* recorded almost thirty years ago. *She's wonderful. I never really knew that, at least not the way I know it now. She captures that lion heart.*

The phone rang, Michael calling from New York to tell her he had arrived safely. He was going to have dinner with her parents the following night. The CD player moved to another disk. "Old Coat" was playing now. As usual, she couldn't remember if the solo voice was Peter Yarrow's or Noel Stookey's. After a while Mary's voice was heard joining on "Roll up your sleeve, life is a hard road to travel, I believe." *A hard road. Yes.* Marcia listened to every syllable, her eyes closed, trying to remember when she had last been completely happy, completely carefree. *Those first few months here. Maybe then, when we first moved here and it was all new and exciting. And Max was just a baby.*

A perfect baby.

A healthy baby.

CHAPTER NINETEEN

When the invitation came in the mail Marcia wanted to call Edie to say they could not attend her dinner— "I'm still not in a party mood, Michael"—but he reminded her this would be the second time in three months they had declined. And so they went to the Andersons leaving Max with Mrs. Grogan, the baby sitter.

Not long after they arrived Todd steered Marcia into the kitchen. To get away from the noise of the crowd in the living room, he said. He was strikingly handsome and attractively confident and Marcia wondered, not for the first time, if he was flirting with her. But, as always, he was a perfect gentleman.

Carmen, the Andersons live-in housekeeper, was busy putting the spanakopita and crab cakes on silver serving platters for the waiters to pass among the guests. Marcia was surprised to hear Michael had been offered a job in the New York office. Todd seemed just as surprised that she didn't know what he was talking about. He filled her in briefly, with enough detail for her to realize it would be a big promotion. He emphasized, more than once, that it was a great opportunity for Michael, "a once-in-a-career chance to leapfrog ahead." He went on, saying it was a terrific job for someone in medi-mal. "Maybe the best job in the country." He concluded by saying more than once that he would miss both of them if they left L.A. Marcia just kept smiling and nodding.

She said nothing to Michael about it until they were in the car on their way home.

"Why didn't you tell me?" she asked, wondering if she should feel angrier than she did.

"I've been meaning to tell you, Marsh," he responded, "I just needed to think it out some more. I needed to figure out what I wanted to do before bringing it up." As they slowed for a stop light he said, "Everything has been so busy lately. I should have told you."

"And?" she prompted, now with a hint of annoyance in her voice. He turned and looked directly at her. *Addressing the jury.*

"I don't have to make a decision just yet. We'll talk about it some more, but I have to say, I'm tempted. I'm really tempted. For a lot of reasons."

"Like what?" She leaned forward to look as directly at him as she could. "You haven't said one word to me about this. Don't I have a right to know?"

"Well, for a start, it's back in New York. In the New York office, which is a much better place to be, career-wise." He paused as the light changed and they drove on. "And money hasn't been discussed yet, but I know it's significant. It means partnership. So it's not something I can just dismiss out of hand."

"But you know how much I love living in L.A. The winters can be so hard back east. And what with everything that's going on with Max . . ."

"I told you, nothing has to be decided right away. Let's just put it on hold for now."

"And?"

"And what?"

"Do I get a say in this? I still don't understand why you didn't tell me."

"I told you. I have not decided to go yet." He emphasized each word. "We'll discuss it again."

Marcia was quite sure that he had, indeed, decided already and she asked, "Is that true? You haven't decided yet?" He didn't respond and neither of them said anything more for the rest of the ride home.

Marcia ran upstairs to check on Max who was sleeping soundly. The babysitter was at the door as Marcia came down. "He was fine, Mrs. Kleinman. He didn't eat much but he was in good spirits. I gave him a bath and he was a little tired after that and was asleep as soon as he got into his bed."

After Mrs. Grogan left Marcia went directly to the piano and started playing a Chopin etude, pounding at the keys, taking her fury out on the notes. She stopped suddenly and put her hands in her lap to control their trembling. She wanted to go upstairs and talk to Michael, to resolve things now, but she was tired and she was sure he would out-talk her so she just sat there.

When she finally went upstairs he was already asleep.

*   *   *

One month later Michael suggested they go out to dinner at a favorite restaurant, Fair Oaks, on the other side of the hill on Beverly Glen. It was a cool evening that got even cooler as they descended the canyon road to the restaurant. She especially liked Fair Oaks because it was so quiet, without the usual high-decibel background noise of most restaurants. There was a slender vase of lilacs on their table. She sniffed at the gentle, sweet aroma. The lamb chops were cooked to perfection. She could sense the succulence even before she put the first bite into her mouth. The mint was unexpectedly and deliciously sharp. Molecules of rosemary, sage, and thyme seemed to discharge with each savory bite of the roasted potatoes. She didn't know if it was the lush romanticism of the restaurant or the excellent bottle of 1995 Medoc they drank, but after dinner, as they stood waiting for the valet to bring the car, Michael suddenly enfolded her in his arms and kissed her. On the ride home he kept his hand on her thigh under the edge of her skirt, every now and then squeezing as if to confirm she was still there. They had not had sex since the surgery. He'd been to New York three times in the last two months and, when in Los Angeles, still came home so late that they hardly ever ate dinner together. This evening felt more like a date than just a night out. She felt herself getting wet as his fingers moved up the inside of her thigh and slipped under the edge of her panties.

Thirty minutes later they pulled into the garage. Michael came around the front of the car as the garage door closed behind them, his zipper already down, and pushed her back against the warm hood of the car, yanked up her skirt, tugged her panties aside and inserted himself into her. She was momentarily afraid her scar would hurt, but it didn't. He didn't bother taking off his jacket or undoing her dress, didn't even touch her breasts, but held her tight in both arms, his tongue deep in her mouth, as his hips moved faster and faster against her. When it was over he was out of breath and she felt his whole body relax. She knew it had been very satisfying for him. She told him how much she had enjoyed it, although she didn't have an orgasm. *I'm getting a little too old for screwing on top of a car.* And then, *what about a condom? I can't get pregnant now. Is that what he wants?*

After that they started having sex again, but only once a week. Either Saturday night if they weren't going out or, more often, Sunday morning unless Max woke up before they did and called to them. Then they might not have sex until the next weekend. A couple of times she awakened in the middle of the night and moved close to Michael and tried to wake him up but he didn't respond. For a couple of weeks, after she tried to discuss with Michael the topic of her being a donor, there was no sex. If she started to reach over him to put her hand on his penis, he rolled onto his stomach. She assumed he was asleep but sometimes she wasn't sure.

She started using an intrauterine contraceptive device.

Once, she woke in the middle of the night troubled by a dream. Michael was with a woman named Lucille. The two of them were just walking. Marcia couldn't identify exactly where they were but she saw sand dunes. Michael and Lucille were smiling and seemed happy. When they came to the edge of a dune, perhaps twenty feet high and quite steep, they stepped over the edge and slid down to the beach on their heels.

Marcia didn't know anyone, didn't know of anyone, named Lucille, unless you counted Lucille Ball or a woman, also a redhead, who had given her dance lessons when she was a child. The woman in the dream was petite, dark-haired and quiet, perhaps even shy. Marcia didn't get back to sleep for some time and lay listening to Michael's slow and annoyingly steady breathing. *Is Lucille really Amanda, the old girlfriend?*

The girl in the dream didn't look like Amanda and Marcia wondered if there was something else she didn't know, something she should know. *What about those long hours when he's in New York? He hardly ever mentions Amanda, but why not? Not that the woman in the dream looks like Amanda, the Gibson girl with the D cups. No, she looks more like me. Maybe Lucille is me, but somehow I don't think so.*

She wanted Michael to wake up and comfort her. She wanted sex, she wanted the warmth, the connection. She wanted to be held. What was bothering her most about the dream was that Michael and the woman, whoever she was, didn't seem to have a worry in the world. They were happy and carefree. No anger, no fear. No illness.

Marcia didn't feel jubilant.

CHAPTER TWENTY

*I*t was a year since Max's diagnosis. As his fourth birthday approached it was clear he was getting sicker. Harvey said the decline was sooner than expected. Now, sick enough to be placed on the donor list, although not sick enough to be high on the list, a different kind of waiting began. After he woke up in the morning Max was still tired. He needed more sleep, often just an hour after a nap. And he was not just sleepy-tired, but every now and then he seemed lethargic. And sleep itself was fitful, restless. The "piggy-snort" they used to love to hear was gone. Worst of all, Max's disposition was changing and he could be short-tempered and cranky. He had always been a little boy who asked question after question, sometimes exasperating Marcia and Michael until he finally got answers that made sense to him. Now the curiosity was gone along with the happy chatter. They no longer heard that contagious belly laugh which erupted if something unexpectedly silly came on one of his favorite TV shows.

Marcia loved to remember a Sunday when the three of them were walking on the Santa Monica Pier. Max was a few months past two and sitting in his stroller. They had just gotten ice-cream cones and his ball of ice cream dropped out of the cone, careening off his chest and landing on his leg. He looked up at his parents, not quite sure whether he should cry or if he was about to be chastised. As Michael leaned down, holding out a napkin to pick up the ice cream, his own double scoop dropped out of his cone onto the boardwalk. Max looked even more startled and then began cackling with glee. Marcia thought it was wonderfully hilarious as well. When Michael started laughing also she deliberately tipped her cone so that her scoop of ice cream plopped down next to Michael's. Max laughed even harder. When they finally calmed down to intermittent bursts of giggles, they heard, "Hey mister," from back at the ice-cream stand. The vendor, a balding man well into his sixties with a gray-tinged, ginger-colored handlebar mustache and mutton-chop sideburns, the name 'Mario" embroidered on his red-striped shirt, was smiling as he waved them over and started preparing fresh cones. "No charge," he said, and leaned down to Max, holding the metal scoop full of ice cream over the cone in his hand demonstrating to Max how he was going to secure it in place. As Mario was saying, "Gonna put yours in first, young fella," the cone cracked and shattered from the pressure he was applying, prompting one more round of hilarity, this time including Mario and a few bystanders. Eventually they each had another very carefully prepared cone, with extra rainbow sprinkles on Max's.

More and more Marcia would remember a time like that and realize they hadn't experienced real happiness in a long while. She wasn't precisely sure when the fun in their lives had started to fade. She was also remembering her dreams more than ever. *My unconscious must be trying to tell me something. I need to keep a pad by my bed so I can write them down.* She went into the garage and pulled one of the unopened packing boxes labeled "textbooks" from a shelf. Her college copy of *Memories, Dreams and Reflections* from Psych 101 wasn't there or in any of the other boxes she searched.

Maybe I should see a professional. I need to talk to someone.

CHAPTER TWENTY-ONE

$\mathcal{P}$atricia Hirsch greeted Marcia with a firm handshake. A tall, slender, slightly angular woman in her late forties or early fifties, Pat had been recommended by Brian, Amy's husband. Strands of gray streaked her long brown hair which fell to her shoulders in a blunt cut. The smell of chamomile tea and chocolate permeated the office. Several friends offered Marcia the names of clinical psychologists and psychiatrists that she considered evaluating before she made a choice but Marcia was comfortable with Hirsch as soon as they met.

Marcia took a seat on the plush dark brown leather couch. The floor-to-ceiling windows opened onto a small enclosed balcony crowded with green plants and potted trees. Behind the desk was a Metropolitan Museum of Art poster of Renoir flowers and there was a photograph of six or eight elephants on the wall next to the door. *Are the big ears African elephants or Asian? Why can't I ever remember that?* "Do I lie down?" she asked, noticing, with the slightest frown, the tissue boxes at each end of the couch.

"No, not unless you want to. It's certainly not necessary. Most of the people I work with just sit where you are and we talk to each other face-to-face. But if you think you'd be more comfortable lying down, that would be fine also."

"No, I'm okay this way. We can try sitting."

"A cup of tea? I'm going to have one." The teacups were bone china, translucent, with a floral pattern that picked up the yellows, oranges and browns in the upholstery of Pat's Queen Anne chair. Marcia took a sip from the cup of chamomile that was given to her and leaned back, unexpectedly and quickly feeling comfortable, at ease, safe.

"Now tell me about yourself, Marcia. What brings you here and, more particularly, how can I help you?"

"Fair enough. Let me see." Marcia shifted to straighten her skirt, pulling the hem down to cover her knees. She inhaled deeply and then slowly exhaled, something she had learned in a long-ago yoga class. "Yes." Another deep breath and then she started speaking, very slowly. "My little boy, Max, is very sick. It's complicated. I grew up in Manhattan with a very successful, very strong and assertive and controlling mother. She was away a lot developing her career when I was young," another breath, "until I was past elementary school. My father is a doctor, a radiologist. Also successful. He is a gentle man, kind, very quiet, perhaps even passive, and sometimes I'm not sure what he thinks, what he feels. I have a brother who's a lawyer. He lives in Europe. My husband, Michael, is obsessed with his work, his legal career, with his cases, and he has little or no time for me, or for Max, and it sometimes seems the only time we talk . . ." She hesitated and sighed, looking directly at the therapist's watchful dark eyes. "We talk when we have sex, and lately that isn't so often. Michael wants to move back to New York and I don't. I've considered that it might be because I don't want to move back to Barbara, my mother, and sometimes I think it might be because I don't want to live with Michael anymore and sometimes I think it's because I haven't really figured out what I want to do." Her smile now was hesitant and sad. "Maybe I've made the wrong choices."

Another long drawn-out breath. Marcia's face contracted as if she was about to cry. Then she sighed again, relaxing her expression. She passed the palm of one hand over her skirt, as if pressing out some invisible creases and then folded her hands in her lap and said, "Where should we start?"

*   *   *

Marcia took Max to the Galleria to get him new shoes. Today he didn't tire quickly and they were able to visit a dozen or more stores. She thought his skin looked almost green rather than yellow under the harsh fluorescent lights, but no one else seemed to notice anything odd about him. In fact, other shoppers walking by also seemed to have a slightly green tinge. After a while Max insisted on being taken out of his stroller so he could walk by himself, which soon wearied him. They went for ice cream—a small cup of vanilla for him and coffee flavor for Marcia.

Max concentrated on the task of eating, oblivious to the drips slowly making their way down his chin. Marcia tried to dab at his face with a napkin but, not wanting to be interrupted, he waved her away with, "No, Mommy, oh-kay." He was asleep almost as soon as she buckled him into his car seat and he slept the entire twenty-five minute ride home.

At dinner Max ate a few peas, a bite or two of mashed potatoes and drank only half of his cup of milk. He moved her hand away when she put a forkful of turkey up to his mouth. *I pushed him too hard at the mall.* Marcia bathed him and was happy when he perked up and played with his boats and his yellow duck in the warm water. After drying him, she clicked the last snap on his pajama top and held him a little longer, a little closer, than she usually did. He generally pushed her away when she did this in the past but now he just rested in the warmth of her hug, his head on her shoulder as she stood up and carried him into his room and tenderly laid him in bed. He only rarely used the pacifiers, his binkies, but tonight he picked one up, shoved it into his mouth and grabbed Pooh in a tight embrace before turning over to sleep on his stomach. She leaned down, kissed him on the cheek and murmured, "Sweet boy." His eyelids fluttered in a vain attempt to stay open but soon he was fast asleep.

Michael got home at nine-thirty and poured himself a half tumbler of Glenlivet before coming into the living room where Marcia was curled up, reading. They shared the usual "How was your day?" before she mentioned she was seeing a psychologist.

Michael waited, then asked, "Why do you want to do this?"

"What I would really like is for both of us to go—"

"Marsh, you know I don't have time for that sort of thing."

"It would only be an hour a week. I think it could really help both of us. She's not that far from your office. And Amy offered to stay with Max."

"Marcia, I don't have time. The answer is no. Period. End of discussion."

CHAPTER TWENTY-TWO

A week after Max was put on the transplant list Marcia called Michael in his office.

"I'd like to make an appointment with you."

"What are you talking about, Marcia?"

"We need to talk about Max, about us, about the whole thing, and you don't seem to want to do that. So let's make a formal appointment. I'll get Mrs. Grogan to watch Max and I'll come to your office and we'll try to work things out." After a brief pause she said, "I'll pay your usual hourly rate."

There was silence and Marcia wondered if Michael was smiling, amused at her earnestness, or if he was frowning, irritated at being bothered in the middle of whatever he was doing and annoyed at having to face what he had been avoiding. Finally, he said, "You're right, Marsh. I'm sorry. I . . . I don't know what . . . Look, we'll talk tonight. I'll be home no later than six and we'll all have dinner and then you and I will talk."

It was almost six fifty when Michael came home, but she was grateful it wasn't later. After dinner Marcia cleared the dining room table and piled the dishes in the sink. She wanted to sit at the table, rather than in the living room, so she could more easily take notes. She made a pot of coffee while Michael was upstairs reading a story to Max. When Max called out "G'night, Mommy" she ran up to give him a kiss and then she and Michael headed back downstairs.

She started to discuss the transplant with him, re-affirming she was the best choice to be the donor. "We don't know that yet," he interrupted, "we still have time to decide. A donor could come along anytime. We'll discuss it when we have to."

Suppressing her anxiety and growing anger, Marcia persisted. "Max is getting sicker. You know as well as I do that getting the right size liver for him, with his blood type, is going to be difficult, that getting any liver at his age is difficult. I just want you to consider it and agree that we shouldn't wait for the last minute, shouldn't wait until he's so sick . . ."

"I thought we were discussing the New York job."

"Isn't Maxie more important?

"Yes, of course he is, but it's not yet an immediate problem. I need to make the decision about the job now."

"You're still young, you don't have to take this job now."

"No, it's now or never," he emphasized, looking directly into her eyes. "This is a once in a lifetime offer. I've worked hard for it. I want it."

"There are other firms," she whispered.

"I don't have a record with other firms, Marsh," he said slowly, his voice louder than before, emphasizing each word. "They don't know me. I would have to start all over building a reputation. You know?"

She told him she loved the house, loved her friends. "You'll have a nicer house," he interrupted again, "you'll make new friends, you'll be fine."

"I do not want to move back to New York. I've loved Los Angeles since I first came here as a child to visit Linda and now I love it even more. I don't want to live in the cold city."

"We don't have to live in the city." He was almost yelling. "You know that. We can live anywhere you damn want."

She repeated she didn't like the winters anymore.

"You'll dress warmly," he shouted, exasperated now. "I'll get you a goddamn fur coat. You'll light the fireplace. We'll get a place in Florida. Jeez, Marsh."

"I don't want a place in Florida."

Michael abruptly stood up, obviously suppressing his fury, knowing he was on the brink of screaming at her. "Okay, I think we've resolved almost everything we can. We're not getting anywhere. We can talk again tomorrow but I need to read some things before I go to sleep."

Marcia didn't move, didn't say anything. She knew she had lost control of the discussion and she wasn't terribly surprised or even that disappointed.

As he was heading out of the room he said, "Do you understand how busy I am at work?"

"Yes I do Michael, but all of this with Maxie is more important."

"I'm aware that it's important. But I don't want you to be the donor unless it's absolutely necessary. I want to wait as long as possible, as long as Harvey and the others say we can wait. A cadaver donor could come along anytime. I don't want to risk either Max or you for a procedure that has more complications. Milt told us. I need to get through the next couple of months, through some really huge cases that are coming to conclusion. After *years* of preparation. Do you realize how much goes into these cases before they're ready to resolve?"

"No, I don't know how much." A pause. "I don't care." She stood to face him. "I'm not sure why we should even be talking about that. Can we just concentrate on Max without the lawyer arguments?"

"Look, as soon as my cases are over, I promise I'll devote more time to you both. Maybe we'll all go away for ten days or so. Hawaii. Tahiti. Whatever."

Marcia was furious, her fists clenched at her sides. "What are you talking about? What trip? Do you think we can take a long holiday and still be on the transplant list?"

"You're right." His voice was subdued now and he put his open hands in front of him, fingers spread, as if to ward off some blows. "That was dumb. I just meant we would spend more time together in just a few weeks." He was partway up the stairs when he stopped and turned to face her. "I want you to know I am seriously considering the New York position." After a deep breath, he added, "But I haven't completely decided yet, Marsh."

"I don't want to leave here. I like it here. I've made close friends here. Amy, Rita, others. My cousin Linda is almost a sister."

"This job may be something I can't refuse. That's really what it comes down to."

"So you've decided."

"No. I haven't decided yet. I'll let you know if and when that happens."

"And what about me?" her voice rising, her nostrils slightly flared.

"I haven't made the decision yet, Marcia. We'll talk about this when I need to make the decision."

"What if I won't go to New York?"

"Marsh, I need to read some things now. We can discuss this another time."

CHAPTER TWENTY-THREE

"*Y*ou've got to be kidding!" Michael jumped up, bumping into the kitchen table where they were seated. The water glasses shook and the silverware rattled. Max's eyes were wide, then his jaw fell, his open mouth releasing a few errant peas. For the moment, there wasn't another sound in the house. Even Smedley looked up from his dish.

Marcia took a deep breath. "What do you mean, Michael? I'm not kidding. I'm serious."

"Without me? You told Val you would be the donor without telling me?" His voice shook with anger. "How could you? What does that mean?"

Max looked from Michael to Marcia, and then sobbed twice. Marcia patted his cheek absently while continuing to watch Michael. "Harvey said Max is almost at the point where we won't have a choice. That this is the stage when living donors make sense. Every time I have tried to talk about this with you—and I have tried—you either say you don't want to discuss it or you change the subject or you go upstairs to your office."

"That's not so."

"It is so, Michael. You don't want to deal with this so you ignore it, just as you ignore everything else you don't want to deal with."

"But we didn't agree. We never decided."

"There was a decision. You decided. Your decision was to not discuss it. Remember? You said you wouldn't let me. You kept saying we could wait. You—" Her voice trembled as Max began crying in earnest. She leaned over to Max and wiped his tears. The sun had gone down and the room was quickly darkening, the long shadows of early evening creeping across the dark red Spanish-tile floor. She walked over to the wall switch

164

and flicked on the lights. "You kept saying Max wasn't that sick." She turned to face him. "You said he could wait. Until when, Michael? Until he's so sick he . . . Until he's almost . . . ?" Her eyes narrowed but there were no tears. "No. No."

"Is this what you're getting out of all those hours with your Dr. Hirsch?" he yelled. "She's not exactly cheap, you know."

Marcia stared at him. *He never worries about money, hardly ever asks how much things cost. This is just one more diversion, but I won't fall for it.* "Harvey says he's declining. He's getting worse." She picked up Max and bounced him in her arms to calm him and continued talking. "It's true. I can see it." Then, lowering her voice, she said softly, "And you can see it, can't you?"

Michael sat down, suddenly deflated, his anger gone. He leaned on his knees and stared at the floor. "But still, it isn't necessary yet. It can't be."

"Harvey says any time now is good."

"I didn't mean . . ." He was still looking down.

Max was no longer crying. He turned his head from one parent to the other and back again as they traded comments.

"Look Michael, you can't do it, my parents can't do it, Frank is the wrong type, my cousins are the right type but I can't ask either one of them, they have their own kids—just what do you suggest? He's been on the list, but there are others ahead of him and we rarely hear about another child with the right size liver and the right blood type." She stopped, waiting to let him respond but he kept his gaze downward. "He's declining faster than anyone expected. Remember they originally thought three or four or even more years? If he wasn't really sick, he wouldn't be on that list. Remember how at first they said he wasn't sick enough to be put on it? Well, he's sick enough now." She cleared her throat and started to turn toward the sink to get some water, but then stopped, her eyes wide, her voice tremulous. "He's sick enough for the list. He needs a liver." Michael's gaze turned to her and, her voice steady and strong, she said, "He needs a liver now."

Michael didn't respond immediately, composing his thoughts. "He hasn't been waiting all that long a time for a donor. It takes time. You know that as well as I do. They've told us that."

"People, children . . . they sometimes . . . The problem is, they sometimes stay on the list until it's too late." *There, I've said it.*

"Not a single person has said that Max is at that stage yet."

"I want him to have every chance."

Michael bowed his head. "Yes," he whispered. "Yes, I know. So do I." He went over to Marcia and Max, who had started sobbing again. Soon Max's sobs became short whimpers with quick breaths and, after a while, he was again smiling at both of them. They smiled back at him but didn't look at each other.

Marcia suppressed a moan and sighed. *This hurts so much. So much.*

*   *   *

She was awake on and off through the night. Her sleeplessness was nourished by the steady anger and dread she was feeling and compounded by Michael's heavy snoring. She'd had a dream, but she couldn't remember it. She kept her "dream notebook" on her bedside table but the dream evaporated by the time she reached for the pen.

At five-thirty she gave up trying to sleep and went downstairs. The kitchen walls were still cloaked in night. It was eerily quiet outside. The sound of her slippers as she shuffled from the counter to the refrigerator to the kitchen table seemed quite loud. Coarse sandpaper on raw wood. She made a pot of coffee and poured herself half a cup, dropping an ice cube into it so she could drink it right away.

When Michael came down two hours later he had on a crisp white shirt and perfectly knotted striped tie. He looked fresh and rested but the first thing he said was, "I could hardly sleep last night because of this, and I'll say it again—I just can't permit you to do it."

She thought about telling him how soundly he had slept but didn't. "What did you just say, Michael? Listen to yourself."

"I said, I don't want you to go ahead with the transplant now. Max can go a while longer. We can keep looking for a donor. We can wait. We can wait until I'm a little less busy."

I must be going mad. Oh, poor Mikey. I know he doesn't mean that.

While pouring himself a cup of coffee he spilled some onto the counter. He grabbed a dishtowel and wiped it up. "I didn't mean that. Fuck it. It's not that I'm too busy. That's not it. I didn't mean that."

He waited for her to say something and, when she didn't, he continued. "You've heard them say it over and over again. It's easier with a whole liver donor. And safer. Safer for Max and safer for you. Even your father says so. All the liver people he's talked to at Sinai and Columbia say to wait for a whole liver donor or else wait until Max is about as sick as he can be."

She faced him to respond, struggling to steady her voice and restrain her fury, making every effort to control herself. "That's not what they said and you know it." She hesitated before going on, gathering her ideas, and held up her hand when he looked as if he was going to speak. "They said we *could* wait, not that we *should*. They never said that we should. The surgeon at Columbia told my father there was no best decision unless there is a cadaver donor liver that is ready right now."

"What the fuck's the difference from what I just said?" Michael hissed.

"The difference is that no one knows the best thing to do. No one can tell us the best thing. There is no best thing to do. There's only trying to do the best we can. The best for Max." She glared at him. "And can we watch the language a little?"

"And what does that mean?" he hissed, ignoring her last comment. "We are doing the best we can. That doesn't mean anything."

"That's because you don't want it to mean anything. We have to make a judgment. We have to make the best judgment we possibly can."

"The best thing to do is to wait, Marcia. That's the best thing. Just wait. I need time."

"That may be, but Harvey says we're—Max—is getting really close to the point of us having to do something, the point of no return." She hesitated and then blurted, "And what if Maxie dies while we're waiting? What then?"

"And what if he dies because of the surgery?" Michael whispered. And then, in a barely audible and tremulous voice, "What if *you* die because of the surgery?"

Marcia felt a wave of relief pass through her. *At last it's out. He's really worried. About us.* "I'm not going to die." His head was turned down again, staring at the floor again, and she walked over to him and placed her hand on his cheek. "Even if there are complications—look at me, please!" After a moment, he looked up. "Even if there are complications, they can almost always be corrected. Milt Spellman said that."

Michael didn't say a word.

"Almost always," her mumble barely audible.

He still didn't say anything for what seemed like hours. "I don't want you to do this, Marsh. Not yet. Besides, you know very well they can't do surgery on Max without both of us giving permission." The phone rang but neither of them moved to answer it. "For Christ's sake, Marsh, I'm a lawyer. I'm telling you this. You can't do it without me. You know that as well as I do."

* * *

"What do *you* want to do?" Pat Hirsch leaned forward, emphasizing the "you." "What do *you* want to do for *you*? Not for Max. Not for Michael. For you."

"I don't know. I really don't. Michael is angry at me all the time and now he won't even discuss the transplant." Marcia reached for a tissue although she wasn't crying. "And I can see Max is getting worse and worse. We can all see that. And I'm furious with him, with Michael."

Marcia looked at the plant in the corner, at the desk, at Pat's face, at the annoyingly parallel pleats of the therapist's skirt. Motionless, Marcia finally said, "I'm really struggling. My head is full of thoughts that don't connect, don't even make sense. Is there something I'm missing?"

"Is that what you think? That you're missing something? That I know what it is you're missing and I'm not telling you?"

"No, no." Marcia waved her hand dismissively. "I know you're trying to help me figure things out. But I can't figure them out. I don't know what to do."

"You know there is no one answer, certainly no answer that's perfect for all of you. Life is messy. It doesn't come with guarantees. We just have to find the best answer."

Marcia nodded. Pat waited, as she often did, to let Marcia talk first. When Marcia didn't speak, Pat asked, "Are you concerned about the effects of the surgery on you?"

Marcia considered the question for a while. "I haven't really thought about that too much. Well, that's not exactly true. I have. I've read everything I can. I have thought about it but no, I'm not terribly anxious about it. At least not consciously. I never know about my subconscious. That's your department."

"My department? Your subconscious is my department?" Pat smiled and took a sip of tea. "I didn't know that."

"Well, no," Marcia smiled back at her, "I realize it's not. I just meant that you seem to understand my subconscious better than I do. And it's not the surgery that I think about all the time. It's more . . ." She stopped and then suddenly her words poured out. "I don't know if I can ever love Michael again. When I'm not thinking about Max, that's what keeps going through my head. I don't think I want to be with him anymore. I don't understand how we can be so different about this."

"Go on. Say more."

"He's not willing to discuss anything. He just pulls this lawyer crap and says he won't give permission. When I point out that Maxie's getting worse, he gets up and leaves the room. I've spoken to a lawyer friend of mine and she says I could challenge him about the permission but, of course, it would take a long time and a lot of legal work." She nodded her head, adding, "and a lot of money."

"What exactly do you want Michael to do right now?"

"I want him to talk to me."

"What do you want him to say?"

"That he is—I just want him to acknowledge that Max is getting worse and that he'll consider it, that he'll let me give a piece of my liver to Max, that he'll at least consider it. That's all I want him to say right now."

"That may not be possible for him, you know. I can't tell you why. I only know him through what you relate to me, but maybe he can't say that."

"Yes, I'm beginning to see that. But I still want him to show that he's willing to do something for me, for Max. I guess I want at least a little bit of encouragement, even maybe a little respite from the arguing. Is that too much to ask?"

"Do *you* think it's too much to ask?"

"No," Marcia dragged the word out, trying to figure out what Pat was implying. "No. What do you think?"

Pat smiled and leaned back in her chair.

"What do *you* think" Marcia repeated, more insistently.

"I believe you know what I think. We've talked about this before." She nodded her head toward the clock on the side table. "It's time." Pat stood up and started walking to the door, her open hand out, encouraging Marcia to join her. "As we've discussed in the past, more than once, I think we are all, to a very great degree, responsible for our own happiness. I also think we can, together, find some solutions for you."

CHAPTER TWENTY-FOUR

When Marcia got home from her appointment with Pat Hirsh she paid Mrs. Grogan and confirmed her for next week at the same time in case Amy was unavailable again. She bent down to kiss Max as he played with alphabet blocks on his bedroom floor, concentrating on piling one on top of the other. Max pushed her away when she tried to hug him, so she went into the bedroom and stood in the walk-in closet. Intending to change from her dress into jeans and a sweatshirt, she just stood there staring at herself in the full-length mirror. *Look at me.* Her almost mid-calf skirt that she first wore ten years ago had a stain and needed to go to the cleaners. A small hole in her sweater was just under the arm. It was mostly hidden but she knew it was there. She had brushed her hair before she left, but there were loose strands here and there that needed tending. *It's been a long time since I've gone shopping just for myself.* A broad smile slowly filled her face as she suddenly recalled going shopping with her mother at Grandpa Morty's.

*　*　*

Marcia's paternal grandfather, Morty, was a jobber in the New York garment district: Mortimer J. Whitman, Inc. He bought high-quality women's dresses and coats from manufacturers and sold them to retailers. His clients included the better stores, such as Bergdorf's and Saks. He also sold directly from his shop on the fifth floor of 491 Seventh Avenue, to women referred to him by others in the trade, by previous customers and, often, by his own relatives. In forty years he had run only one paid classified ad— "Coats, suits, dresses, sportswear, knits. For that special lady."—in *New York* magazine. Barbara would take Marcia along when she went to Grandpa Morty's for new clothes.

Morty's shop was far from glamorous. An ancient thirty-cup stainless steel coffee urn with a toggle spigot sat next to the reception desk. A mammoth, glistening, brass National cash register, with the genuine ivory shelf just above the cash drawer, had been in the same place on a counter close to the entrance since he opened the shop. It was hardly used even when Marcia was a little girl. Morty let Marcia push the keys of the archaic cash register to open the drawer and sound the bell as much as she wanted and he usually remembered to hide some coins inside for her to keep.

Renowned for his good taste and the high quality he carried, Morty always pulled out two dozen or more dresses and coats that he thought would look well on Barbara. While she was trying them on he would take Marcia to a diner on the west side of Seventh Avenue and the two of them would share an ice-cream sundae or a banana split.

Marcia used to run in and out of the clothing racks when she was very young. She mostly remembered the fun they had at the diner and the time they had giggled together after Morty had ordered a second scrumptious sundae, including six extra maraschino cherries for her alone, not to share. The styles Morty carried were definitely too mature for Marcia until just before she went to college, when she got one coat and a few skirts. Morty died during Marcia's first year at Smith and the business disappeared.

Marcia thought of Grandpa Morty often when she went shopping for clothes or when she stood in her closet trying to decide on something to wear.

One side of the closet was filled with Michael's suits, dark blue, gray, black pinstripes, and dark blue blazers. Some of the attorneys in the Los Angeles office wore more casual clothes, even sports jackets and slacks instead of suits, but Michael still dressed like a New York attorney. She used to think of that as a reflection of his commitment to propriety, his dedication to the long, well-honed traditions of the law. Now she saw it as evidence of his rigidity, his resistance to change.

*   *   *

Marcia was in the bathroom brushing her teeth when Michael called to her from the bed. She had to strain to hear him over the eleven o'clock news.

"I've decided to take the New York job. I'm starting in July. Four and a half months from now." He put aside a pile of depositions he'd been reading. They had not discussed the topic in over a week, by mutual consent. She hoped they would eventually talk it over and find common ground, but she never expected a *fait accompli*.

She stared at the bar of soap in its seashell dish on the bathroom counter. *Is this for real? Maybe it's some kind of strategy.* She finished brushing her teeth and rinsed her mouth twice. Then she came out and sat on her side of the bed, twisting around to face Michael.

"When did you decide?"

"Today. I spoke to Hal Bell in New York. They're pushing hard and I had to decide. It was a now or never situation. They'll get us a condo in the city, if we want it, Upper East Side, or a house in the suburbs. Whichever."

"Even though you know how strongly I feel about this, you still decided?"

"Marsh, I just can't turn this down. Can't you see that? Saying no isn't an option. Not if I want to accomplish important things." He peered over the rim of his glasses and held his hand out to her, as if it contained an offering of some kind. "You pick—East Side, or Tenafly, Short Hills, Mamaroneck, whatever. I'd rather be in the city but I can commute. I'll live wherever you say we should live. In time you'll see this is the best thing to do."

Very quietly, keeping her voice as even as possible, she said, "Is this retaliation for my wanting to be the donor?"

He took off his glasses and peered at her. "Don't be ridiculous. Of course not. Really, sometimes I just do not understand you."

"What you don't understand is that I don't want to move back to New York. I like Los Angeles. This is where I live now. This is home." She paused, inhaling deeply. "And especially, I don't want to start with a new transplant team."

"I considered that. We'll stay the course here for however long it takes. If necessary, I can move and then come back here every other weekend or whenever. We'll work it out. I don't have to move now, in any case. Not until July. Or even the end of the summer."

"Yes, I heard that."

"So?" He looked quite stern and his tone was flatter than usual. "By then we'll either have a new liver or we'll use a living donor." He hesitated and started to reach over to her but then, looking directly into her eyes, said, "If necessary we'll use your liver. If the donor pool doesn't turn one up soon we'll use your liver."

Finally. Finally he acknowledged that she could be the living donor. She felt what seemed to be a chill, perhaps a wave of gratitude, for the concession. Not thankful to Michael, just thankful. *But remember, I am being manipulated. He's a master of debate, of coercion.* Michael had been unwavering in every discussion about the transplant, determined they wait for a cadaver donor. Until now.

All those times when she tried arguing with him, pleading with him, imploring him, telling him at one point how insignificant he made her feel by being so intransigent and ignoring her. One time he had snarled, "Damn it, Marcia, I need to work on this case without any more interruptions. That's just the way it is. Live with it."

Live with it.

Since their last argument, more than four weeks ago, they had not had sex. Neither of them seemed interested. They had a hard time just looking at each other.

One Tuesday, when Michael was still not home at eleven, Marcia thought of Amanda Martinez. *Is she in L.A.? Are she and Michael together at the Biltmore or the Peninsula or maybe close by at the Marriot on Ventura*

Boulevard? Did they spend nights together when he worked out of the New York office? I'm not sure I care anymore.

The next morning she poured his coffee and, as he took his first sip, said, "Michael, I'm wondering if maybe we should separate."

He sputtered and coughed. "What are you talking about? I don't know what the fuck it is with you, Marsh, but I can't have one of these conversations now. I have to be in court today and . . . and we'll talk about this later."

Immediately after he left for work she pulled yesterday's shirt and undershirt out of the laundry bag and examined them for evidence— the smell of perfume or a lipstick stain. She found nothing and felt ridiculous and ashamed of herself. *I won't do that again. Amanda's most likely 3,000 miles away right now. And besides, Michael wouldn't be careless enough to wear evidence of an affair. He's too smart for that.*

She went to bed that night before Michael but again had trouble sleeping. Her persistent thought was that he was now using her liver as a chip in the bargaining process to persuade her to follow his script, the script that featured their friends throwing them good-bye parties, garage sales to get rid of things they had never really needed, things that weren't to be part of their new life back East. Calling the moving company. Shipping the cars. Would she like to sell this rebuilt piano and get a new one when they settled? Why don't they go directly to the Steinway showroom across from Carnegie Hall? Michael would steer the finishing touches of leaving, the taking care of whatever might be left after the movers packed everything, the dealing with realtors and contracts. Even showing the house to prospective buyers. Then doing things in reverse once they arrived in New York. Where she didn't want to be. She would be expected to obediently pick out some co-op on East 72nd Street or a broad-lawned, three-story Greenwich home or a contemporary waterfront estate on the North Shore. Michael, as usual, would want her to overspend on whatever she selected for them to live in, which would then justify him working those long billable hours to pay for it.

And she would definitely be expected to not bring up the subject of separation or divorce.

*   *   *

"Sweetie, you may just have to live with it."

Marcia stopped tugging Max's sweater down over his chest and stared at the phone, which was on speaker.

"That from you, Barbara? You're telling me I should just 'live with it'? Pick up and move back to New York?"

"Marcia, your choices are not so terrible."

"I've got to go now," Marcia said and hung up.

Why don't I want to go back to New York? Do I really love Los Angeles that much? She asked herself if the winters were really that bad. She tried to measure, to calculate, what part of her feelings had something to do with weather, with Michael, with Barbara. With herself.

Alan viewed Michael almost as a second son, becoming both surrogate father and friend to Michael. She wasn't surprised when her father called him. She didn't know exactly what they discussed, didn't ask, but Alan told her it had been a good conversation and Michael was trying to see both sides. "To tell you the truth," her dad concluded, "and you know this Marcia, I would be very happy if you all came back to New York. You know that."

Marcia cried after that phone call. They were all ganging up on her. Michael didn't even mention he had spoken with her dad. She needed to discuss her feelings, even before her next appointment with Pat, but that was six days away. She wasn't able to confide the same way in anyone else, not in the same way she could talk to Pat. No one was as objective, as non-judgmental. Her parents were not offering her the support she'd become accustomed to getting from them, especially her father. They weren't telling her what she wanted to hear and she hesitated to burden them with her pain. Amy was away with Brian at some medical meeting. She could call for an earlier appointment but Pat probably wasn't going to tell her what to do either.

She could almost picture the appointment before it happened. There would be too many "What do *you* want to do?" questions.

"Pat, I really need your help!" she would say. "If I knew what to do, I wouldn't be here, would I?"

Pat would fill both of their teacups, taking an extra moment to place a biscuit on Marcia's plate, before responding. "I can help you find that answer but I cannot give you the answer. You just have to trust there is an answer for you." Marcia was sure she would hear the usual "together we can find it."

Marcia would pull a tissue from the box next to her. "I know, I know. I'm sorry," she would say, but what she would feel was that she had no allies.

She would still feel she was alone.

Now, considering the likely next session with Pat, she cried even more. Then she thought she might show up for the appointment with a placard saying, "Just tell me what to do." Inexplicably, Marcia immediately felt stronger, felt better. She laughed out loud at how ridiculous the scene was.

CHAPTER TWENTY-FIVE

*W*hen Max was an infant Marcia loved taking walks with him in the carrier that held him so snugly against her chest. She and Michael took great pains making sure the different size adjustments were right for when he carried Max and when she carried Max, marking the strap "Ma" for her and, at a different position, a "Pa" for Michael. Michael was reluctant to permanently mar the carrier's inner lining with their notations until Marcia teased him, saying, "Come on Mikey, it belongs to us. We won't be breaking any law." He smiled at her, but it was a forced smile and she knew it still bothered him.

As soon as Max could hold his head up by himself they put him face forward in the carrier. Marcia never understood parents who carried their children facing their own chest, the child unable to see anything but shadow and cloth, when there was a whole new world out there for them to look at.

She recalled the many times her father carried her on his shoulders for Sunday afternoon strolls through Central Park on spectacularly beautiful Spring days or, even better, glorious New York Fall days. The autumn colors would be erupting all around, the free falling golden and rust-red and brown leaves carpeting the paths. She could almost feel, and more than once pined for, the invigorating first hint of winter in the air, brisk but not quite cold, days that Alan always used to say made you realize you were really alive. She enjoyed New York, or at least her memories of New York, but she loved living in Los Angeles even more.

She and Frank would happily endure the questions their father rattled off on their walks encouraging them to be aware of their surroundings, to observe. "Don't turn around," he would say. "What was the color of the jacket that little girl was wearing?" Or, "How many squirrels were climbing that tree we just passed?" "Were those men playing checkers or chess?" By the time they were approaching their teenage years Alan had a hard time tripping them up and was delighted when he was able to do so, sometimes almost cackling with glee and a triumphant, "Touché. My point!"

Marcia did the same thing with Max when they went to Griffith Park. But now he was weary all the time. He noticed very little of his surroundings. At least he wasn't as yellow as he had been, the result of one of the many pills he was taking. Harvey emphasized the importance of making sure Max ate well. "He's a growing child, and you need to compensate for his loss of appetite. And don't worry about healthy food or smart food. He mostly just needs food."

But Max wasn't growing anymore. He had always been only slightly above the median in the growth curve scales, something they'd attributed to Marcia being so petite. But now his height, even more than his weight, had dropped almost to the 35th percentile. Harvey increased the dose of the vitamins he was taking, explaining, "He needs the fat soluble vitamins, especially A, D, E, and K."

Harvey was concerned because Max's spleen might be enlarging. "I think I can feel the tip. That's not good, it could mean cirrhosis is developing. We'll check his platelet count next appointment," he'd said. But the ultrasound didn't show any appreciable change in the spleen since Max had been tested three months earlier and the platelet count was still in the normal range. "That's a good sign. But even without overt cirrhosis he is declining, as we can see." Whenever Max had a fever—every month or so, sometimes two or even three times a month—Harvey would order a white blood cell count and a blood culture to look for circulating bacteria. The results were almost always normal but, when the white count was even slightly elevated, he would prescribe an antibiotic, even without an obvious infection and even if there weren't any organisms in the blood. "If he becomes cirrhotic he can start accumulating fluid in his belly, what we call ascites, and that can get infected without any obvious cause. Also he can get infected in the liver where his bile ducts don't drain well. The bile that backs up becomes a good medium for bacterial growth. We need to watch for both of those and keep ahead of them with antibiotics."

180

At first Marcia would be very anxious, very sad, when Harvey talked about one possible complication after another. Also, at first, Michael would listen very attentively when she passed the message on to him. Now they were accustomed to Harvey's extra concern, his deliberate caution, and they didn't react as strongly. Marcia still worried, at least until she saw Max seemingly unchanged the next morning. Michael just nodded or, at most, said, "Okay. Thanks."

*   *   *

Michael was gone another week in New York. Whenever he left, Marcia felt freer and able to practice as much as she wanted since she didn't have to be concerned about preparing dinner for him. Cereal and yogurt or a couple of scrambled eggs were just fine for her. Marcia had two or three hours almost every morning when Max napped, and again in the afternoon, for practicing or reading. She was enjoying *Jean-Christophe* again, hoping the novel inspired by the life of Beethoven would afford her some special insights. She had even more time in the evenings after Max was tucked in and she would practice or read until she had to struggle to keep her own eyes open.

Amy sometimes made dinner for Marcia and Max while Michael was away. One Thursday Marcia and Max spent the day at her cousin Linda's Laguna Beach house. Watching the gradually shifting shadows carefully, she made sure Max didn't get too much sun. After dinner, with Linda's urging, she decided to spend the night rather than drive the sixty or so miles in the dark.

Friday morning, after a full breakfast, Marcia headed home on the crowded 1-5. Max was asleep within minutes of leaving Linda's house, as he now usually was even when they drove short distances. The radio was playing "What I Did for Love" from *A Chorus Line*. Alan took her to see the Broadway production when she was twelve. It was one of her first Broadway shows and remained her favorite. She wished she could have the song repeat, but a tune from *Grease* began to play and she turned the radio off.

I guess moving back to New York is one of those things you do for love. She repeated the words a few times. *That's what you do for love. That's what you do for love,* and then she started to cry. Letting the traffic rush by, she pulled the car onto the right shoulder of the freeway as the tears gushed out. As she was slowing down the gravel kicked up under her car, a noisy syncopated tap dance. Max let out his piggy-snort once, something he had not done in a long time, but didn't wake up. She made sure the front passenger window was slightly lowered, made sure all the doors were locked, turned off the ignition, put her arms over the wheel and allowed herself a good cry, stifling the sound of her sobs as much as she could so she didn't wake Max.

What if I really, truly, don't love him anymore? What do I do then? How do I do something for love if I don't love him anymore?

A sharp rap on the car window startled her. Her heart pounded and she had to catch her breath. A highway patrolman towered above the car and then leaned down to observe her closely while looking back at Max who, now awake, was rubbing his eyes.

"Are you all right, Miss?" His sunglasses were perched on top of his head and his round peach-fuzzed face was expressionless.

"Yes, Officer, I'm just fine." She reached for the keys, but he rapped sharply on the window again, waving his index finger admonishingly at her. "No."

"I need to start up the car so I can lower the window some more," she explained.

"No, you don't want to do that. I just want you to step out from the car. Would you mind stepping out, Miss? Don't turn the car on."

"What?" Was this some sort of trick, a con, to lure her out? But his patrol car was parked directly behind them, its lights swirling, and the freeway was filled with morning traffic. Max watched it all silently, curiously. She thought of the many times she had pointed out a policeman to him, saying "See the nice policeman, Max? Policemen and policewomen are your friends."

"Get out? Yes, of course, Officer." She eased the door open just enough for her to step out as the officer moved aside. She made sure the door was ajar in addition to the window slightly down so there definitely would be plenty of air for Max.

She explained that she had been at her cousin's for the night and was heading home, that she started to cry because of a personal matter and thought it best to pull over to the side of the road rather than driving in the heavy morning traffic while she was weeping. "I can give you her phone number, if you like. My cousin. In Laguna. You can call her."

"No, that won't be necessary." He regarded her from head to foot. A professional assessment, not sexual—he was merely trying to figure out what file she belonged in: crazy, drunk, dishonest, druggie, battered, what? "You been drinking, Miss?"

"Drinking? At this hour? Drinking what?" She smiled nervously, her voice tremulous.

"Alcohol, Miss. Have you been drinking alcohol? Beer, wine, vodka? Anything like that?"

A Mayflower moving van zoomed by and she felt her car shudder in its wake. She was leaning on the front fender and wobbled for a second or less. She wondered if the officer thought she was losing her balance. She felt her cheeks flushing and worried that it made her look guilty of something. *Do I look as if I'm covering something up?* She was determined not to give him the details of her sad story, determined not to use her tale of woe to her advantage.

"Alcohol? No, of course not. I mean, it's not even lunchtime." She looked at her watch before showing it to him, as if to prove her point, after which she felt foolish. "I have a child in the car." She half-turned and gestured toward Max. "And besides, I'm not a drinker. I don't drink except for wine with dinner once or twice a week." *Shut up, Marcia.*

"I believe you Miss but I wonder if you would do a few simple tests for me anyway, just so I can be sure. I'm thinking of the baby in the backseat." He leaned forward to take a closer look at Max, who stared wide-eyed at the officer. "A real cute little guy. Glad to see you left the window open a crack"—still no expression on the trooper's face— "just wantin' to make sure you're okay for him."

"His name is Max."

"You go bye-bye, Mommy?" Max said, as she started to walk a straight line. *Thank goodness I'm wearing sneakers and not heels.*

"I certainly hope not, sweet boy. I don't think so." She threw a hesitant smile at the officer.

"That's just fine, Miss. Now if you could just close your eyes and touch your index finger to your nose. Both index fingers, but just one at a time."

Marcia dutifully, steadily, and one after the other put an index finger to the tip of her nose.

"That's just fine, Miss. You're not sick, like diabetes, are you?"

"No. Really. I was just having a little cry."

"Well, then, that'll be all. You can go now." He opened the car door for her and waited until she had fastened her seat belt before closing it. "Hope things work out okay. Sorry to trouble you."

She turned on the ignition and lowered the window. "Thank you, Officer. You've been very kind and thoughtful. Max and I appreciate it." She pulled her license and registration from her wallet and offered it to him.

"Won't be necessary, Miss. You drive carefully now and have a nice day." He leaned forward, smiling for the first time, and waved to Max. "You be a good boy for your momma, Max."

*   *   *

Marcia and Max went to the airport to pick up Michael on Saturday afternoon. Max was more energetic than he had been in a while, repeatedly asking Marcia "Where is Daddy? Where is Daddy?" They waited in the LAX cell phone lot until Michael called. Max leaned forward as much as he could in his car seat as they drove to Terminal 7. Max couldn't control his enthusiasm when he heard the sound of the trunk opening and squealed, "Daddy, Daddy home!"

Michael threw his suitcase, briefcase and raincoat into the trunk and climbed into the backseat to give Max a big hug. When he got into the front seat he offered a non-committal "hi" to Marcia and a kiss that grazed her cheek.

On the ride home Max recounted the week's activities, telling Michael, "Mommy bought me my best movie at Costco," and "I got a new coloring book 'bout Nemo" and "We went to the g'lato store and I got strawberries" and "We saw Dr. Harbey and he gave me a blood test and it didn't hurt" and "Mommy made chawky chip cookies in the kitchen" and "We had melted cheese for lunch and it was really good" and "Lexie got a new dog and his name is Benny," and "Mommy had to talk to a policeman."

The tsunami of words from Max elated Michael but, after less than ten minutes, Max's eyes closed and he was asleep. Marcia made succinct comments about most of the things Max had said, dismissing the policeman episode with, "it was nothing, it was all a mistake," before going on. "He was really excited to see you," Marcia said, keeping her eyes on the traffic.

"I guess so. But he seems exhausted now, doesn't he?"

"It's that way a lot now. Good trip?"

"Yes. We settled the Creavitus case without too much damage. It could have been a lot worse. Everybody was happy with the result."

"That's good."

"Yes."

They drove on, mostly in silence, Marcia often checking in the rearview mirror to see how Max was, then they came to the off-ramp to Encino.

"Did you sign the contract?"

"Marsh, for the last time, I can't turn this down." Michael kept his eyes straight ahead, looking at the traffic backed up before them on Ventura Boulevard. "I can be a senior partner in just a few years and you'll be able to do anything you want, live anywhere. You know the contract they're offering—I've told you all this before—it's very generous. The partners, Phil, Bill Douglas, Dick and the others, they have big plans for me." Finally, he turned his head to look at her, to gauge her reaction. There was none. "I've thought about it a lot," he continued, his brow creased but a tentative smile on his face, "a place in Europe somewhere, Paris, London, would be terrific, wouldn't it? We could rent it or just keep it empty for us to use whenever we want to hop over there."

Marcia concentrated on the traffic.

CHAPTER TWENTY-SIX

*M*ax slowly walked to the play corner in Harvey's office. He usually ran over to the pile of toys, played for a while and then went to sleep. This time he shuffled, his energy spent after having his blood drawn. He laid down, sucking his thumb, and soon dozed off. Pooh, with his own mid-paw band-aid in place, was tightly wedged under Max's left arm. Marcia noticed Pooh was upside down and she thought about righting the stuffed bear but decided to leave him the way he was rather than risk disturbing Max.

Marcia and Michael stared at the decorated wall behind Harvey's chair—at the all too familiar framed diplomas and the letters from children—waiting for Harvey to appear with the test results.

Harvey's nurse came in, left a file on his desk and adjusted the blinds, redirecting the mid-morning sun. "Harvey will be here in a few minutes," she said as she headed back out of the office.

"I guess those are the results," Michael tilted his head toward the file and whispered to Marcia.

"Yes."

"He may need the antibiotics again."

"Yes."

"Harvey could be calling Milt and Val, don't you think?" Michael rubbed the back of his neck.

"Yes, I suppose."

"What do you think they're discussing?"

"I don't know."

"I guess you're never going to talk to me again."

Marcia almost smiled—this was what Michael used to say whenever she was very quiet after a big disagreement. The phrase had become a familiar way for them to bridge an angry chasm, as well as a kind of code signaling a readiness for compromise, even flirtation. He used that very phrase on their third date, the first time they'd made love.

*   *   *

He called the day after they met at a party at Helen and Charles Fleiss' loft in the Meatpacking District in lower Manhattan, the neighborhood still in the early stages of gentrification. Charles was a law school classmate of Michael's and Helen, formerly Helen Witt, and Marcia had been friends at Smith. Their last names were alphabetically close, Whitman and Witt, and Marcia and Helen were paired for the introductory tour of the campus soon after they arrived. They remained close friends ever since.

Three years after they graduated from college Helen was getting a Ph.D. in physiology at Columbia. She met Charles in the law library where she had gone for the quiet in order to study. Marcia had earned her Master's by then and was on the junior faculty of the music department at Montclair State in New Jersey.

Marcia was starting to get bored at the party and was thinking of leaving when Helen grabbed her arm and steered her across the loft to meet Michael, who had arrived a little late. "I think you will really like this guy," Helen promised.

His hair was light brown, even a little blond then, and although it looked as if it hadn't been combed in a long while, it seemed perfect just the way it was—Robert Redford in Hubbell Gardner mode. Later she would learn Michael spent considerable time cultivating that tousled look and he suffered greatly when his hair started to thin and his hairline began receding.

For their first date Michael offered, with a chuckle, "an evening of informal dining and light entertainment" when he came to her apartment to pick her up. They went to a Rangers hockey game at Madison Square Garden. Dinner was hot dogs and lukewarm beer. When he asked her if she had enjoyed it, she confessed she'd never been to a hockey game. "I usually go to concerts and lectures and movies." Then added quickly, "But this was great fun. I really liked it. The hot dogs and the beer, although the beer wasn't that good." Feeling even more reassurance might be in order, she took a deep breath and said, "I'd be willing to try it again sometime."

When he called for a second date, two days later, he asked, "How about a real dinner and then a sort of concert?" When she hesitated and questioned, "What kind of concert? It's a school night," he told her she would have to wait to find out but promised they would be home before midnight.

He took her to an Italian restaurant in Chelsea, Da Umberto, stating unequivocally she would eat the best tiramisu. Then they went down to Greenwich Village for a ten o'clock performance by Gato Barbieri, the jazz saxophonist.

As Michael was hailing a cab to take her home she commented how much she'd enjoyed it, especially since it was not exactly the type of concert she usually went to.

"You don't like jazz?"

"No, no, I love jazz. My dad loves jazz. But I think I'm more of a traditional jazz sort of girl. Errol Garner, Charlie Parker, Clifford Brown. You know." She stopped to compose her thoughts. "I guess I wouldn't have gone to this concert on my own so I'm really glad you brought me." She paused again, leaned to him and lowered her voice, as if to divulge a state secret, "I think I liked the hockey more than the Gato."

On the ride uptown they kissed twice. When he put his hand on her breast she moved it away, saying, "It's really late and I do have to get ready for my classes tomorrow." She hurriedly got out of the cab when they came to her building. "Good night." Then she leaned into the cab through the open window and kissed him again. "Call me."

When he called her the next night he said, "How about dinner this Friday? Just dinner. A nice place. You'll like it and there won't be any surprises." Before she could answer, he added, "And there are no classes on Saturday."

"Dinner's fine but don't assume too much, Michael. I'm just signing on for dinner," she teased him, laughing.

After they settled in the back seat of the cab to head to the restaurant they kissed, a longer kiss than previously, and then another. "Whew," she said, "but don't forget. We're just having dinner."

"I'm a lawyer. I never make assumptions." His head was in shadow, but she was sure he was smiling—she wondered if his shallow dimple was showing—and she knew then they would have sex this night.

This time they went to the restaurant Daniel, on East 65th Street. "That was a wonderful dinner. And I loved the rhubarb cake." She leaned close to him as the waiter cleared the plates, "it was at least as good as the tiramisu the other night." She already had two and a half glasses of red wine, a Pomerol, the best wine she had ever tasted. Then Michael pointed at something on the menu for the waiter. A dessert wine in a tiny glass arrived, with just enough for them to each enjoy a couple of sips. Almost instantly, as the smooth amber liquid touched her tongue, Marcia's eyes widened. *Now I know what nectar of the gods means. Good grief, I'm starting to think in clichés. I better get control of myself.*

After Michael gave his credit card to the waiter he asked Marcia, "Do you know what that dessert wine was?"

"A sauterne, wasn't it?"

"Yes, that's right. Did you like it?"

"It was luscious."

"I have to tell you, bad form though it is, that little thimbleful of wine cost eighty dollars." He tipped his glass up to his mouth to drain the last few drops. "That's a Chateau d'Yquem. Half-bottles of some vintages of it sell for, I don't know, I'm guessing, five or six hundred dollars, maybe even more. This vintage is at least a couple of hundred dollars a half-bottle. It's made from grapes that have been deliberately infected with some bug. A fungus, I think."

Marcia sat back in her chair and stared at him. "Why on earth did you order it? This restaurant is expensive enough without having that, don't you think?"

Michael looked surprised. "What do you mean? I wanted to come here tonight. I wanted to take you." He leaned closer to stare directly into her eyes. "And I wanted it to be special."

She kissed him on the cheek. "It was special. It was very special. But you don't have to spend all that money to impress me."

"Look," he put his hand over hers, "I'm not going to do this all the time. I don't have a lot of money, you should know that. Law school tuition is scholarships, loans, and working." His broad smile disappeared for a few seconds. "But I wanted to impress you." A nervous cough before saying, "Guilty, your honor," and then the full smile again.

This time when the cab turned onto West 84th Street she took his hand, half giggled, and said, "Come up for a while."

When she opened the door to her tiny studio apartment, stacks of sheet music piled on the floor and a Kenneth Noland poster on the wall, he said, "Quite a place." He pushed the door closed behind them, took her in his arms and began kissing her while unbuttoning her blouse and simultaneously shaking off his jacket. With equal urgency she worked at his belt buckle, feeling the growing hardness inside his pants. "Do you have a condom?" she whispered, her breath coming faster and faster. "Yes," he said, "yes."

After they made love and lay in each other's arms for a few minutes he exclaimed, "Wow, that was great!" and hugged her tightly. Marcia didn't say anything at first, just moved even closer to him, her right arm pressed between them, her left arm draped across his chest. The sheet was only up to waist level, but she felt more than comfortable—the idea of being covered by thousands of warm rose petals came to mind—and she breathed a sigh of contentment. *Yes, that was wonderful. A wonderful evening and wonderful lovemaking.*

After a few more minutes, Michael half sat up and she moved slightly to lie flat on her belly. She hoped they would make love again. Instead he announced, in a cross between a growl and a John Wayne drawl, "I'm hongry, ma'am." He smiled down at her and said, "What say you hop round the corner to that little deli and get me a nice side o' beef?" and then he slapped her buttock just hard enough that it smarted.

Marcia jumped out of bed, pulling the sheet around her, and flipped on the wall switch. "What are you talking about? Who do you think you are? That hurt, damn it."

She glared at him.

He stared back and that smile, complete with dimple, returned to his face. "I guess you're never going to talk to me again."

"You're damn right I'm not. Now I think you'd better leave."

"I wasn't serious, Marcia! I didn't mean to hurt you. It was just a stupid joke. Come on. We had a big dinner. I'm not hungry at all. I'm sorry." He leaned forward, his expression now grave. "It was just for fun. And I guess not funny. I'm not the cowboy type. I don't even like John Wayne. And I am really, really sorry. But you can't think I was serious. Come on." He thrust his lower lip out in an exaggerated pout. "I guess you're never going to talk to me again?" he repeated, this time a question rather than a statement.

She stood silently, her back pressed against the bathroom doorjamb, starting to feel embarrassed at overreacting, the corners of her mouth turning up in a smile. She watched his beginning erection and, mollified, said, "Just don't ever do that again." She dropped the sheet to the floor, waited just long enough for him to look at her very slowly, head to toe and back again, his erection getting fuller and fuller, and then she turned off the light and slid back into bed.

*   *   *

"Sorry to keep you waiting" Hirakawa plopped down in his chair. "I just checked with the procurement people to see what the availability is. Max is still not near the top of the list. There are other kids up there. Some have been on the list for many months, some started out sicker than Max. Some with more common blood types. Getting him a liver is just not likely, at least not right away. Unless the unpredictable happens and we are really lucky. Maybe not until he's in full liver failure and he gets bumped up a few notches on the list."

"Oh," Michael said, slumping in his chair

"He's got cholangitis, infected bile ducts, again. His white count is up. We'll get him a bed and give him IV antibiotics overnight."

"I thought repeated cholangitis moves you up the list."

"That's true Marcia, but there are still a lot of kids ahead of him. There are times when you have your choice of livers—young, old, whatever—and there are times when you're just in the middle of the Gobi Desert. As you know all too well, it has to be the right blood type. The blood type you and Max share is uncommon. You know that also." He scratched his cheek, "I guess I said that more than once, didn't I? And the liver has to be the right size. Sometimes it seems as if there's neither rhyme nor reason regarding when a liver becomes available. It's just the way the cards fall. Especially with little kids."

Michael sat up straight. "Okay, all right. Let's go ahead with it. Let's use Marcia's liver."

When did he stop discussing decisions with me? Marcia's irritation momentarily overshadowed her relief. *Maybe he never really discussed them at all.*

Finally, she was going to take care of Max, make him well again.

Harvey immediately walked them to Val's office to set a date for the surgery. While Val made some notes, Marcia looked at Michael sitting beside her and reached over and touched his hair, pushing a few wisps from his forehead.

As soon as they got home they made phone calls to people who needed to be informed and, since it was the middle of the night in London, sent an email message to Frank. Michael's mother, Margit, immediately started crying and said she would fly out whenever they needed her. Barbara cried also and said she would fly out the next day, until Marcia reminded her they still had a few weeks to go. There was much to do to prepare before they would need the family.

After dinner, as she was loading the dishwasher, Marcia watched as Michael played with Max and his blocks, Max's favorite game. Michael stacked them high until they fell over or until Max pushed them over. Each toppling brought shrieking peals of laughter from Max, more happiness than Marcia had heard from him for too long a time.

Dropped ice-cream cone happiness.

"Time for bed, you guys," Marcia called out to them as the water started whooshing into the dishwasher.

After she pulled the cover up under his chin and waited until Max was fast asleep she went back downstairs and played the *Andante con moto*, the second movement of the *Appassionata*, stopping twice to make short notations on the score. She thought about the three variations of the second movement's theme, and about its tranquility and serenity, in contrast to the first and third movements. Barbara once told her Beethoven wanted to calm nerves with the second movement. "He wants to ready us for the whirlwind of the final movement, its heroics and passion," Barbara had said. "That's how he plunges us into the third."

Nadia Olenko, Marcia's long-ago teacher, had emphasized, her hand chopping the air in front of her, "Beethoven is definitely talking with God in opus 57," echoing what Marcia had heard as a child.

Marcia played it through once more and then sat still, hands loosely open in her lap, staring at the music. She played a few bars of a Joplin piece to ease the tension from her shoulders. Then she walked slowly upstairs, smiling, hearing the last few bars of the third movement of opus 57 in her head, the thunder, the unbridled spirit.

She stepped into the bathroom to wash up. For the past few weeks she had been changing into flannel pajamas in the bathroom. Now she slowly took off her clothes in front of her dresser. Not looking in the mirror, she was sure Michael hadn't moved. Convinced his pencil was still poised above the yellow pad, she was positive his eyes were now on her. She could sense him staring over the rims of his reading glasses. She knew he was looking at her the way he used to when they were first together.

She put on her robin's egg blue chiffon nightgown and walked back to the bedroom door to switch off the overhead light. She was mindful that the glow from his bedside lamp now outlined the silhouette of her body. She slipped into bed. Not turning to look at him she was confident his position was still unchanged—his book still propped on his knees, his glasses down on his nose, the pencil motionless—and that his eyes were fixed on her every move. Knowing the rest of the evening was in her control she let the corners of her mouth move slightly, the beginning of a smile, but she didn't turn toward him.

Slowly, deliberately, he put the pencil, the pad and the law journal on the floor, placed his glasses on the bedside table, turned off the lamp, and, as his hand rubbed her firm nipple, said, "I guess we're talking again."

Yes. At least for a while.

195

CHAPTER TWENTY-SEVEN

*B*arbara and Alan arrived four days before the scheduled transplant. Michael's mother would arrive in two more days. At that point the family would move to a hotel near the hospital but, until then, Marcia's parents were at home with her. Frank called from London almost every day and she insisted there was no reason for him to fly all the way to California. "We're going to be fine. They do this sort of thing all the time. We'll see you for the holidays," she cheerfully intoned.

The day after her parents arrived Marcia and her mother were sitting in the kitchen having a mid-morning cup of tea. Her father had gone out for a walk. Michael was already at work and Max, after a good breakfast, was napping. "I never really appreciated how controlling Michael could be," Marcia said. "I don't really understand him after all. I never realized he could be so oblivious to, or maybe uncaring about, my feelings, about my needs. About me. He will listen but if he doesn't like the topic he'll just ignore it, ignore me," Marcia's voice began to rise. "Sometimes he won't respond at all, won't even acknowledge what I've said."

Barbara reminded her they had actually discussed this very thing a few weeks before the wedding, but Marcia didn't recall. "I guess you couldn't see it at the time. That's part of being young and in love, isn't it?"

"I suppose so," Marcia conceded.

"He's a driven man, you should realize that by now," Barbara continued. "He wants to be the best lawyer in his field." She paused and reached over to pat her daughter's hand. "I understand about wanting to be the best. How it consumes you. He wants to be a big success and," she wagged her finger, "don't forget that he also wants to make a lot of money."

"He makes a decent living already. As you may have noticed, we live quite well. Encino is not exactly a slum."

"Marcia, he's one of those men who will always want more if more is available. Money, status, reputation. Control. He'll want it even if it's not available." Barbara held her breath for a few moments. "I know," her voice was much softer. "I can relate."

"What do you mean? You were never interested in money."

Barbara stood and held out her cup for a refill of tea. "Let's go sit in the back. It's such a lovely day."

"Well, just for a while. I need to see if Max is awake for lunch. He has even more vitamins than usual to take and I'm supposed to start an antibiotic tonight in preparation for the transplant." She looked up at the sky as she opened the screen door and they stepped across the threshold. "And it gets very hot out here when the sun's overhead."

They sat close to the house, under the eaves. The gardener had come earlier and the sweet smell of freshly mown grass prompted Barbara, after a deep inhalation, to say, "We don't get that marvelous aroma very often on the Upper East Side."

Marcia nodded, inhaling deeply.

"Marcia, you said I wasn't interested in money. Every one is interested in money, it just wasn't my first priority. I knew I had a security blanket since my father would always take care of me if I needed help. I was driven by the music, by the need to perform, but I knew that having money was important. I dreamed of making big contributions to Juilliard, to the Phil, to public schools for music appreciation classes. Scholarships. I really wanted to be able to dole it out. And champagne. I wanted champagne, the good things. But more than any of those things you can buy, that you can pay for, I wanted to be a pianist. That was always first. Not a pianist playing in Lyons or Liverpool or Albany or any of the other places I gave concerts. I wanted the top. Paris, London, New York. Vienna. I would have given anything for that. I wanted the fame, the reputation. I wanted to be sought after. I wanted to be desired just as much as any sultry siren, but for my hands and my fingers, not my body. I saw others of my generation where I intended to be, playing where I wanted to play. Men and women, Americans, Europeans, Latinos, whatever. But I didn't have whatever it took for that next step, the big step. And I never really learned what it was. I was close, but not quite there. I had the background, the talent, the right teachers, a good manager, the repertoire." She cleared her throat. "Good Lord, I had the repertoire. In those days I could play everything, I had everything in my head. And I thought I played as well as anyone."

"You did, I heard you."

"Maybe the problem was I wanted it too much and couldn't hide it. Maybe I was too aggressive. Too pushy. Sometimes Michael is like that."

"Yes, I suppose."

"But my point isn't to give you a long diatribe mired in the past. It's that I would have done anything," she lowered her voice and leaned forward, "*anything* to get what I wanted. I wasn't going to get married and have children because that would have interfered with my concentration. Gotten in the way of my going forward. I was like a shark, always moving forward, or else I would die." She stopped and smiled. "Although I did almost marry a European, did I ever tell you that?"

Marcia sat up straight, her face showing surprise. "No, you definitely never told me."

"Yes, well, it didn't happen. But almost." Barbara smiled again, momentarily lost in thought. "He was from Lichtenstein, of all places. Very handsome, very charming. He adored me. Lots and lots of money. Old family money. He followed me all over Europe that season after we met. Took me to the best restaurants. I was twenty-six, no, twenty-seven. I told myself I couldn't imagine calling Lichtenstein home, that no matter what he said I would have to give up my career, I would have to have twelve children and probably get fat. He was Catholic, but I knew religion wasn't the problem, wasn't the big problem." She blew on her tea and took a long swallow. "I wanted Théâtre du Châtelet, not Lichtenstein, I wanted Salle Pleyel, Carnegie, Wigmore. And I also knew that if I had children, I would neglect them . . ."

"How long did you date him? How did it end?"

Barbara's voice was deeper, almost guttural, as she shifted in her chair to directly face Marcia, "Look at me now, this is important. I hope you know that I didn't marry your father as a compromise. Not at all. He was my Lancelot, my Mr. Right, my Mr. Big. I was still playing concerts when we met, but I was a little more mature then, a little smarter, wiser, whatever. Possibly I was just a little tired of it all. I probably had already accepted—at least deep down inside of me—that I wasn't going to get to the very top of where I wanted to be, although I don't remember ever saying that to myself. I just knew here was a good and decent man and I would have a good life with him. I loved him as soon as I met him. He was the smartest, the funniest, the gentlest man I had ever met. I knew I wanted to be with him all the time. I didn't want to leave his side. You know, perhaps better than I do, what a good human being he is. I knew I would have a really wonderful life with your father. And I have, I really have." She moistened her lips with one quick swipe of her tongue and went on. "It was a few years before I met him when I started to tire of all the traveling and of the loneliness and the every-now-and-then awful orchestras when I played a concert." She laughed. "God, I once played in some small city in Germany—Mannheim, I think—yes, I think so. Or maybe someplace else, maybe it was Wiesbaden, I'm not sure. It was the Brahms second, always a good piece to play in Germany, a good piece for a pianist, but the orchestra was so bad. They had a new conductor that year and the orchestra members obviously didn't like him and were waging their own Cold War." She laughed again at the memory. "And I was so angry that I ended up playing that piece better than I ever had before, but the orchestra was only periodically in time with me. Almost as if I was in West Germany and they were in East Germany. We barely managed to finish together. I think that was when I started to seriously consider I wasn't going to make it. Not the way I intended. My next few concerts were all solo piano and I was really good. I remember a small hall in Amsterdam, smaller than I had expected, almost intimate, but it was wonderful. And full. Not an empty seat. Even then the smell of marijuana was everywhere, but they were glued to me. Rapt. I could tell they were listening to every note. And I was good that night. More than good. I didn't always do encores but that night I did the Chopin A-flat major, the 'Heroic.'" She closed her eyes, the lids fluttering two or three times before she squeezed them tightly shut. "The applause was . . . thunderous. That's the word, thunderous." Marcia stared at her mother, eyes still closed. When Barbara looked again, her cheeks were rosy, her eyes sparkling, and she continued. "I would have played another encore, but how do you follow the A-flat major? It was wonderful, that night. Magical."

Marcia recalled the first time she stood in the wings for one of her mother's concerts. She was six. Barbara hadn't yet limited the number of trips she made out of the country and it was one of her rare recitals in New York. Marcia was used to seeing her mother practice and was accustomed to her deep concentration. This time watching Barbara in front of a full, live audience fascinated her, especially when all the people stood up to applaud at the end of the first piece.

"I wish I could have heard that Amsterdam concert," Marcia whispered, her own eyes widely open with a look of wonderment, a gentle smile on her face.

"You know," Barbara leaned forward, almost whispering. "Before that encore, before the Chopin, I played opus 57, your opus 57. And opus 13, the *Pathétique.*" Marcia nodded. "It was beautiful. No one was breathing. They wouldn't let me go after that and the Chopin was the only thing I could think of, the only thing grand enough, extravagant enough, to follow Beethoven that night."

She grasped Marcia's hands in hers. "Can I tell you something? About the *Pathétique?*"

Marcia nodded yes, expectant. "You once played the slow movement of the *Pathétique* for your junior high school talent show. That's when I knew. It's not so terribly hard to play. But to capture the delicacy, that's hard. It's lace in parts. Most people play it as if it's wool or even corduroy. The second movement is, is . . . it's the sound of silver coins slipping from a velvet sack onto a silk pillow." She breathed in deeply, her eyes shut. "It's the trickling of an undiscovered stream in a deserted winter forest." She paused as if listening to the woodland sounds. "When you played it, you captured something I hadn't.'" She squeezed Marcia's hands. "And I cried. I'm not sure if I cried for you, because of how well you played and how proud I was, or," she said, looking straight into Marcia's eyes, "or . . . at that stage of my life, I'm sorry to admit, perhaps because I was jealous, because I was sad for myself. I wanted to be where you were. I wanted to be that good at that age. I wanted my career still in front of me."

Barbara stood and stepped into the full sunlight, pacing back and forth on the lawn. "Michael hasn't had his Amsterdam yet. He hasn't done the 57 or the 14, or even *Für Elise* in front of people who would be ready to die after hearing it. He's still going full steam ahead to his Paris, his London. Except it's on Park Avenue. I don't know about the law. Maybe there is no Wiesbaden orchestra for him or maybe there will be lots of Amsterdams."

"Yes, I know that," Marcia said. "But maybe he isn't as wise as you. Sure, you put marriage and family on hold. But Michael wants it all. And there isn't enough left of whatever his 'all' is for me at the end of the day. Lawyers say that a lot, don't they?—'at the end of the day.' Well, at day's end I never see him." Marcia took a deep breath, her face still. Sad. "I cook and serve his meals. He tells me what he wants to tell me. I keep his house clean. I fill his bed but, truth be told, he works there also. The floor on his side of the bed is sometimes a mini law library until I nag him into cleaning it up." She fiddled with a loose strap on her sandal. "What I've been thinking is maybe he could have it all with someone else. Not me. This is not what I signed up for, is it? Or maybe I just ignored the realities. Perhaps I imagined myself content to be a housewife, to have a career as a teacher, to have children." She paused and looked straight at Barbara. "At this day's end it may not be enough for me. I don't have the satisfaction I expected. I need more. Perhaps it's like you not being satisfied on the road anymore." She halted searching for words. "In the end, I'm your daughter, aren't I?"

Barbara didn't respond and then walked over to Marcia and hugged her tightly. Before letting go she kissed Marcia's cheek. "Yes," her voice was husky, "yes, you are."

"I've been discussing all this with my therapist. I often feel . . . I'm not sure what. I guess *unfulfilled*. That's the word. Maybe I'm looking for something thunderous." Marcia's mouth and her eyebrows were downturned and her forehead was creased. "With Max sick I realize it's normal to sometimes feel trapped, unable to do things for myself because he needs so much attention. There's so much worry in my life now. But I used to feel trapped even before he was sick. I just didn't understand it that much, didn't acknowledge it." She tugged ineffectually at the sandal strap that had by now come undone. "I guess that's what therapy does for you, it helps you recognize things that have been there for a long time."

Barbara knelt down in front of Marcia to buckle the strap. "I listened very closely last night when you practiced. I hope you know how good a pianist you are. You've always played well enough to be onstage if you wanted to be . . ."

Marcia cocked her head to the side, one eyebrow lifted. "We haven't had this particular conversation for a while."

"That's not the point. I'm not lecturing you or hectoring you or badgering you. Not this time. I just want you to know that now, right now, you are not just another capable pianist. You are my daughter and you will never know how grateful I am for that. Because, among many, many other things, you are bright and decent and honest. But more than that you are also a very gifted pianist. You have the talent. You've always had it. And I'm grateful for that, also. The rest, the drive, the insatiable need, only you can decide what to do about your talent." She hesitated, as if forming her thoughts. "And maybe you need to ask yourself, or discuss with your Dr. Hirsch, why you are so focused on the piano now. Why you feel you have to master opus 57? More to the point, it's ready. The piece is ready. You can play it now. Today. Yesterday. Last week. Why isn't it ready enough for you?"

Telling me what to do again? Controlling? Again?

This time Marcia hugged her mother, squeezing her very tightly. She kissed Barbara's cheek. "Maybe you're right."

CHAPTER TWENTY-EIGHT

*I*t was still dark at six a.m. when they arrived at the hospital. After they registered there was a wheelchair for Marcia and one for Max. The night before she had told him, "We're going to give you a little piece of Mommy's liver and then you'll feel much better." The first thing Max said to each of his grandparents when he saw them at the hospital was "I getting Mommy's libber and 'bout time!" They all laughed until Margit began crying and walked away from the registration desk. Alan and Barbara didn't cry until after the elevator to the operating rooms closed behind the wheelchairs.

Michael was allowed to stay in the pre-operative area with Max and Marcia, but he had to put on a blue paper coverall. He and Marcia watched the pediatric anesthesiologist start an IV in Max's arm. "That hurt!" Max said, sounding more surprised than angry, then he was immediately fast asleep. Marcia grabbed for his fingers as he was wheeled past her to go to the operating room, but she wasn't close enough and couldn't connect.

Other patients were in cubicles awaiting their surgeries, their curtains open or half-drawn. Michael was the only visitor except for one other family member, a mother with her teenage daughter. The girl was doubled over clutching her belly. The nurses were all with patients and the phone rang five times before a clerk finally ran over to the desk to pick it up. "There's a delay for room 6," he held the phone out for one of the nurses. "Can you talk to them?"

"Michael," Marcia whispered.

"Yes, hon," he stepped a little closer and tried to hold one of her hands, but she kept them clenched across her chest.

"Michael, I still don't think I can move back to New York."

"Of course you can. You'll feel better when this is all behind us. We'll have plenty of time to figure it all out. To make it work."

"No, I need to tell you now. I want you to know."

"Marcia, this is crazy. It's hardly the time to discuss something like this. Right now I just want you to be well and for Max to be well. We'll discuss the rest tomorrow."

A second anesthesiologist walked over to the foot of Marcia's gurney and introduced herself. Pamela something. Strawberry-blond hair worn in a ponytail. *Good grief, she's awfully young.* Marcia tried to read her ID badge but it was constantly in motion. Lowering the rails on the left side of the gurney she told Marcia, "They're just about ready for you. I'm going to start an intravenous line and you'll soon be asleep. The next thing you know, you'll wake up in the recovery room."

Marcia was told to start counting backwards from one hundred as the anesthesiologist injected something into the access point of the IV tubing. Marcia almost giggled as she felt the first effects of the anesthetic. *Didn't hurt at all.* "One hundred, ninety-nine, ninety-eight, ninety—"

* * *

Marcia woke up with a little more discomfort in her belly than when her FNH had been removed. But this time her throat was burning, hot and raw. It hurt each time she took a breath. Breathing through her nose helped, but she didn't always remember to do that. She understood that she hurt more because the surgery this time was more complicated and the breathing tube in her throat had been in so much longer. She wasn't concerned, although she thought her lack of concern was strange, disconnected.

She heard a voice. "You're doing fine, Marcia. Just take some deep breaths and that'll help you wake up."

She took two slow, deep breaths, then went back to sleep.

When she woke up again she immediately said, "Max?" but wasn't sure she made any sound.

"He's good, Marsh." It was Michael, sitting at the side of her bed. He took her hand. "Max seems to be doing just fine. You're in the recovery room. Max is in the pediatric recovery room. I just saw him a few minutes ago. He looks fine, but he has lots of tubes and wires hooked up." She was sleeping again and didn't hear him finish the sentence.

It was dark outside the next time she woke up. For a moment she felt like peeing then remembered the catheter and her discomfort went away. She looked up at the monitor slightly behind her head and then at the one to her left. Both sets of sharp squiggly lines seemed to be moving consistently and nothing was beeping. It was uncommonly quiet outside her room and then she saw the big white wall clock indicating it was just before four in the morning. She fixed her gaze on the fluid in the IV bag, hoping to hear a drip-drip-drip sound, but it was silent and, almost instantly, she returned to a deep sleep.

The next time she awoke it was daytime and the hall outside her room was busy with a steady hum of conversation and activity. Her throat still bothered her and she groped at both sides of her body until she found the call button by her right hip and pushed it.

"Well, good morning. Did we have a good sleep?" A new nurse seemed to appear out of nowhere. She had a big smile. Her hair was in cornrows and her turquoise-rimmed glasses dangled from a red-beaded chain around her neck. Marcia blinked a few times trying to focus on the nurse's name tag. Delia Reynolds.

"Yes, thank you, good. Good sleep." Marcia's voice was rough and raspy and, at first, she spoke slowly in order to form sentences. "My little boy? Do you know how my little boy is?" She craned her head forward.

"No, I haven't heard anything, so that's a good sign. He's in a different unit, he's in the pediatric I.C.U., but I'll call over and check. You just lie back and relax." The nurse adjusted the pillows and pushed a button at the foot of the bed to elevate Marcia's head. "How about some ice chips? They'll make your mouth and throat feel less dry."

Marcia nodded, closed her eyes. *Everything's fine. Doing okay.* She thought about turning on the television but decided to try to rest a little more even though the unit was bustling with activity. She dozed on and off all day as patients and staff, some pushing various pieces of equipment, streamed past her doorway. Racks of meal trays went by as well as rolling shelves of orange-capped plastic liter bottles filled with clear fluid. Men and women in dark blue shirts pushed brooms and mops. Every hour on the half hour visitors, anxious or smiling, downcast or laughing, rushed in to the various rooms only to be herded out after a too-short ten minutes of visit time.

She had her own mini-parade of care-team visitors. The nurses and the nursing assistants—their badges labeled "Care Partner"—came by in the morning at the change of shift. Then the transplant resident saw her before he went off for another day in the operating room. The dietitian stopped in, then left when she realized Marcia was recently out of surgery and still not eating. At ten o'clock the entire transplant team, on morning rounds, squeezed into her room. Medical students were relegated to the back only able to peer in through the glass from outside the cramped area, some with masks still hanging around their necks or blue tissue-paper caps left on their heads. Dour Dr. White, stern as usual, put a stethoscope on her belly and said, to no one in particular and to everyone within earshot, "She's got bowel sounds, let's start feeding her. Liquids." A resident typed something on his BlackBerry and a nurse scribbled something on her pad.

"When is Max going to be up and awake? When do I start walking?" From the first day she'd had no trouble calling Dr. Spellman "Milt," but she didn't feel that connection to White. She was confident of his medical acumen and his technical skills but he didn't invite a warm relationship. He even answered the phone with a brusque, "This is White." It hadn't been a problem for Michael, though. Right away, he'd asked, "Do I call you John or Jack?"

"Marcia, your surgery was just as complicated as Max's. We had a lot of work to do on your bile ducts and your blood vessels. The big difference is we have an easier time figuring out pain levels for aftercare with adults." He checked the monitor over the head of her bed. "You're doing well. We would have moved you out of the I.C.U. already but your blood pressure was a little low for a while. It's fine now."

After he left she realized he hadn't answered either of her questions. Val stayed on after the others left, patted her hand and said, "The nurses will probably take you for a short stroll after lunch. You're doing great, and Max is just fine." Marcia smiled up at Val and, much relieved, said, "Thanks, Val. You know how much I need to hear that."

Marcia's lunch tray included clear soup, tea and Jell-O. Her throat was much less sore and she was hungry. When the care partner came in to clear the tray, she asked, "How about a couple more of these?" waving the empty Jell-O cup at him.

Michael called at twelve-thirty, just as she was finishing the second Jell-O, to ask how she was.

"I'm good, Michael, I'm fine . . . No, no reason to rush over. I'm mostly sleeping. I'll see you later."

He said he'd been there until eleven the previous night, going back and forth from her room to Max's. And he had checked on both of them this morning before going to the office. He also talked to Spellman who assured him that she and Max were just fine, were both doing great.

"Yes, I think I saw you once . . . Yes, four-thirty is fine, no rush . . . Yes, I'm fine. I'm getting a lot of attention . . . I think I remember Val told us they keep children a little more sedated than adults, or maybe one of the nurses said that, but they say he's doing well . . . I'm really anxious to see him, but they just keep telling me 'soon.' I want to hear 'now.'"

Barbara and Alan came in every hour, as permitted, usually with Margit. They hardly talked and left promptly when the allotted ten minutes were up. Most of the time Marcia dozed. Once, Alan turned the television on to get the news and woke her briefly.

When Michael came in that afternoon, Marcia tried to sit up, leaning on one elbow, and asked, "How's Maxie?"

"Great." Michael leaned forward to kiss her forehead. "He's doing just fine. I spoke to him before coming up here. He's still a little groggy, a little silly, but he seems great."

She smiled and, with her eyes closed, remained smiling for a while.

"You know I'm really happy things went so well, Marsh." The bell ending the time for visitors rang.

"So I'll see you later?" Marcia reached her hand out to hold his, her face expressionless.

"Yes, of course. See you later." He turned before he crossed the threshold, "I love you, Marsh."

"Yes, I know." She slipped into another dreamless sleep.

* * *

At the end of her second post-operative day Marcia started worrying that Max was going to hemorrhage before the 48-hour time period passed and no one would notice. A little after midnight she insisted her nurse, Adele, call the pediatric I.C.U. to check on Max. Adele returned within minutes and warmly said, "All of his vitals are good. He's doing very well. He had some ice cream about two hours ago and is now sound asleep."

In the months before the surgery Marcia read over the list of complications so many times she had memorized them. *Hemorrhage, usually first two days; bile duct strictures, not uncommon, lots of causes; bile leak, not uncommon; chronic rejection, usually a year or more. Or not at all.*

When she got tired of thinking about complications, she plagued herself with questions: *What if my liver doesn't work well? What if he needs a new liver? Will he be high on the list then? If Maxie needs a new liver who can donate? What if I have a bile leak and die? What will Michael do? What will happen to Max? What if Max gets one of those overwhelming infections?*

Linda, her cousin from Laguna, visited the third day after Marcia's surgery. Marcia was grateful for her chatter about her kids, about a shooting at the new luxury hotel in Dana Point, about the Marine jets that buzzed the beach, about the show at the Laguna Museum, about a charity dance she and Teddy were going to, about her new shoes. The continuous babble almost kept Marcia's mind off Max.

When she got the word she could finally visit Max later that day, getting there seemed to take an eternity. Marcia didn't want lunch, she didn't want a bed-bath, she couldn't understand why getting her chart together took so long. *I thought it was all electronic these days.* She knew she couldn't take the stairs and the elevator took another forever to arrive.

Finally they wheeled her into Max's room. He seemed to be sleeping peacefully, although Marcia knew the sleep was likely induced by sedatives. Marcia anticipated he would be sleeping a lot of the time for the next couple of days. She watched his chest move up and down in even rhythm. She was relieved just to be with him, a little less anxious now that she could see for herself that he looked all right.

A week before the transplant she and Val visited the pediatric I.C.U. where Val explained the monitors and all the wires and tubes and medications. Marcia read the articles in medical journals she had gotten from Harvey and looked many times at anything and everything that was available on the internet that even remotely dealt with pediatric liver transplantation. She prepared herself for what Max would look like after the surgery. But, as close as she was to him now and as much as she could see he was doing well, she was still sadder than she expected to be, than she wanted to be.

She thought at this point many of the monitoring lines would have been disconnected. There still seemed to be a lot of wires and tubes. Dr.

White told her they usually maintained the arterial line and the central venous line for a while to allow open access for fluids as needed, as well as for any medications they might want to administer in a hurry. "We want to be able to draw blood whenever we want to check his chemistries without having to stick him over and over again. You know as well as I do that getting blood from little kids isn't so easy. Isn't fun for them."

After Marcia persistently asked, Val described Max on his first day after the transplant as being flat on his back and completely flaccid, his little arms and legs splayed to the sides, with many wires and tubes. With the tips of her fingers Marcia gently touched bruises that were still at his wrists and ankles. That she hadn't seen him those first days had been easier in some ways, but she still felt she should have been here.

The next day the bruises were fading, the angry look of them gone. Max was awake, propped up on some pillows, watching his favorite movie, *Finding Nemo*.

"Mommy, Mommy, come see Nemo."

Max's nurse was there. "Hi, I'm Lainey. He's a sweetheart, you know." Lainey said Max already ate some applesauce. She described the most recent blood tests and told Marcia about Max's wetting the bed just after the catheter was removed. "Lord love him, he was not happy when that happened. But after that he did fine using a urinal. And he really likes that urinal. Once he used it he thought it was great fun to pee. I think he likes the sound, sort of a soft drum roll you know, of the urine hitting the plastic."

Marcia backed her wheelchair up to sit beside Max as he followed Nemo's journey. She tried holding his hand but he pulled it away, saying, "I'm watching, Mommy." Then he just put his head back and went to sleep. Lainey covered him with a light blanket. Marcia sat another twenty minutes until someone came to transport her back to her room. But she was happy to wait. She was content just to be near Max and to watch him. *My sweet little boy.*

Her parents and Michael's mother were in her room when she got back. As soon as she was moved to a regular room at least one of them was there almost all the time. There were four vases of flowers, a fruit basket and a couple of boxes of candy. Even an orchid and a get-well card from Lina Padilla, the first specialist they saw. Alan had already picked through one of the candy boxes for the dark chocolates.

Amy Levy and Linda each called that evening as did Frank, long distance at five in the morning London time. There were calls from Pat Hirsch and Edie Anderson. More flowers were delivered and Harvey Hirakawa stopped by with a small vase of tulips from the gift shop.

"Harvey, that is so sweet of you. You're not supposed to do this. You're our doctor."

"Yes, well, these are from Harvey the friend, not Harvey the doctor."

There had been some confusion in the transfer from the I.C.U. to a regular room and a dinner meal had not been ordered for Marcia. It finally arrived at about nine fifteen and she ate it seemingly without stopping to breathe.

The next day Marcia began walking up and down the halls. She walked as much as she wanted as long as someone was with her. She had much less pain than she expected, just a dull, persistent soreness at her side under her ribs. She visited Max as often as she could and when the staff was too busy to escort her there, one of her visitors wheeled her to the pediatric unit.

On the fifth day Jack White came to Marcia's room. The resident and Val were three steps behind. "You can go home tomorrow or the next day if you want to. You're doing great." He tapped something into his BlackBerry as he spoke. Val came in and sat at her bedside.

"What would you do if you lost that thing?" Marcia was sitting up, the back of the bed raised to a 45-degree angle, *Los Angeles* magazine splayed face-down at her side.

White looked up at her, obviously surprised. "My BlackBerry? Probably have to end it all. My whole life is in here." He didn't smile at all and went back to tapping. "Val will give you some instructions and some prescriptions. I want you to take the antibiotics a few days more. I've given you some pain meds and a sleeping pill, as well as a stool softener so you don't have to strain."

"Thank you. When can Max come home?"

"Not too long from now, but let's keep watching him another few days before we pick a date. You still need some time to mend without running around after him."

"I don't need that much time. My parents and my mother-in-law are here to help me. When they go home I'll have a twenty-four-hour caretaker for a couple of weeks. Actually, she's ready to start anytime." She nodded toward Val. "Val is helping arrange all that and . . ." She hesitated and White raised his eyes, peering over the rim of his glasses. "I want to have Max home as soon as possible."

"Fine, that's all fine," White said, his voice back on automatic pilot. "I want to see you in a week. And if you have any problems or questions, anything at all, call us, anytime. Twenty-four seven. Someone will get back to you within fifteen minutes of your call."

"That's reassuring, very reassuring. Thank you. What about Max?"

He looked at her again, this time taking his glasses off to emphasize that he was listening. "A couple more days, as I said. Then we'll decide." He paused, daring her to bring the topic up again, and then put his glasses back on. "You can't lift him up, you know. Not for many weeks."

She nodded, "I understand. Yes."

"No driving until I tell you. No tennis or jogging or any other sports until I tell you. No exercising at all until I tell you. No alcohol until I tell you. No sex until I tell you." He didn't look up, as usual didn't smile, and didn't look to see if she was listening.

"You know I didn't have a strong period a few weeks ago. I didn't tell you because I thought it was just anxiety." She paused. "I'm usually pretty regular." She watched as White arched his eyebrows, then glanced at Val. "Actually," she went on, "I was due a few days ago, the day after the surgery, but I just figured the surgery and all the fuss may have thrown me off-kilter."

"So this would be your second missed period?"

"I'm not sure that other one was really missed, it was just very light. But, okay, yes, I guess so." She wiped the corner of her mouth with a tissue. "Maybe."

"Could you be pregnant?"

She flushed a little and half-closed one eye, squinting at him. "I'm not sure."

"What does that mean?" He pulled up a chair and sat down. Finally, she had his full attention.

"Is there a problem?"

"No, no. I guess we might not have gone ahead if we'd known you were pregnant, but not for any good reason. We've certainly done pregnant mother-to-child transplants in the past without a problem. I do have to tell you there has been a miscarriage in one case but that mother had some other post-op problems. Most of the time it's not an issue."

"What about that day, the first day after the operation, when they said my blood pressure was low? Could that affect my periods? What if I really was pregnant?"

"I wouldn't expect any problem. It wasn't that low. We were just being cautious. So you're not having any bleeding now?"

"No, not at all."

"And what do you mean when you say you're not sure? You haven't used the pill since we took out the FNH, have you?"

"No, no, I haven't."

"Are you using any other contraceptive?"

White's phone rang. He looked at the monitoring display behind Marcia's bed and then walked out of the room to take the call.

Marcia turned to the bedside table to get a cup of water but before she could reach it Val stood up and poured it for her from the pitcher. Marcia looked at her, downcast. "It's just that Michael and I have been having some . . . we haven't been . . . we've only had sex once in the past few months." She gnawed on her lower lip. "And that was two months ago. Maybe two and a half. So I think if I was pregnant from that I'd be showing by now. Right?"

Val leaned forward and whispered, "I guess we would have liked to know that also."

Marcia sat up straight now. "Why is that an issue?"

"We usually like to know about psychological—interpersonal—issues, especially with the adult recipients. Not so much with donors, but we still want to know." She tapped her pencil against her cheek. "That's just my knee jerk response. Forget it, we can't do anything about it now. You know the psychologists sometimes question a transplant if the home setting isn't up to par." Marcia thought Val sounded a little annoyed.

White came back into the room, holstering his phone. "Maybe we should do a pregnancy test before you go home?"

"I really don't think I'm pregnant. I mean it's unlikely. I don't see the point unless you think it's medically necessary." Marcia paused, then said. "Actually, I guess we should know. So, yes, we might as well find out. Do the test."

"It's not medically necessary at this stage. You just might want to know."

"Yes, of course. Let's do it. I want to know for sure."

The next day, before she was discharged, Marcia visited Max for two hours. The nurses insisted she use the wheelchair as long as she was a patient despite her repeated, gentle protestations telling them she was sure she could walk to his room.

Even though Max slept most of the time Marcia thought he was more alert in his waking times than he had been before the transplant. All the blood test results were rapidly returning to normal values. The daily ultrasound was always reported to her as "okay, just fine." And the blood test indicated that she wasn't pregnant.

She didn't want to go home without Max but she was resigned to the fact it was going to happen. She asked Margit and Alan to stay at the hospital with Max until Michael came for them at dinnertime. "Mom can help me get settled at home."

Margit had prepared a brisket with all the trimmings: onions, carrots, potatoes, the works. She even baked a blueberry tart for dessert. Although Marcia thought she would only eat enough to be polite, she devoured everything on her plate and even had a second thin slice of the luscious tart.

She didn't talk much during dinner and excused herself right after she finished eating. "That was really a delicious dinner, Margit. I never think to cook brisket. Thank you so much. Please save me a piece of the tart for tomorrow. It was wonderful." She walked over and kissed her mother-in-law on the cheek and squeezed her shoulders.

Barbara offered to help her upstairs and Michael said, "Need help?" at almost the same time. She waved her hand dismissively. "I'm okay. Just don't eat all the dessert," she smiled. She went up the stairs slowly, one step at a time, feeling Barbara's eyes following her progress. Even Smedley, on the top step, imperious as ever, kept watching her. She was out of breath by the time she reached the landing. "I'm fine," she called down to her mother, "really. Just a little weaker than I thought I'd be." She bent down to pet Smedley. "You haven't been getting much attention lately since I've been away, have you?" He arched his back under her touch and meowed his agreement.

Jack White told her to take a sleeping pill the first night home, even if she felt she didn't need one. She was swallowing the pill when Michael came into the bathroom.

"Everything good?"

"Yes. Really. Thank you." She rinsed her mouth out and walked over to the bed and climbed under the covers. "I just need some sleep. I'm really tired. I'll see you in the morning."

He leaned down to kiss her forehead but she coughed and turned her head away. "Sorry, really tired." He stayed bent over as if he were about to say something, but then straightened up and switched off the light.

Michael had been very attentive while she was in the hospital. For the first two evenings after the surgery he stayed at her bedside reading various case documents while she slept. Once, when she woke up at two in the morning, Michael was standing there, his briefcase in his hand, ready to leave but discussing something about a medication—she heard him say a drug-like name but couldn't tell if it was one of hers or related to one of his cases—with a woman doctor she didn't recognize. The woman, probably in her late thirties, was tall and very attractive, a slender blonde in high heels and a red dress under her long white coat. *Is he hitting on her while I'm lying here with a big gash in my belly? Why did I think of that? He wouldn't do that here.* Marcia hadn't been able to stay awake and when she woke in the morning she was sure it was all a dream. The entire memory slipped from her mind until just before she was being discharged and that same doctor accidentally came into her room looking for another patient. Marcia decided it wasn't important enough to mention to Michael.

The continuing fatigue she was feeling surprised her. She expected to have more energy by now. Her thoughts shifted to Max alone in the hospital without her. She wanted to call but decided it might just remind him she wasn't nearby.

She slept very soundly that first night home, grateful to be back in her own bed and happy Dr. White had convinced her to take a sleeping pill.

CHAPTER TWENTY-NINE

*M*arcia's period came seven days after her surgery. She stared at herself in the bathroom mirror, a little sad she wasn't pregnant but mostly relieved her body was returning to normal.

She felt overwhelmed with so many family members hovering over her. She knew they only wanted to help but she wanted to do as much as she could on her own. She wanted her house to herself again and, most of all, she wanted Max home.

Barbara played the piano every day for at least an hour or two, usually early in the morning, wanting to keep it available for whenever Marcia might want to practice. Barbara never played any of the Beethoven sonatas. Mozart, Chopin, Brahms, others, but never Beethoven. Marcia knew that was deliberately done for her benefit, although she wasn't quite sure she understood the reason.

Listening to Barbara play was a form of therapy for Marcia. She could escape into the music, letting it block out everything—her problems with Michael, her concern for Max. *I'm good, I know it now, but she is amazing.* When she had listened to her mother play in the past, she had concentrated on the music itself, on the overall sound of it. Now she concentrated on her mother's technique. All the various intonations, the phrasing, often just staring at Barbara's fingers in their confident, shimmering, flawless traveling up and down the keyboard. *A master class. And just for me.*

Val called to tell her about the live-in helper who would stay with them for at least a couple of weeks. Victoria Mayaguez was a physician in the Philippines but, already in her fifties, hadn't pursued the difficult goal of getting a medical license when she moved to Los Angeles five years ago to be with her son who was an undergraduate at UCLA. She also had a daughter who was studying medicine in Chicago. A nurse before going to medical school, Victoria easily earned her California nursing license. Now she mostly worked with hospice cases but also helped post-transplant patients. And she liked working with children.

When she took over the housekeeping, the laundry, the shopping, the whole house, Marcia began to believe Victoria had been dropped from heaven. She took Marcia's temperature and blood pressure at least twice a day and made sure Marcia napped in the morning and afternoon. She would have done all the cooking but the grandmothers would not allow that. Victoria had an innate ability to adjust to everyone's personality and consequently was never intrusive.

*   *   *

The second day home started well for Marcia after a good night's rest. Michael tried to anticipate her every need and she felt quite cheerful. She and Michael arrived at the hospital at noon expecting to take Max home. Instead the charge nurse paged Dr. Spellman, explaining that the surgeon wanted to talk to them.

"He's got a little fever," Spellman said, his hand on Michael's shoulder. "Nothing to be alarmed about, but we're going to look for rejection and infection. Let's rule those things out first. We've already drawn some blood and the results will come back within the hour. Sometimes children have a fever after transplant and we don't know why and nothing comes of it."

"But what do *you* think, Milt?" Michael stood with his arms crossed and his feet widely separated in what Marcia thought of as his courtroom-attack stance. They were outside Max's room, Marcia looking more at Max than at either Milt or Michael. All the blips on the various monitors seemed to be regular and steady, but Max appeared flushed, his cheeks a little pinker than usual.

"Well, Mike, he's covered with antibiotics and an antiviral for the common transplant infections, although kids don't always have the common ones. The ultrasound and the Doppler show good flow in his blood vessels. They're not a hundred percent reliable but they're pretty good."

He stopped to clear his throat before continuing. "I think he probably has some mild rejection. His enzymes were starting to increase slightly yesterday, but that's not completely conclusive at this stage. We usually see rejection between one and two weeks, so this fits. You would think he wouldn't reject his mom's liver, but it's common and it's usually transient and very easy to control. We do the blood type match but that doesn't mean that you," he nodded toward Marcia, "and Max are identical people in every regard. We'll do a liver biopsy right now and find out for sure before treating it."

Spellman continued talking but Marcia lost track of what he was saying. She was silently reviewing the list of complications she had memorized, including signs and symptoms. *Yes, the only things that fit are infection and rejection.*

Spellman gently touched Marcia's elbow to make sure she was listening. "If he's rejecting, we'll boost his immunosuppression a little. It's usually not a problem. If the liver biopsy is normal, which is also a possibility, we'll just watch him for a while." He waited for their questions but they had none. He smiled encouragingly. "Not a big problem, really. This happens to a lot of kids, and we usually get it under control pretty quickly."

*　　*　　*

When the nurses wheeled Max back into his room after the biopsy he was fast asleep and Michael said, "Let's grab a cup of coffee."

The hospital café was chilly and Marcia headed for a table near a window that was in sunshine. After they ordered, Michael nervously tapped his fingers on the table, an uncommon act for him, and said, "I sure hope this is nothing serious."

Marcia rested her hand on top of his. "He's done so well up till now. Milt said it was likely just 'a little rejection.' Nothing that serious."

"I guess." Michael started to put his other hand on top of hers but she pulled her hand away and dropped both hands into her lap. "Michael, in the last couple of days I've called around and there are a couple of teaching jobs I'm sure I can qualify for. There's a position at Santa Monica Community College that sounds right for me. I've already spoken to the head of the music department and she wants to see me whenever I can manage to get over there. They need someone like me. And there's also an open position at Cal State Northridge. The salaries are not too bad. I'd like to stay in the house if possible but will certainly understand if you want me to look for a smaller house or an apartment. I'd love to keep the piano, but that's entirely up to you."

"Do we need to discuss this now?"

"Max seems to be doing well and I'm doing well and, I guess, this whole other issue is more on my mind now."

He just looked at her, started to speak twice, then finally said, "You do know I can't turn down this job, don't you?"

"Yes. I do. I'm sorry. Truly. This is not an easy time for us, for either of us, but I just know what's the right thing for me. I don't feel the way I used to. On the one hand I feel I've become a new person. A stronger person. And—at least for now—I need to be in California as I figure it all out. And," she brought one hand up and briefly put it over his, "it's not the same for us. There's something missing for me. There's no sense ignoring that."

"For you?" He raised his voice, looking around to see if anyone noticed, and then spoke in a scratchy whisper. "For *you?* What about me?"

"I'm not sure I can explain it." She concentrated on keeping her own voice soft and even. "I don't completely understand it yet, but I don't think I can be the wife you want. The wife you need."

Their coffee came and she put two teaspoons of sugar in his cup with some milk and then a little milk in her own. He said nothing but kept tapping on the table until Marcia again put her hand over his.

"I'll always love you, but I'm just not in love with you anymore. Once I realized that, everything changed. Can you understand? I need to find myself again. I don't feel like a Mrs. Kleinman anymore. And I don't feel like the old Marcia. I'm not exactly sure of all of this yet, but I know we don't belong together." He stared at some point beyond her, his eyes unfocused. "I'll never stop caring for you," she continued, "I hope you know that." Her tears were flowing now and she pulled a packet of tissues from her pocketbook. "I'll always want to hear from you, to keep in touch with you," she was sobbing now, "and . . . and . . . I will make it easy for you to see Max whenever you want. Here or New York or wherever, but I don't want to live with you anymore. I know it won't be easy, but I promise I will do my best to make sure you and Maxie see each other as much as possible." She cried a minute or two longer and then wiped her eyes dry.

After paying the check Michael walked to the gift shop to get a *New York Times*. She followed a step or two behind him, neither of them talking.

Just before they went into the pediatric unit he turned, put his hand on her arm, and said, "It's not that easy, Marsh."

"I know, Michael. Really. I know." She wanted to hug him, show how much she cared for him, but she didn't move at all, keeping the space between them.

"I'm not ready to give up that easily."

"I know that also." Marcia felt a tightness in her shoulders and wanted to cry again, but she just followed Michael to Max's bedside.

* * *

Max continued sleeping for a few hours after the biopsy. When he did wake they were hovering over him. They all briefly spoke, but he was quickly asleep again.

A few minutes before seven in the evening Spellman and some members of the liver team came into Max's room. "He's got a little rejection.

Everything else is fine. His wound looks terrific and he looks terrific. We'll give his immunosuppression a tiny boost and he should do well. We'll look at his enzymes tomorrow and probably let him go the day after." Spellman was mostly looking at Marcia and half-smiled when she frowned. "Maybe tomorrow."

*   *   *

The next day Max was chatty and happy and they were ready to let him go home. "The enzymes are good today," the nurse told them. The nurses gave Max a new plastic urinal, still in its plastic bag, with a wide red bow tied around the flask's neck. He had been walking to the toilet in his room for a few days and hadn't used the urinal at all, but he giggled and put the plastic flask under his left arm, the right occupied, as usual, by his buddy, Pooh.

"What do you say, Max?" Marcia prompted him.

"Thank you." He put his right hand across his waist and tried to bow a little, even though he was seated in a wheelchair. It must have hurt because he quickly straightened up, grimacing as if he might cry.

Max received ten get-well stuffed animals and the nurses put everything in an extra large plastic bag for them to take. Marcia wanted to leave some of them for other sick children, and convinced Max it would be a good idea, but the nurses said they couldn't allow another child to have a toy that came from a patient's room. The obvious favorite was a large Tigger that Todd and Edie Anderson sent. Max insisted that Tigger, who was a little taller than Max, ride in the wheelchair on his lap between Pooh and the urinal.

When they got home Max slowly and steadily walked from the driveway and, as he had been repeatedly instructed, did not run. When the front door opened he dashed ahead, squealing, into the arms of his grandmothers and his grandfather all of whom were laughing and crying at the same time. Through all the hugs Max held tight to his three most important possessions—Pooh, Tigger and the urinal.

Four days later Barbara, Alan and Margit returned to New York, confident Victoria would manage well. Barbara had been invited months earlier to speak to the high school students at what she still called 'Performing Arts,' her alma mater. Scheduled for the following week, she didn't want to disappoint her friends there.

Marcia and Michael hardly spoke. Instead, he decided to move out of the house until it was time for his relocation to New York. He signed a four-month lease for a furnished executive apartment in Century City, close to the Caney, Wheeler offices in Westwood.

CHAPTER THIRTY

*M*arcia sat at the piano and played *Greensleeves*, and then two Chopin nocturnes, some Clementi exercises and the first movement of the *Pathétique*. Then she played a Kabelevsky sonata faster than it needed to be played, enjoying the stretching and bending and arching of her fingers flying so quickly over the keys that they blurred even to her. Then she returned to the *Pathétique* second movement thinking about what Barbara told her about when Marcia played it so many years ago. Now, she listened very closely to her own sounds. She wasn't sure she caught every nuance the way Barbara had, but she knew her playing was good. *Maybe even very good.*

She pulled out the score for the opus 57 and followed the notes as she listened to the first movement from the Berman recording, the last movement of the Ashkenazy recording, and the slow movement from her mother's recording. A couple of times she touched the pages with her fingers as the piece progressed and, for some passages, moved her fingers as if she were playing the music herself.

It was almost midnight when Marcia finally went to bed. She left the CD player on, with the slow movement of her mother's recording on repeat. She visualized the score as the music wafted up to her room, hearing each and every measured and precise note and chord. Laying in bed she closed her eyes and moved one foot, then both feet, to the rhythm, turned her head to better hear the *pianissimos*, and then was asleep.

*   *   *

"I spoke to Nick Drury—the senior attorney in the divorce division? You know him, right?" Michael didn't wait for her answer. "He suggested we start with Janet Healy, who's a mediator. Do you want to see Nick or some other attorney? You don't have to feel obligated to use somebody from Caney. Probably you shouldn't since I'll be using somebody there.

Or should we just start with Janet and see if we can manage without lawyers?"

It had been more than a week since Michael moved out. He called for two nights in a row imploring her to reconsider. Those calls each lasted more than an hour. During the first call she cried a number of times, particularly when she had to repeat, "Michael, I just don't think I love you any more." He finally ended that call by slamming the receiver down. The second call was calmer, easier, more reasoned. Michael was more accepting. Now was the third call.

She felt like sighing but didn't. *Here he is picking my lawyer. Still in control.* "Michael, I think the mediator will be fine. I'm not looking to be difficult. I want us to be happy and I want us to be friends. I trust you."

"I spoke to Janet already. She'll probably suggest a period of separation even before we try to settle." He paused and Marcia could hear him sipping his coffee. "I guess that's already happening," he said softly, before speaking up again. "Look, I didn't make any commitments about what we will likely do, I didn't make any deals. I can come over if you want to discuss it in person. I want to pick up some things anyway."

"You can talk to Janet all you want. You know I really do trust you, Michael. I don't believe you would hurt me. If I think you are hurting me without being able to recognize it, I will ask around and find an attorney." She hesitated. "I hope you know—I think you do know—for me, this isn't about money. I want to be self-sufficient as soon as possible. Until I start working regularly and can support myself I just want some help for child support and house expenses and things like that. I'll probably take the Santa Monica job. Alan and Barbara have offered to help also." She waited for a comment, but there was none. She tried not to sound as glum as she felt, saying, "If I can't afford the house with their help I'll find a smaller place." Still, only silence from Michael and she thought it was time to change the subject. "And of course, yes, please come for dinner." Marcia acknowledged to herself that she was weary, but she wanted Michael to spend time with Max. "I'll grill some salmon. Max will love that you're here. He misses you. I told him you were thinking of moving to New York. He didn't say much, but may even think you're there now. I can give him more details and you can talk to him when you get here."

"Yes." Another pause. "Look, Marcia, I still don't understand this completely. It's all happening too quickly. I don't know why we can't make it better."

"What time can you be here? I don't want to overcook the fish."

"Is eight too late?" he said, in a lower, sadder voice.

"Max will be asleep by then."

"Of course." She heard his deep sigh, "I'll be there by six-thirty. For Max." A few seconds of silence.

"I'll plan on seven for the fish," Marcia said.

*   *   *

Despite his Century City lease, Michael moved to New York earlier than originally planned. Before he left he came for dinner twice more, bringing Marcia flowers each time, along with toy cars and a fire truck for Max the first time and a big box of Lincoln Logs the next. "I'll do anything if you'll change your mind," he said as they sat in the living room after dinner. He held his red wine, the glass still half-full, and she sipped a Pellegrino. "Whatever you want," he said very slowly.

"Michael, please, we've been through this."

"I just can't understand this, Marsh. It seems so arbitrary."

"I'm not sure I completely understand it either, but I know it's the right decision. It's right for me and it's right for you, even if you can't see that yet. I'm not completely happy about raising Maxie without you here, but I know how much you love him and I will make sure you see him as much as possible."

"I can't see him if I live in New York and you live here."

"Michael, I'm really happy here. I don't want to go back to the cold and the snow and the slush and the kind of life I'd be living there. But it's more than that. A lot more. Please try to understand. I need to create a new me and I just feel I need to do that here. I don't have all the answers yet—ha! I'm not sure I have any answers yet—but I know I need to be on my own."

"Maybe it's that you don't want to move back so close to your mother."

She started to respond but hesitated, suppressing her initial feelings of annoyance at the question. "Maybe. That's possible, I've certainly considered that. But I really don't think that's it. We've become close friends through all of this. I really don't think that's it."

"Did you ever discuss it as a possibility with your shrink?"

She searched his face for any trace of his usual skepticism when discussing Pat Hirsch, but saw none. "Yes, of course we have. That's part of what I mean when I say I've considered that, along with everything else. I've thought about it on my own and I've also spent a lot of time discussing it with Pat." His expression began to sour but she ignored it. "Pat might be a little dubious about my denials of that as a reason but, at least for right now, I," she emphasized the word and then repeated it, "I don't think Barbara is a big factor. In any case, I expect she will visit us even more often now. They've both—I mean Barbara and Alan—they've emphasized that Max and I can stay with them as much as we want to so I'll definitely bring Max to New York for holidays. And you'll be out here too, for business, so you and Max will see each other a lot, one way or another. I'll be on a schoolteacher's schedule and I promise I will spend as much time as possible in New York so you can see him. And in another few years, he'll be big enough to be put on a plane by himself."

"What does your Pat think about this arrangement?"

"You know how it works. She doesn't tell me what to do or what to think, she just helps me understand what it is *I* really want to do." She took a long swallow of water. "Who knows, maybe I'll learn more about myself someday and decide I want to move back. Anything's possible." Deciding she had to change the subject, Marcia hesitated before saying, "I'm thinking of taking lessons again." Michael didn't respond so she went on. "Piano lessons. Serious lessons. I'm exploring the idea." Another pause. "But right now, for now, I need to stay here."

Michael nervously ran his fingers through his hair. "I'm still not sure how I get to spend time with Max if he's so far away."

"We just went over that, Michael. If Harvey says it's okay, we'll come for Thanksgiving and you can take him to the parade. And we'll spend another couple of weeks there in December so you can take him to see Santa and have as much time with him as you can spare."

"This is all that therapist—"

"No, it's not," she interrupted, her voice raised and sharp. "It's me. *I* need to do this. *I* need to take care of me."

He put his wine glass on the coffee table and she stood up to put a coaster under it.

"Okay, I know I don't pay enough attention to the house, to things like coasters," he moved his hand toward the empty glass, "for example. But if we live in the city, I'll come home earlier, I'll pick up my socks and do all the other stuff I haven't been around enough to do."

She laughed, smiling warmly, careful not to sound as if she were laughing at him. "No, that's not it. Really. It's not about coasters and socks or anything like that. It's me. I've changed. I'm not the person I was when we married. I need to be on my own."

She walked over and brushed his hair back from his forehead, noticing once isolated strands of gray becoming patches. *Poor Michael. He could go gray* and *bald at the same time. That will be so hard on him.*

Michael stood up and grabbed her by the shoulders, almost knocking her off-balance. He put his arms around her, held her close, trying to kiss her, but she pushed him off. The idea of having sex with him was briefly tempting, but she told herself it was too complicated and she turned her head to the side.

"Fine. Whatever." He picked up his jacket from the piano bench. "Fuck it," he muttered, closing the door hard behind him as he left.

CHAPTER THIRTY-ONE

"He looks sick, Harvey. I'm really worried." It was the fifty-sixth day after the transplant, almost two weeks after Michael's move, and Max's temperature was almost 101.

"Bring him in."

Marcia sent a text message to Michael: *M looks sick. Fever. taking to Harv. # 2 call u? cell? other?*

He phoned as she finished buckling Max into the car seat. The engine was running and she pushed "Accept" on the dashboard screen. When Michael's voice came out of the car's speakers Max sat up straight. "Daddy! Where are you?"

"I'm in New York, Max. I'm going to have dinner with Grammy Margit later on."

"When are you coming home?"

"Soon, Maxie, soon. Let me talk to Mommy now."

"Oh-kay."

"I love you, Maxie."

"I love you too, Daddy."

"What's happening, Marsh? I thought everything was good."

Marcia stared at the screen. She had never quite figured out how to cancel the car Blu-tooth so the conversation was not broadcasted. *I could ask Michael but what's the point?*

"Daddy, Daddy."

"Yes, Max. What's up?"

"Mommy got me new blocks with alphabets on. I'm learning alphabets."

"That's wonderful. Mommy is a good teacher, isn't she?"

"Yes. And Daddy?"

"Max, let me talk to Mommy for a little while. I really need to talk to her. Is that okay?"

Marcia stared into the rear view mirror. Max was frowning. She reached back and picked Pooh up from where he was, just out of Max's reach, and handed him to Max. "We'll call Daddy when we get home so you can talk to him all you want later. Okay?"

Max kept frowning, but nodded and began talking to Pooh, only glancing up when he heard Michael say "So?"

"He's been fine. Last week Harvey said he could go to his play group again and mix with other kids. Also, he said that we could probably come to New York for Thanksgiving. They've adjusted the immunosuppression down a little and Harvey says he can mix with kids the way he used to. I think I told you that, didn't I?" She went on when he didn't respond. "I was going to take him to a movie this afternoon. But he didn't look that good today and his forehead was warm. Definitely a little fever and then I used the thermometer and it was more than I thought." Marcia was surprised at how calm she felt. "Maybe it's some more rejection but you know that Harvey said to come in with any fever at all. I don't know. Look, I've put him in the car and I just want to know where I should call you this afternoon if I need you."

"My cell. Anytime. If you want, I'll take the first flight in the morning. Just tell me."

"Yes. Okay. I will. I'll let you know." She reached back and eased the zipper of Max's sweater up a little. "Michael, thank you," she said, grateful to share this information before pushing the "end talk" icon on the dashboard screen. She would call her mother after they saw Harvey.

The early morning traffic had already let up when they got on the 405. Trees and bushes were starting to wither and turn brown after the long, dry summer and the early *Santa Ana* winds. She opened her window for a little fresh air as they passed the Getty Museum exit.

She parked in the hospital garage and pulled the stroller out of the trunk before unbuckling Max. He had gained enough weight after the surgery that he was almost too heavy for her to carry. She watched him climb out of the car seat and scramble into the stroller. *He doesn't look that sick, does he?*

She and Harvey watched the ultrasound screen together as a nurse moved the hand-held detector over Max's upper abdomen. Every now and then Harvey changed the magnification of the image and leaned a little closer to the screen. Max's temperature was greater than 101 when they got to Harvey's office. Much less active than at home, Max just lay there, mostly watching Harvey, only stirring occasionally to look at Marcia. He didn't say anything.

After the nurse wiped the gel from Max's abdomen and left the room, Harvey pushed some buttons and retrieved some of the screen images. He pointed to one and said, "See? There."

Marcia never understood what it was she was supposed to see in the various ultrasounds of Max. Today, there were parallel arcs of variably gray shadows emanating from a focus at the bottom of the screen and radiating out. Harvey indicated a clear area, larger than a walnut, interrupting the arcs.

"I don't know what I'm looking at, Harvey. What is it?"

Max turned his head to look at the image but didn't even try to sit up.

The nurse came back with the results of the blood count, "Twelve thousand."

Marcia looked at her and then back at Harvey. "That's high, isn't it. What does that mean? How does it match with what you see in the ultrasound?"

"Let me look at your eyes, Max." He leaned over Max and gently placed his fingers on Max's eyelids, spreading them a little. "I think they're a little yellow, Max. What do you think?"

Max looked puzzled. "My eyes blue, not yellow. You silly, Dr. Harbey," he said solemnly.

Harvey looked at Marcia. "He's a little jaundiced. His white count's up. The ultrasound looks as if he has a small liver abscess. We need to treat him," he patted Max's hand, "in the hospital. We'll give him i.v. antibiotics right after we get a blood culture specimen. We'll try using one of his peripheral veins but we might need a central line again. And we need some images more sensitive than the ultrasound."

A wave of anxiety spread over Marcia and she could feel herself beginning to perspire, suddenly very warm despite knowing the room temperature had not changed at all. She wanted to scream at first but then felt like talking to her mother and her father, to Pat Hirsch, to Michael. She wanted to talk to someone right away, somehow who could take away this sudden pain, but she knew she would have to wait a while.

After Max had been admitted and was asleep in his hospital bed, Marcia was asked to come to one of the small conference rooms. Milt Spellman, Jack White, a new transplant resident, and Harvey were already seated around the table. Marcia tried to feel at ease as she pulled out a chair and sat.

"Well, he almost certainly has hepatic artery thrombosis." Spellman paused, seeing Marcia's puzzled expression. "A clot in the artery that feeds the liver. Ultrasound is not always optimal to pick up on that. It's hard to be sure in children. Lots of false positives." He explained they needed to study the blood vessels with more sophisticated techniques, that this complication wasn't as common as it used to be but it was still a problem for children or even adults when a split liver was used. "And he may have some degree of portal vein thrombosis." Spellman patted his pockets looking for something not there. "Clotting. Portal vein clotting."

"He was doing so well. Perfect. He was great."

"Well, yes. As Harvey may have told you, it's unusual for these to develop more than thirty days after surgery. Max is a little later than usual, but, unfortunately, it happens."

The surgeon's voice softened, but Marcia's escalated. "And the abscess you showed me on the screen?" She turned to Harvey.

"Yes, that could reflect bile duct injury because of the reduced portal blood flow. A complication of the thrombus," Harvey responded slowly.

"I don't understand any of this," Marcia turned from one to the other, but there was no response.

Val came in with coffee for everyone and sat in a chair against the wall, directly behind Marcia who felt a little more secure seeing her. Only Jack White reached for a cup and started sipping, the steam billowing out of the little opening in the cover.

"Well? What changed? Milt? I'm still confused," Marcia pleaded, her hands shaking a little, her anxiety obvious.

"Well, when he had that first episode of rejection he may have had increased resistance to blood flow, which possibly contributed to the thrombus formation."

Marcia shook her head and closed her eyes for a few seconds. "I'm sorry. I still don't get it. That was weeks ago, more than five weeks ago. Maybe more. Yes, more." She pulled her notepad from her purse and waved it at them. "I have my notes," she said, knowing how useless the gesture was and, more, how powerless she felt. How confused. How desperate.

"Yes. I know," Spellman continued. "This is not so easy and I may not be explaining it clearly."

Marcia twisted around. "Val, I'm sorry to trouble you. Could you get me some water? I'm really dry for some reason. It just happened all of a sudden." As Val stood up, patting Marcia's shoulder, Marcia added, "I need to get myself together. I need to concentrate."

"Of course, I'll be back in a minute," Val said, and patted Marcia's shoulder again.

"I'm sorry, Milt. Please go on."

"With rejection, the portal areas—you know them by now, don't you?" She nodded affirmatively. "The portal areas get filled with inflammatory cells. And maybe some edema, some swelling, and then blood flow is compromised. When you change the usual flow of blood it's more likely to clot, especially where we hooked up Max's native artery, his own artery, to the graft, to your artery."

Val put a bottle of water and a cup in front of Marcia who immediately unscrewed the top and gulped more than half of the water down right out of the bottle, suddenly feeling a little cooler.

"Well, Max's artery, any child's artery, is tiny to begin with. The opening is even smaller than the size of the lead in a mechanical pencil. You know?"

"Yes," Marcia responded in a low, flat voice.

Spellman patted his pockets once more, again to no avail. "We can see collateral vessels start to develop as early as two weeks after the transplant but they may not always be enough."

"Enough?"

"For some reason the liver may need the hepatic artery flow but the collaterals don't quite compensate."

"I still don't understand this." Marcia rubbed her brow and frowned. "So what do we do now?"

"There's a little more to talk about before we discuss next steps."

"Oh, *great*. What more?" Marcia couldn't keep the edge out of her voice.

"The artery feeds the bile duct. When the artery is thrombosed, that is to say completely closed off, you sometimes get bile duct stricture, narrowing, or bile leak. Max is jaundiced and his bilirubin is increased, so we need to look at the bile duct also."

"It could explain why he has that small abscess," Harvey added.

A shiver ran down Marcia's back. "Look, this is all easy for you to understand, but I really don't know what you all are saying." She clasped the water bottle with both hands, just to have something to hold on to, something to still the tremor that she could feel coming. "Do I, do I . . . should I call Michael and have him fly out? Is Maxie going to be okay?"

By now, they all knew about the separation. Only Harvey and Val, at different times, had commented that they were sorry to hear the news and repeatedly offered to listen if she needed to talk. Val suggested therapy and offered to give Marcia the name of a therapist. When Marcia told Val she had been seeing Pat Hirsch for some time, Val commented, "I'm surprised you never told us," and then touched Marcia's knee and added, "That's good. I'm happy to hear that."

Spellman leaned forward. "Calling Michael is up to you, how you feel. If the abscess responds to the antibiotics, as I expect it will, then Max is going to be okay for now and there is no reason for your husband to fly back here. I think you can both wait until tomorrow to make that decision. Max can be okay for quite a while."

She sighed and leaned back in her chair. "Okay, yes, I'll fill him in after we're finished. Thank you." Then she leaned forward and looked directly in Spellman's eyes. She could sense how tight her eyebrows were and how firmly her jaw was locked. "What does that mean? What do you mean that he'll be okay for a while?"

"I'm afraid there's a chance, a possibility, at some time in the future—I can't tell you when—it's possible Max is going to need another liver, Marcia." He moved his chair as if to move closer to her, although the table was between them. "I'm not saying this is definite," he spoke a little slower than before, "but I just want you to know about it. A lot of times, if his own vessels don't compensate enough, we end up needing another liver. But that could be quite a while from now." Now he did lean over the table, getting a little closer to her. "Might not happen at all."

"What?" feeling light-headed, she stared wide-eyed at Spellman.

"In fact, when this occurs in children it can be quite difficult to resolve the thrombus."

"I thought you said children usually do well. Isn't that what you told us?"

Now Marcia felt the room moving and she was warm again, sensing beads of sweat on her forehead. "Yes, of course." Spellman reached across the table to try to take her hand in his. "But remember we discussed the potential problems that can occur with a living donor transplant. We didn't expect this, but we knew it was a possibility."

Marcia flinched and put her hand over her mouth, "Oh no," feeling a lancing, fleeting pain under her breast bone.

*   *   *

Michael picked up after the first ring. "Marsh?" His voice sounded muffled.

"This a bad time?"

"Can it wait twenty minutes? I'm in the middle of a meeting. If you need it, I'll step out." She realized he was cupping the phone in his hand to suppress the sound.

"Yes. Not exactly an emergency, but it is urgent. I need to talk to you soon." She inhaled deeply. "Today."

"Let me call you in less than twenty minutes, no, thirty, less than thirty minutes. Is that okay?"

"Yes. Please."

Marcia had stayed in the conference room after the others left in order to call Michael. Now she still sat there, just staring at the wall. Val looked in and Marcia signaled that she was all right.

She flipped up the cell phone cover and checked to see that her phone was still charged. *Yes, thank heavens.*

Less than thirty minutes later the phone rang.

She told him as much as she could remember of the meeting, checking the few notes she had made after everyone left. "You don't have to rush out here just yet, unless you want to . . . Yes, he's staying in the hospital. He's got some problems but they're taking care of them for now. They think he'll be okay soon . . . 'For now' means for now. Give me a chance. I'll tell you everything you want to know. Just don't raise your voice. Please . . . They think Max has a thrombosis of his hepatic artery. Maybe also the, the, ah," she hesitated, looking at the notes she had scribbled to make sure she was relating what had been discussed correctly, "the, ah, portal vein, yes, the portal vein. At least partially. It may be related to that rejection episode he had before. I don't understand this all that well but he's developed an infection of the liver, an abscess . . . Yes, that's what I said . . . Stop yelling. I don't know how he developed it exactly. It may relate to his hepatic artery, which takes care of the bile duct." She again looked at the notes she had scribbled on her pad. "The artery is very small and this is sometimes a problem in children. He may also have something with the bile duct."

He was yelling even louder now and she could easily hear him when she held the phone a foot in front of her.

"Please, Michael, I know you're upset. You don't have to tell me that. I'm very upset also. Milt said you could call him anytime if you have more questions . . . Do you have his cell phone number? . . . Good . . . Yes. He's getting medicine intravenously. Antibiotics . . . No, not necessarily. He'll probably come home in a day, or a couple of days, if he responds to the antibiotics . . . Harvey thinks he'll respond. It also depends on what they find on the x-rays . . . It's up to you if you want to come out . . . Yes . . . Yes, I'll call you tomorrow morning, but seven your time is four here . . . Yes, ten would be better for me, or even nine . . . Okay. Ten. Thanks. Thank you."

She heard a siren passing by in New York. She wondered where Michael was when he called.

"Michael? Here's the thing." She didn't say anything for almost ten seconds. "He might need a new liver. It's too early to know, but it's a possibility." She hesitated and blinked rapidly to dissolve the tears that were forming. "I can't donate again."

There was a prolonged period of silence as Michael digested this news.

"They say another partial liver transplant is too difficult after a living donor, they would probably have to replace the whole liver this time. So we'll have to wait for a donor to come along . . . A cadaveric donor? . . . No, I really don't know. I forgot to ask. I think they mentioned it. But I don't know how high he is on the list yet. I don't know why. It's the rules they have to follow." She started scribbling some questions for Milt. "I'm writing down some things to ask him. I'll contact Val or Milt as soon as we finish talking . . . Michael, I don't make the rules. Why don't you talk to Milt? . . . It could be months and they said that we could even end up doing okay without a new liver. They're not absolutely sure yet. But, also, it could get worse before that . . . They said they have to look for a bile leak, but I didn't really understand that either. They're doing a lot of testing today . . . He is getting antibiotics. Did I say that already? But he might not respond to antibiotics."

Silence.

"Michael? Are you still there? . . . What? We should have waited? What do you mean? Waited! Waited for what? . . . *What? My* fault?" She moaned but felt like screaming as loud as she could, as loud as anyone had ever screamed. "Oh, Michael. How could you? How could you say that to me?"

After hanging up she cried very hard for a few minutes, trying to suppress her sobbing as much as she could, swallowing her tears. One of the office assistants came in to clean the table, took one look at Marcia and backed out. Marcia's phone rang twice but she didn't even look at it. She blew her nose into a paper towel and cried again, until Val came in. "Michael?"

Marcia nodded but still couldn't talk. Val sat in the chair close to Marcia, reached over, hugged her tightly and whispered, "Sorry." They huddled together while Marcia sobbed, letting the tears pour out. Finally spent, she wriggled out of Val's arms and wiped her eyes. She pushed her chair back and stood up. "Thank you, Val." They hugged again and Marcia said, "I need to see Maxie."

She went to Max's room and sat by his bed as he slept, letting another torrent of tears flow. This time she didn't try to stop them. She didn't even dab at them with tissues. She didn't acknowledge the nurses who came in to ask if she needed their help. She stayed in the chair all night, only sleeping for a couple of hours after midnight, physically and emotionally exhausted by her almost continuous weeping, weeping, weeping.

CHAPTER THIRTY-TWO

"Here's the good news." Harvey pulled in one of the rolling chairs from the nurses' station to sit with Marcia in Max's room. "He hasn't had a big bleed, although he probably has had some bleeding, possibly from an esophageal varix—"

"What's that?" Marcia interrupted.

"The portal vein blood can't get through the fibrotic liver the way it does in the normal liver so the blood backs up into the spleen, which can enlarge, and into veins, the esophageal veins, which can bleed. I'm pretty sure we discussed this at one time, but," he patted her arm, "we've discussed a lot of things, haven't we?"

She knew her face had turned ashen.

"Max's problem now is the portal vein itself, not the liver, not cirrhosis. The vein is at least partly blocked by a clot, the thrombus. Remember, those esophagus veins drain into the portal vein."

"And Max doesn't have the other complications?"

"Actually, yes and no. He probably has had some small bleeding, we saw evidence of blood in his stool, but, as I said, no big bleed. We didn't find any dilated veins." He paused and smiled as widely as he could, making sure she was looking at his face. "Which is good."

"And the bad news."

"The bad news is, even though the thrombus is letting some blood through now, it probably won't go away all together and the vein may close up completely. And, as Milt and the others told you, the limited blood flow can also affect the bile ducts, along with the artery, and the ducts can get inflamed. Probably giving you too much detail, as usual." Marcia smiled wanly. "In any event," he continued, "we could have another abscess. Abscesses can be really hard to control. Antibiotics don't always clean them up. And if the portal vein obstruction stays or gets worse, we're effectively back where we were before the transplant."

After he got home two days later, Max ate with considerably more gusto. He hadn't asked for a chocolate chip cookie since before the transplant but when he saw a television commercial he said he'd like some. Marcia baked three dozen, surprising him after his nap, and he devoured the better part of two cookies with a full glass of milk, even picking up the crumbs that had fallen on the table. Marcia felt happier than she had for the past few days.

Marcia took Max in to see Harvey Hirakawa every other day for the first week he was home. Max was still on antibiotics and the ultrasound studies showed the abscess getting smaller and smaller each time they looked. She was at the piano during most of the many hours when Max slept during the day. In addition to the 57, she was working on the 21, as well as the 13, the *Pathétique,* but neither of them with the intensity of the 57. She also studied some Brahms pieces, some Liszt pieces, and others. In the evening, after dinner and after she and Max played some games or read together, when he was tucked in for the night, she played again, often with Victoria sitting on the sofa leafing through a newspaper or sewing.

She asked Victoria to stay as long as possible so she could devote all her time to either Max or her music, letting Victoria take care of most of the cooking, the vacuuming, the laundry and other chores. Marcia's parents were giving her money for the mortgage and Michael had no objection when she told him about the additional cost for the nurse. He told her, more than once, that he could take care of all the expenses, but she was happier with, and grateful for, her parent's help. Victoria arranged for a cousin to stay when she took time off. The cousin was capable and efficient, but Marcia always felt most comfortable, more secure, safer, when Victoria was there.

If she wasn't playing music herself, she continuously listened to music. She played Judy Garland's *Palace* album for a couple of days, over and over. Then she switched to Karen Akers, an album of Harold Arlen songs and one of Puccini arias. Also Glenn Gould's *Goldberg Variations* and Hillary Hahn's Bach partitas. *South Pacific*. The *Firebird*. The music from *Henry V*. Often there were different CDs playing in different rooms. Victoria brought in some recordings of Phillipino music that Marcia genuinely enjoyed, but not as much as listening to her favorites. There was hardly a moment when there wasn't music filling the air and filling her mind.

Listening to Judy Garland singing, "You Made Me Love You," she was reminded of Michael and felt sad when she realized how infrequently she thought of him and how little she missed him

Every now and then she would sit at the piano and play parts of the opus 57 for Barbara, either over the phone or when Barbara visited for a few days every other week. Marcia now looked forward to those visits, especially to hear what her mother had to say about her playing. It was consistently useful, always insightful and always constructive. Marcia also found that when she played the piece after discussing it with Barbara it would often sound better, richer, fuller, closer to what she hoped for, closer to the Beethoven spirit she struggled for so long to discover. She knew these subtle differences in the way she played from one time to the next could only be appreciated by a very few, but she could hear them. And her mother could.

Once, during the second movement, Barbara whispered "yes," stretching the word out, prolonging that last "s" until it evaporated, and Marcia felt as if she had just beaten Navratilova at Wimbledon or hit a bases loaded home run at Yankee Stadium. As if she had just enjoyed a schnitzel and a beer with Ludwig himself.

Michael apologized to her many times, almost every time they spoke. He said he didn't mean to blame her but she knew he would never stop thinking they should have waited for a whole liver donor. She was sure he would never be completely able to stop thinking it was her fault. As painful as it was, as disappointed and angry as she felt, she had to admit his blaming her was actually serving her well, guaranteeing she could never go back to him, even in a moment of weakness. And she often asked herself if they should have waited, but reminded herself of Milton Spellman's imperative to never look back.

Unfortunately, late at night when she had trouble sleeping she couldn't always contain her self-doubt and couldn't always hear Spellman's words in her head.

When she saw Pat Hirsh and, more than once, questioned the decision she'd made, Pat would ask, "If you had to do it again, would you make the same decision or a different decision?" before reminding her she couldn't control what had happened afterward, couldn't go backwards. Marcia would think about it for a moment or two, sigh, and then reply that she would indeed make the same decision. To some degree her own occasional misgivings made her more tolerant of Michael's anger about the transplant, allowing her to be less depressed when she heard hints of his still barely contained wrath.

When Michael called to tell her he had a meeting in the Los Angeles office and would like to see Max and also see her, she was surprised at how much that pleased her. Max hadn't seen his father in almost five weeks and she knew that he would love being with Michael. If she couldn't really go back to before Max was sick, to before the transplant, to before their separation, she could at least enjoy the three of them being together again while Michael was here. The ice-cream cones on the Santa Monica pier came to mind and she was even more cheerful about the visit.

"Will you stay in town for the weekend? Max needs time with his daddy. Come for dinner Friday night, if you can."

Michael showed up before five on Friday evening. They hugged awkwardly, touching cheeks. He handed her a large bunch of Gerber daisies and a box of dark chocolate truffles from La Maison du Chocolat, her favorites. He also brought a set of model trains and a six-foot tall stuffed giraffe for Max.

And his suitcase. She looked down at it and at his rental car in the driveway but didn't say anything. *Michael doesn't like to leave things in the car, he probably doesn't mean anything by this.*

"I thought I'd either stay here in the extra room or I could run over to the Marriot, if that's easier for you. I have a reservation."

Before Marcia could respond Max yelled from the top of the stairs, "Daddy, Daddy, Daddy," and started coming down as Smedley fled in the opposite direction. Michael handed the flowers and the chocolate to Marcia, dropped everything else onto the welcome mat where he stood and rushed in to sweep Max into his arms as Max reached the fourth step from the bottom.

"I really, really missed you, Maxie."

"Me too, Daddy."

Max's arms were around his father's neck, his legs clamped around his waist. They clung together until Michael sat down on the stairs, Max on his lap, and said, "Let me look at you," as he tenderly brushed the hair from his son's forehead.

Marcia discussed the separation many times with Max, stressing his mommy and his daddy both loved Max very much and their need to be apart had nothing to do with him. "We just have to learn to accept this is the way it is and make the best of it. We can't go back in time," she said, knowing she was using the same phrase over and over again. She promised Max he would see his daddy as much as possible, especially on holidays. One day he might even spend the whole summer with Grammy Barbara and Grampy Alan and Grammy Margit. Then he would be able to see his daddy almost every day. And Daddy would visit every time he had work to do in Los Angeles— "which is a lot of times, sweetie."

As Michael and Max walked hand in hand to the door to bring in the trains and the giraffe, Max looked up and said, "I really miss you, daddy." Michael looked at Marcia, the momentary pain they both felt almost palpable.

When Marcia came downstairs from putting Max to bed, Michael was in the living room sipping a glass of wine.

"Go up and tuck him in, Michael. He's waiting for you. You can give him his antibiotic. One teaspoon. The spoon is next to the bottle on the bathroom counter." She thought about what she said and then added. "My bathroom."

When Michael returned more than fifteen minutes later Marcia had her own glass of wine and was sitting in a chair opposite the sofa, leafing through *The New Yorker*.

"I read *Make Way for Ducklings* to him."

"We haven't read that one in a long time. I'm sure he loved it."

"What do you say we go to Disneyland tomorrow? I'm all finished with whatever I needed to do."

Marcia looked at him quizzically, a half smile on her face. "You have the time? You want to go to Disneyland? You know it takes an hour to get there and an hour back. And it's pretty busy on weekends."

"Look, I have a two o'clock flight Sunday afternoon. Other than that, I have no obligations. Todd invited us for dinner at his house tomorrow, Edie would really love to see you, but I told him you probably wouldn't want to leave Max with a sitter." He looked around. "Is what's her name still with you?"

"Victoria. Yes, but this is her weekend off. She's probably going to leave at the end of the month. I can manage most of the time, but it's still nice having her around. She'll be back Sunday evening. And you're correct, I don't want to go. But I'll call Edie and thank her."

"Okay, I needed to mention it. I'm sure she'll appreciate the call."

"But Disneyland sounds marvelous," Marcia said. "Let's leave early to try and beat some of the crowd."

"Good idea." Michael stood up and started to carry his glass into the kitchen and then turned to her. "I guess I'll head over to the Marriot." He waited for her to say something, but she barely moved her head up and down. And then he asked, "Do you want me to help with the dishes?"

"No, thank you. I'm fine. I'll take care of it. If you're here a little before nine we can get on the road."

Max fell asleep before Michael maneuvered the car out of the Disneyland parking lot. It was just past two and Marcia was surprised and pleased Max had lasted so long. It had been overcast and not too hot and he hadn't starting yawning until they were almost finished with lunch. Max was wearing a brand-new Mickey Mouse cardigan and had dropped Pooh to the floor when his eyes closed. His Mickey Mouse hat was turned on his head, with one ear tilted onto his forehead just over his left eye. Marcia almost laughed out loud at the resemblance to Charles Laughton's Captain Bligh in his admiralty hat. Max's face was slightly flushed and Marcia kept looking back at him, worried, until the flush faded after about ten minutes. She told herself it was just due to the excitement of the day.

Marcia and Michael didn't say much of anything until they were well on the I-5 heading toward Los Angeles. She reached over and patted his arm. "That was great fun, Michael. Max had a wonderful day. We both did. Thank you."

He grinned. "Yes, I did too." He looked over at her and said, "Maybe it's not too late for me to learn to relax a little," but she just smiled without responding. Michael concentrated on the road for a while, moving into the diamond lane where there was less traffic. "I guess the Teacups were his favorite." Marcia nodded. "Or Pirates. Maybe Pirates."

"Yes. He did like that, didn't he?" she agreed. "I didn't remember how much fun Disneyland can be. I guess the last time we were there was when we first moved to California." She instantly regretted opening a door to discussing the past, but Michael didn't seem to notice, keeping his focus on the traffic in front of them.

"And he wasn't frightened at all, was he?" Marcia went on.

"No. No, I don't think he was."

The density of cars on the road increased the closer they came to Los Angeles, but then it was much less congested when they moved onto the 101. Soon they were turning into the long driveway at home, gliding past the azaleas and into the garage.

Michael carried the still sleeping Max up to his bed and then came down as Marcia was looking at the mail. She turned to him. "Do you want to run off and do whatever you need to do until dinner? I thought we'd have dinner about seven."

He looked at his watch and then at the grandfather clock near the stairs. "Yes, okay. That'll be fine. I'll go over to the hotel and take a look at my e-mail and probably shower before dinner. I'll come back at about five, five-thirty, and play with Max. Will that be all right?"

"Yes, perfect."

He stepped closer and leaned forward and she let him kiss her on her cheek. "See you about five."

"Yes." As he turned and walked to the front door he said "I'll call you before I leave the hotel to see if you need anything at the store."

"I'm sure I don't need anything, but that's fine. Call. Lamb chops okay?"

Michael brought six bottles of red wine back with him and put them into the small wine rack she kept on the floor in the hall closet. He opened a Pomerol and let it stand, airing, on the dining room table which was already set for dinner.

Later, as she cleared the dinner plates from the table, he said, "That was wonderful, Marcia. The chops were cooked to perfection and the asparagus was just how I like it, almost crunchy."

"Very good, Mommy," Max said, nodding enthusiastically.

"Thank you. Unfortunately, all I have for dessert is ice cream and chocolate chip cookies."

"That's great."

"Great, Mommy, great. Great." Max started clapping his hands and Michael joined in, intoning "Compliments to the chef, compliments to the chef," as he picked up his wine glass and said it once more, "Compliments to the chef."

"Chef, chef, chef." Max was almost hopping in his chair with excitement, clapping his hands and grinning with delight. Marcia laughed out loud at the two of them.

By the time Michael bathed Max, read him a story and put him in bed for the night, Marcia had the dinner table and kitchen all cleaned. The dishwasher was humming. The wine bottle was empty and, after briefly considering, she decided to not open another. She walked into the living room and checked to see all the pillows were plumped. The yellow glow from the corner lamp cast the room in muted colors and shadows. She poured herself a small glass of sherry, sipping it down before pouring a tumbler of Glenlivet for Michael. She could hear Michael and Max talking, but couldn't tell what they were saying.

She intended to go to the foot of the stairs to eavesdrop but felt a little wobbly when she got to her feet and, kicking off her shoes, sat back down on the sofa. *I've had enough wine for one night. The Pomerol was wonderful but I probably shouldn't have had that glass of sherry.* She giggled. *I definitely shouldn't have had the sherry. I'm not letting him in my pants tonight. We're past all that. I think he knows it. I hope he knows it.*

She burped, covering her mouth belatedly. *I know what he was up to with those chocolates. And the Pomerol. And the daisies. But it won't work. I'm definitely not letting him stay tonight. Brunch tomorrow and then he's off to the Big Apple.* But she couldn't suppress another giggle.

Michael stopped at the liquor cabinet on his way into the living room and brought the sherry bottle to refill her glass. "I stayed with Max until he was fast asleep. We had a nice talk." She started to put her hand up for "halt" but then changed the gesture, opposing her thumb and index finger, and said, "Half."

As he leaned over to pour, she turned her face toward him and murmured, "No."

He looked at her, quizzically at first, and then he smiled, put the bottle on the coffee table, and embraced her as she started to stand up. They were kissing before she was on her feet. He pushed his tongue into her mouth and she eagerly reciprocated. He backed her up toward the stairs as she started unbuttoning his shirt. By the time they had reached the first step her sweater was on the floor and he was unclasping her bra. When they reached the top step both her skirt and bra were off. He clutched the waist of his unzipped pants so they wouldn't slip below his knees and cause him to stumble. He had to steady her a couple of times so she wouldn't fall, so they wouldn't fall together.

She stepped out of her panties as he closed the bedroom door. She admired his leanness and thought *lithe,* then smiled at the word. She clasped his rising penis, walking backwards until she fell back on the bed and let go of him, her arms and legs wide, ready to accept him, ready to take him, ready to envelop him.

She giggled once. *So much for not letting him in your pants tonight.* And then he was inside of her.

He woke her when it was still dark and forced his arm under her shoulders, pulling her close. They kissed as he stroked her breasts until her nipples were firm and high and she began to moan. He moved his hand to massage the inside of her thighs before pulling her onto him, letting her set the pace and the rhythm of their lovemaking.

After it was over, and they were both wet with perspiration and gasping for air, she lay contentedly in the crook of his arm, her head on his shoulder, not entirely comfortable but not moving, as he smoothed her hair. He started to stroke her nipples again but they were still too tender after their lovemaking. "Don't," she whispered, "it hurts."

Until they both caught their breath, they didn't talk. Then Michael whispered, "We could try being together again, Marcia. Just give it a try."

Marcia put two fingers over his lips and said, "This was wonderful, Michael, but it doesn't change things for us. I told you I would always love you and care about you, but I really don't want to be married right now. I'm going to start teaching again in January. I got the job at Santa Monica Community College. It suits me. I think I can make a good life here. I think I'm going to start playing . . . well, never mind that. It's just, I'm a different me now."

"Marsh . . ."

She leaned over and kissed him on the lips, caressed his cheek. "This has been marvelous, Mikey, a marvelous weekend. Everything. Being with you. Seeing you and Max together. Disneyland. Teacups and pirates," she smiled, their noses almost touching, "and," she kissed him again, "definitely the sex. But I can't go back. I know it won't work. I'm not the same person. I think we had something good and then we lost it. That's all. It's gone."

As she stood up and walked toward the bathroom, pulling her robe over her shoulders, he propped himself up on one arm. "Is there someone else?"

She turned, startled, and then, seeing his worried expression, she started laughing. "Oh, definitely not, no. That's really not it. Since you've left I haven't even thought about sex. Definitely. I haven't looked at another man. Haven't thought about one. Wouldn't want one. There's no one else, but," she came back and sat on the edge of the bed and caressed his cheek again, "I hope there is someone in the future, for both of us. I hope we each meet someone we care for, who really cares for us and . . . and that you and I are happy and stay friends." She put her hand around his. "I do, I really do."

CHAPTER THIRTY-THREE

*B*arbara called almost every day and Margit called almost as often, although she and Marcia had very little to talk about other than Max. Margit did tell her once how sad the separation made her, how she didn't understand it and how she wished they would reconcile. Since that one painful conversation they almost never discussed anything but Max. Barbara and Alan invited Margit for dinner in their New York apartment a few times, but Margit always declined.

One afternoon Barbara asked Marcia if she could hear the *Appassionata* slow movement. Marcia gingerly set the phone on the piano bench, earpiece facing the keys, and started playing. Once, in the first twenty bars, she hit a wrong note, but she ignored it knowing it didn't really matter that much. She could tell that the full and penetrating and wondrous sound she had been striving for was there this time. She knew her playing of the piece was still changing, still improving, but it was almost the way she wanted it.

Barbara confirmed her thoughts, saying, "That's excellent, sweetheart. It's much better than the last time you played it for me and I thought it was wonderful that time. Let me hear it again next week. I really have nothing special to say about it except it was lovely. In fact, I'm not sure I've ever heard it played better. Different, of course, but not better." There was a period of silence, and then "Are you still there?"

"Yes," barely a whisper.

Barbara's next words were at first hesitant but soon in her usual, firm tone. "Don't get too comfortable with it. You still need to work on that last movement, but this was really wonderful. Perfect."

Marcia realized, more than ever before, how much the music filled the spaces in her heart. How much she needed it. Music gave her time away from her anxieties about Max, from the sensations of deep pain often coming without warning or provocation, from the awful worries with her when she woke in the morning and when she went to sleep at night.

Before hanging up, Barbara said, "I love you my darling girl."

CHAPTER THIRTY-FOUR

*M*ax was excited about wearing a Pooh costume for Halloween, but Marcia was thinking more about Thanksgiving and was leafing through *The Joy of Cooking* to get some ideas for the meal she was planning to prepare. The entire family was coming out, all three grandparents and even Frank, who was bringing his Dutch girlfriend. Amy, Brian and Julia were coming, as well as Amy's mother, who was visiting from Hawaii. Marcia invited her cousin Linda and her family, but Linda declined saying this was the year to have Thanksgiving with her in-laws. Victoria would be coming also, with her son from UCLA and her daughter, the medical student in Chicago. Although Michael would be in Los Angeles the first week of November, two days after Halloween, Marcia invited him back for Thanksgiving dinner.

"Yes, that would be perfect. I have to come twice in November to Los Angeles. The second time is for an arbitration just before Thanksgiving. I was going to call you to set up some time to be with Max." He cleared his throat twice, hesitated, and then said, "Would you mind if I brought Amanda? Amanda Martinez? For Thanksgiving? She's also involved in our case and will be in L.A. that week." Another short period of silence. "We're not dating again. Just colleagues."

Marcia didn't say anything at first, and then, in a raspy voice, "I guess," following which she forcefully said, "No, I mean yes. I didn't intend to say 'I guess.' Please, just ignore that. And yes, please bring her. Bring Amanda. I mean it. I would love to have her join us. I am really looking forward to seeing her again." When Marcia hung up the phone, she wondered why she had reacted that way. *I really do want him to find someone, don't I?* And then she thought about the first time she met Amanda, at that retreat so long ago, and how beautiful she was.

Maybe it's time for me to start thinking about dating. No. Not yet. I'm not ready yet.

Then Max broke her reverie, calling out from the den where he was playing with his Lincoln Logs. "Look, Mommy, look. I got a log cabin."

*   *   *

Marcia ordered the turkey from Gelson's to be picked up two days before Thanksgiving. The rest of the menu was all planned. Dressing, yams, turnips, onions, peas and carrots. Cranberries and pumpkin pie and pecan pie. Fresh apple cider and more. The whole dinner was outlined on a sheet of paper on the refrigerator door and reverberated in her head. This would be the first time she cooked a real Thanksgiving dinner, stuffing and all, on her own and she kept telling herself, sometimes aloud, that she had so much for which she was thankful this year.

Max was resuming more and more of his pre-school activities three mornings a week, much to Marcia's delight. She called the grandparents almost every day to relate Max's progress, the joy obvious in her voice. They always had questions about Max's increasing number of activities. Jack White frowned when she mentioned gymnastics and said, "Maybe let's skip that until after Christmas. No special reason." Marcia didn't think the kind of gymnastics four year olds do would be in any way traumatic but she also didn't think it worthwhile arguing with White, who, although he never really cut her off, still managed to communicate that he was too busy for conversation. Overjoyed watching Max playing with other children again, Marcia was relieved they were fascinated rather than repulsed by his scar, which he delighted in showing, jerking up his shirt and saying, "My mommy's libber." There were also the expat get-togethers every couple of weeks and Marcia enrolled Max in a music class. Marcia didn't have time anymore to practice in the mornings except on weekends. She did have Max's afternoon naptime and evenings after Max was in bed. She was slowly but surely expanding her repertoire by playing more pieces she didn't know well. Three or four mornings a week she jogged, pushing Max in his carriage.

Michael arrived in town on a Wednesday. He had meetings to attend, including working dinner meetings Thursday and Friday.

When Michael came to the house on Saturday Max wanted to show him how he looked in his Halloween Pooh costume. He brought out all of his remaining trick-or-treat candy. Michael took Max to the zoo that afternoon. After Max's nap, Michael and Max went to Jerry's Deli on Ventura Boulevard for dinner. Just the two of them.

All three of them went for a late brunch Sunday morning in Santa Monica and then Marcia and Max took Michael to the airport for his flight. After he yanked his suitcase from the trunk Michael opened the door and hugged and kissed Max in his car seat. Then he came around to Marcia's side of the car.

"You know the door's still open, Marsh. There's nothing going on with Amanda and me, and I'm not yet as over you as you are me."

She smiled warmly up at him and said, "Have a safe trip home. We'll talk to you tomorrow." As he walked toward the terminal she lowered the passenger side window and called out, "And we'll see you in a couple of weeks at turkey time."

CHAPTER THIRTY-FIVE

*M*arcia made an appointment to audition with Evelyn Kurtin, a former Juilliard classmate of Barbara's who now taught at the Colburn School in downtown Los Angeles. Kurtin's reputation as a teacher had steadily grown as a number of her former and current students established careers as soloists.

Marcia played Bartok first. Barbara had told her Kurtin particularly liked Bartok, Rachmaninoff, Chopin and Mozart.

"Your mother tells me you don't know how well you play."

"She has ideas about me I don't completely share," Marcia smiled hesitantly.

"About concertizing?"

"Well, yes. I'm not sure I want to—or even could—follow in her footsteps. I think it's too late for me. Don't you think?"

"I don't have to tell you how tough that life is. Barbara tells me you have a youngster. I have no idea what to tell you about a concert career at this stage, except to suggest that it's not impossible for you." She hesitated, then stood up and walked to Marcia's side and looked directly into her eyes. "You have the talent, you know." Kurtin shook her head up and down. "It wouldn't be impossible." And then, sitting down again, "you have the talent."

"Yes, well, it's something I haven't really allowed myself to think about until now"

"Let me ask you something. Why are you here?"

"What?" Now Marcia stuttered. "What do you mean?"

"There are lots of piano teachers in Los Angeles. Why me? I mostly teach people who want to give concerts. People who want to earn a living playing the piano."

Marcia didn't respond, holding her breath.

"You know that, don't you?"

"Of course."

"Didn't you ask Barbara to call me? She didn't force the issue, did she?"

"No," Marcia smiled, and then chuckled. "Not this time. I asked her."

"So?"

"So I really don't know if I want to be out there. I don't know if my life, my little boy, will allow that. I am grateful for what you said but, deep down, I'm not quite convinced that I'm good enough." She took a deep breath and noisily exhaled. "Mostly I don't know if I want it enough."

Kurtin turned to her desk, picked up an open package of sunflower seeds and, moving her hands to be far from the keyboard, poured some into one palm. "Please," she offered them to Marcia, who waved them off. "You know that's the key. You have to want it more than anything. You have to want to be out there. You have to be willing to accept the exposure, the sometimes terror of being alone on a stage. The hard work, the travel, the occasional screw-up in the plans, the loss of luggage—you know this as well as I do." She leaned forward. "If you do want it enough, the rest, even raising a child, will fall into place. You only need to want it."

"Yes. I know. I just figured I ought to get started with studying—studying with you—so I'm ready if and when I decide I do really want to perform. I need to begin studying now, while I'm deciding."

"I'm only going to tell you once more how much talent you have." Now Kurtin was sitting at the edge of her chair, her eyes fixed on Marcia's, her head nodding up and down again. "You do have the talent. You do. Perhaps you're not ready to believe me. So I will just tell you that I think you should begin. You should come work with me."

After Marcia put Max to bed that night she played opus 57 from beginning to end. *I'm getting close.*

That night she dreamt about her mother playing in front of a large audience. When she woke in the morning she remembered it was Rachmaninoff's Third Piano Concerto, but she wasn't sure that it really was her mother. *Was it me?*

CHAPTER THIRTY-SIX

Ten days before Thanksgiving, a week after Michael returned to New York, Marcia found Max lying in his bed with his eyes half-open. His pupils rolled lazily toward her when she came into his room to get him ready for his music group. *Maybe it was just too full a weekend for Max.* She had taken him to visit his cousins at Linda's beach house and he had played outside with them for hours, maybe too many hours. But this was more than weariness. He was sick. She sat at his side, put her hand on his forehead and then kissed him just above his eyebrows. He was hot. She got a glass of ginger ale for him and called Harvey's office.

She started talking over the operator who was telling her the transplant team was not in yet. "Yes, I know that. Could you please contact Dr. Hirakawa and tell him Mrs. Kleinman is bringing Max in right now? . . . Yes, to the office . . . Yes, but I am sure he'll respond. I have his cell number and I'm going to call him next but I want to make sure he gets a message in case his phone is off or he's still in the shower or whatever . . . Yes, of course. I'll give it to you," and she recited her own cell number.

Harvey picked up the cell phone call right away as he usually did. After she described Max he told her to come right in to emergency and to call him as soon as she parked her car. He would be in the ER when she walked in.

With Max in his car seat and heading down the driveway she called Michael, punching the easy-dial number onto the car's monitor screen. "Thank God for Blu-tooth," she whispered aloud.

"What, Mommy?"

She looked in the rearview mirror and Max was smiling. *Is this a false alarm?* But he looked flushed and was blinking more than usual.

"Is this worse than before?" Michael asked. "You sound more concerned than last time."

"I don't know. I can't tell."

"I'm a little busy today, this week really, but if you tell—you just have to tell—I won't hesitate and I will come. I will."

"Michael, he does look sicker to me than last time." She glanced back at Max again. "But I'm not sure. Maybe I'll just call you after I see Harvey."

"Call me."

Max's abdomen was slightly distended and the ultrasound showed two small abscesses. "He's got some fluid buildup from the portal hypertension. The abscesses don't help," Harvey said. Max's temperature was almost 103 and he was panting.

Harvey started an I.V. at Max's ankle—Max did not respond to the needle stick—and they began treatment with IV antibiotics, as well as a diuretic to get rid of some of the belly fluid. Then they brought him to the pediatric I.C.U. By then he was only responding when Marcia poked him or shook him. He didn't answer her when she spoke to him. It was almost eleven, not yet noon on a morning that, to her, was beginning to feel endless.

She called Michael and told him about the abscesses. He said he would book the first morning flight. "I'll take a cab directly to the hospital as soon as I land."

Max's abdomen was even more distended than when they had arrived. Harvey, with the assistance of a pediatrics resident, stuck a needle in the abdomen and withdrew some green-tinged, slightly cloudy fluid. "He might have a bile leak. We'll get the surgeons to look at him right away. We may need them to put in a drain. This looks as if it's infected. We'll send it to the lab, for culture."

Marcia felt herself shivering but wasn't sure it was obvious. The shivering was mostly in her shoulders and her knees were weak. Her own breathing became labored and fast and she leaned on the edge of Max's bed to make sure she didn't fall over. The shivering was making her shake now and she realized it was obvious when the resident stared at her. Harvey looked up and put his hand on her arm. "Marcia, sit down for a minute."

"We've been through this before," she said as a resident pulled a chair over for her and a nurse moved close to Max. "I still don't know what's going on."

As Harvey put his hand on her wrist to feel her pulse she felt herself returning to normal. "I'm okay now. I think I'm okay. It's passing." She took a deep breath, holding it in before noisily exhaling. "Thank you. Thank you both. I'm okay."

Harvey said, "Why don't I get a Xanax for you? It'll steady you," but Marcia stood up, steady again, and firmly said, "No. I'm really okay." She took a few steps, emphasizing the point. "I'm really okay now and I don't want to take anything. Thank you."

Michael arrived a few minutes after ten the next morning. He put his suitcase against one wall, out of the way. Max looked very sick, almost the way he looked immediately after the transplant, except this time he didn't have an endotracheal tube or a nasogastric tube. There was an arterial line, a central venous line and a bladder catheter. A nasal oxygen catheter was also in place. Max didn't react to any of this. Each breath looked as if it was hard work.

Michael almost walked by Marcia when he came into the pediatric I.C.U. She was standing huddled in the corner of the room, wearing his old gray Columbia Law sweatshirt and maroon sweatpants. She wore no makeup, her hair was tangled and her eyes were red.

"Oh, Mikey." She folded herself into his arms, her knees briefly bending a little so he felt the weight of her until she regained her footing, "Oh, Mikey."

"There, there," he stroked the back of her head, trying to straighten her hair a little, taking frequent sideways glances at Max.

They agreed to call the grandparents, all of whom said they would be there tomorrow.

At midmorning on the fourth day the monitor started beeping loudly. Two residents rushed in and asked Marcia and Barbara to step outside. After ten minutes one of the residents came out and said, "He's okay now. His blood pressure dropped but he's better now. He's stable. We'll let you in soon."

Marcia watched the clock closely, her eyes fixed on the second hand as it staggered in perfect rhythm from one black hash mark to another. She knew exactly how long it had been since they had asked her to step into the hall. She did not know how long it was before Max's blood pressure was restored. She wanted to know but didn't ask. Michael, who was downstairs getting coffee, hurried in as the curtains opened. A nurse was straightening the corners of the bed sheet. Marcia explained what had happened.

On the fifth hospital day Max was again fully responsive. He sat up and talked with Michael and played with his toy cars. He listened to Marcia read a story for a few minutes before dozing off and then later let Michael feed him some ice cream. They brought in some of Marcia's chocolate chip cookies but the nurses didn't want Max to have any for fear he might choke on the crumbs.

On the sixth day, his blood pressure was difficult to maintain and they kept adjusting the medications going into the central line. He was still responding to their caresses, their pushing his hair into place, and their kisses, but only slightly. His temperature was elevated again. Harvey said he had an antibiotic-resistant strain of bacteria and they were testing it against other antibiotics. "The abscesses are getting a little smaller, but he's still septic, still has a circulating infection."

That night the beep-beep-beep of a monitor went off again and a nurse injected something from a syringe that had been previously prepared and taped to the back of the bed, once again stabilizing him. After that he was completely unresponsive. It was increasingly difficult—"almost impossible" they said—to maintain his blood pressure and he now required a continuous infusion of "pressors," as Harvey called the drugs. "It's the sepsis," Harvey explained. Max developed countless tiny hemorrhages in his skin, on almost every part of his body, some of them just pinpoints and others, small splotches. There was no urine in the tubing leading to the plastic collection bag.

Marcia now sat at his side non-stop, holding his hand, her face frozen. She hadn't gone home for the last three nights, except once to shower and change clothes. On the way home she thought about taking a soothing bath with lavender salts for the delicious smell and pink bubbles for the frivolity, although she hadn't bathed in a tub since high school. Instead she jumped from the car and ran directly up to the shower. She packed a small bag with extra clothes and, in less than thirty minutes, was heading back to the hospital.

The nurses now allowed the whole family to come in at the same time. There was no longer a two-person limit and they could stay as long as they wished. When Madeline, the charge nurse for the day, told them about this change in restrictions, Michael looked startled at first, hissed "shit," and then started to leave the room so no one would see him when he started crying. Marcia and Margit embraced him, crying with him, Margit repeating words in Yiddish over and over again, *mamela, mamela,* and *kinderlekh,* and *gottenu,* and *meshugas,* and, more than a few times, *klog is mir.* Marcia couldn't understand most of what Margit was saying and didn't ask her father to translate.

On the seventh day, just before Alan was going to take Barbara and Margit down for lunch, Max had a cardiac arrest and couldn't be resuscitated.

CHAPTER THIRTY-SEVEN

The wires and tubes were disconnected and the bedclothes straightened before the nurses opened the curtains. The monitors were now turned off and disconnected, grimly dark and silent. Marcia kept looking at the black, unlit screens, longing for just one blip, one wave, one flickering numeral, but all she saw were tombstones. The formica-covered counter, usually cluttered with supplies, was empty. The plastic bags of intravenous fluids waiting to be hung, the boxes of injectable medication ready to be administered, the sterile gauze packages, the disposable thermometers, the mint-flavored swabs for when Max's mouth was dry, were all gone. The staff outside lowered their voices when they walked past the doorway. The bed sheets were almost completely smooth and wrinkle-free, the top sheet pulled up to Max's neck. One of the nurses had put Pooh next to Max.

Marcia kept staring at Max's body. *He's so little, he looks so very little, so still, so pale.*

Michael stood against the wall, silent. Alan's arms were wrapped around Barbara and Margit, all still crying. Barbara held two tissues up to her cheek to blot the tears and Margit dabbed at hers with a time-yellowed lace hankie.

Harvey Hirakawa arrived first. Val was followed by Milt Spellman and one of the residents. After murmuring words of condolence and support for Marcia and Michael, for all of them, Spellman sat opposite Marcia, with Michael standing behind her chair, and asked for permission to perform an autopsy.

Marcia leaned back against Michael, his hand resting on her shoulder. She didn't say a word but her fury was obvious in her tightly shut jaw, her flaring nostrils, her unfocused red eyes. Her fists clenched. She wanted to scream at Spellman. *You cold, insensitive bastard!* She wanted to scratch out his eyes. Then she blinked a few times, stopping the first tears. *What am I thinking?* She never, even as a child, thought of scratching out anyone's eyes. *Oh, my sweet little boy.*

"We can learn from this, Marcia," Spellman whispered, putting his hand on Marcia's arm.

"He's had enough, Milt," she barely whispered.

"You know he can't be hurt anymore."

"What for?"

"We'll learn from this."

She looked up at Michael and then across the room at her mother, tears still streaming from eyes as red as her own, and at Alan. Grammy Margit had not stopped weeping even for a moment. She endured the camps, the loss of so many loved ones, the slow passing of her beloved husband and this was one pain too many. Harvey leaned on the doorjamb. Then Marcia looked at Max once more. "I don't know! Daddy? Harvey? Michael?" Her words came out in bursts, separated by sobs. "What should we do?"

"I think it's okay, Marsh," Michael kissed the top of her head. Harvey and Alan and Barbara nodded yes, as Margit walked out of the room, her shoulders in spasm with her sobs.

"I want to talk to the pathologist, Milt. Arthur Warner. I want to talk to him first. Can I talk to him?"

Warner came rushing into the I.C.U. in less than fifteen minutes. Half a sandwich, apparently hastily rewrapped, was stuffed into his coat pocket. They all went to a small conference room just across the corridor. Over her shoulder Marcia could see one of the nurse assistants going into Max's room and she started to turn back, but Harvey said, "They won't do anything until you say it's okay, Marcia. Max will still be there when we come back."

Barbara and Margit sat at the table on each side of her while Michael and Alan stood back against the wall. Spellman and his team had left, but Harvey was still there. Warner held the door open for Val, who had gone out for a few minutes, and then he threw his unfinished sandwich in a trashcan in the corner.

Warner looked even more unkempt than when she had last seen him. His white coat was quite rumpled, as if he had slept in it, although it looked clean. *He needs a haircut*, Marcia thought. She focused on his tie, which had a music motif, the clef symbol in gold repeated over and over against a red background. She remembered the Bach violin partitas playing in his office the first time she visited him. *I ought to be discussing music with him, not an autopsy on my little boy.*

Hastily, without considerable thought, Marcia had scribbled a short list of questions for Warner while waiting for him to arrive. As she read them aloud, paraphrasing her notes, he answered them one by one.

"When will you do the autopsy?"

"This afternoon."

"How long will it take?"

"Two or three hours at the most. And then three or four days before we have the slides back, the microscopic slides. But we'll be able to tell a lot even before we have the slides."

"Can you give me things to read about autopsy?"

"Now?"

"No, no. Soon."

"Yes, of course."

"Will you do the autopsy yourself?"

"I promise." He looked directly into her eyes, taking both her hands in his. "I will do the autopsy with a resident assisting, beginning to end, and I will tell you everything we find. Either today or tomorrow or whenever you are ready." He paused and looked around the table at everyone. "And I promise that you will be better off for this. Knowing what the autopsy shows will help your healing, will ameliorate at least a little bit of the pain. The autopsy will help you all." He stopped and looked at them individually, waiting to see if anyone wanted to say anything. "And I promise we will learn things that will help the next child, the next Max, who has this condition, who needs this surgery."

Michael signed the permission form first and then Marcia signed it, her tears splashing onto the paper, making the ink from Warner's pen run.

Marcia insisted on meeting with Arthur Warner the next day, even though he reminded her the results would be just his observations and that he wouldn't have the slides for microscopic study ready until the following week. When she continued to plead, "I really need to know as soon as possible, I can't tell you why, I just do. Please," he agreed to meet at four the next afternoon. Services and burial for Max were scheduled for the next morning after that, although Margit expressed concern that they weren't following Jewish law, that they would not be burying Max before sundown today.

"Margit," Marcia gently held both of her mother-in-law's hands in hers, "I don't mean to offend you, but I honestly don't care. I shouldn't be burying him at all, no one should have to bury their little boy. So it doesn't matter about Jewish law. Or any other law. I just don't care."

Margit put her arms around Marcia, hugged her tightly, and whispered, "Of course, my darling, you're right. It really doesn't matter. You're right." And then they cried together for a few minutes, rocking back and forth.

Michael and Alan went with Marcia to see Arthur Warner, all of them with eyes red from a long night of crying. Harvey had planned on joining them but his assistant called and said he had an emergency and probably would not be there.

Warner gestured for them to sit. A young woman in a white jacket was seated already and she stood as they entered the room. "This is Lotte Strauss. She's the resident who helped me with the autopsy and I wanted her to sit in, if that's okay with you."

The Beethoven third piano concerto was playing in the background and Marcia wondered if it was on for her benefit, but she didn't remember telling him she was a pianist, just that Barbara was. Or maybe she had.

"Of course," Michael said, and they all shook hands before taking their seats.

The tabletop was perfectly clean, not littered with papers and journals as it was when Marcia was last there. Warner started speaking again. "I really don't want to show you the photos yet. We can do that in a few weeks. There's nothing terrible about them, and I promise I won't keep anything from you, but you need a little time before we review them. It's just not what you are accustomed to seeing. I hope you will indulge me on this. You can come back in a few weeks or a month or so, and I can show them to you along with the microscopics and then you will have a more complete picture. We'll try to make it a time that Dr. Hirakawa can join us also."

Marcia started to object but then looked at him, at his downturned eyebrows and, almost parallel to the eyebrows, the down-turned corners of his mouth, the warmth and sympathy and even personal suffering plainly visible in his open, pale blue eyes. His beard was badly in need of a trim, shaggy at the neck, and the hairs in his nose and ears needed trimming as well. Marcia took three slow and deep noisy breaths, her mouth closed, and, suddenly calmer, more at ease, than she had been since Max died, murmured, "Whatever you say."

"Thank you." He leaned forward slightly and placed both hands flat on the table. "The portal vein was obviously thrombosed, we could see that even without a microscope. He had infarcts, that's what we call necrosis, or we can call it cell death. They were in his spleen, his liver and his kidneys."

"Why his kidneys?" Michael asked.

"He had an abnormality of his blood clotting mechanism, caused by the sepsis, the infection. Earlier in the day, yesterday, a little before his heart stopped, his platelet count had dropped and some other tests were consistent with that diagnosis."

"What does that mean?" Marcia asked, noticing that her father was nodding his head in agreement before murmuring, "Makes sense."

Warner looked at Alan before turning back to Marcia. "Sometimes when people, adults and children, have infections or cancer or some genetic defects in their coagulation mechanism, they get tiny clots, thrombi, in their small vessels. The blood flow stops and cells die, what I referred to as infarcts. It often affects the kidneys. We call that whole complicated abnormality D.I.C., disseminated intravascular coagulopathy. Max's adrenal glands showed almost complete hemorrhagic necrosis, complete death of all the cells. Typical Waterhouse-Fridrichsen syndrome, or at least that's what we used to call it years ago."

"Waterhouse-Fridrichsen?" Alan leaned forward. "Haven't heard that term in a long time. From medical school days."

Warner said, "Yes, not a term used very often nowadays." He continued, "It's essentially the same as D.I.C. It used to occur in children mostly in association with meningitis that was almost always fatal before the days of penicillin. We still see it every now and then, not necessarily with meningitis, but often with other forms of infections. When Max's adrenals failed his blood pressure couldn't be maintained."

"Could we have prevented it? Or treated it?" Marcia asked.

"Remember a long time ago, when we first met? I suggested Max would probably need a new liver on the basis of his liver biopsy changes. In a very real sense we lost some control of events as soon as we were on that track, as soon as Max developed a condition that needed a liver transplant. The disease took over. We expected," he deliberately looked directly into Marcia's eyes before going on, "a better outcome than this. I know this is no consolation, and probably hurts you more than I would ever want to do, but most children we transplant do well. We don't see this often." Marcia took a tissue from her purse, her eyes glistening. Warner resumed, "And then once he developed the bile duct problems and the abscesses and all the rest, there just wasn't that much to do. As Spellman and his team probably told you this is one of the untoward events that happens after pediatric transplants, whether donor liver or cadaver liver."

They didn't say anything for a while and just sat there. Warner ignored the ringing phones. His secretary came in and silently handed him a note.

"Do you need to go?" Marcia asked while Warner read the note. "We probably only have a few more questions."

"No," he waved the note at her before wheeling his chair to his desk and adding it to a small stack of papers. "You take all the time you want. I assure you. No rush." Warner wheeled himself back and leaned toward her. "I mean it."

Alan spoke up. "The liver and bile ducts?"

"Yes, well. Where should we start? There were three obvious liver abscesses. I would expect we will find microscopic ones as well. We took a culture but I doubt if we'll be able to grow any bacteria because of all the antibiotics he was on, but we'll see. I suspect that we'll find lots of microscopic inflammation throughout because the liver was softer than usual." The resident leaned over and pointed to something in Warner's notes. "And there was peritonitis which I think you already knew." He paused and looked at Marcia, then at Michael and Alan, and then back at Marcia. "You doing okay?" The resident was taking a few notes every now and then and, with her pen in midair, looked up at Marcia.

Marcia's voice was scratchy as she whispered, "No, I'm not okay." But after a pause, she shrugged and said, "I mean, yes, I'm okay. Let's go on."

Warner picked up the phone and pushed one of the buttons. "Gloria, can you get us all some water?" He looked up and asked, "Anyone prefer coffee or tea?" There was no response and he continued, "We didn't see a bile leak. It might just be so tiny we can't see it or it might have sealed over with the inflammation. There certainly was plenty of exudate, um, what you would call pus, that is what we call exudate. You all know that means infection, right? We'll want to see the micros on that also."

Warner's assistant came in with a bottle of water for each of them. Alan unscrewed the top of one bottle and passed it to Marcia. "Thanks, Daddy," she whispered, and then took a long, slow drink. "Please," she looked at Warner, "please, go on."

"The only other important thing to discuss is the lungs. They were heavy with fluid, very congested, what the clinicians call 'acute respiratory distress syndrome.' This is something we see in very sick patients with sepsis. And there was a small abscess in the right lung and some pneumonia surrounding that."

Now, after five, the sounds from the corridor had appreciably diminished. Marcia, facing the door, noticed small groups of younger physicians heading in the direction of the exit. She abruptly stood up, suddenly wanting to get out of the office, out of the hospital, as soon as possible. "You've been very kind. I really appreciate your time and your skills. Thank you. Again, you've been so kind."

Michael, and then Alan, shook hands with Warner. "Will we get a copy of the final report?"

He tilted his head toward the resident. "Lotte will make sure we finish the case as soon as possible. You can come back and we can review it together and then you can take a copy with you. Call Gloria to make sure it's been typed up and she'll make an appointment for us all to get together. I'll try to round up Harvey. I doubt if there will be any big surprises, but it will still be good, and useful—it will be decidedly useful—for you to discuss this again. Also, at that time, we will have answered the questions that need a microscope to resolve and we'll know if we were able to grow any organisms."

Marcia felt exhausted, as if she had been pummeled. For the first time in her life she felt much older than she had been just a few days ago. The weariness permeated her flesh, her bones, her very being. She felt like sleeping. For a long time.

CHAPTER THIRTY-EIGHT

They're probably already over Iowa. She looked at the dashboard clock. *No, more like western Pennsylvania by now. I don't know. Somewhere. It's more than four hours, they're probably getting close to home.* She turned off the ignition. The car lights stayed on until she was inside her home.

Frank had flown in from London. Friends, including the Fleisses who had introduced Marcia and Michael, flew in from New York. Margit had wanted them to sit *shiva*, the ritual of keeping their home open seven days for visitors to share in the mourning, but they only sat for four days, beginning the day after their meeting with Warner. Margit didn't insist on the wooden benches but did, quietly and on her own, cover all the mirrors, according to tradition, to discourage vanity at a time reserved for introspection. Amy came all four nights, as did Linda and her husband, Brett, but their children only came the first night. Two other cousins flew in from the East Coast. Todd Anderson and Edie and others from the Los Angeles office came by. Harvey came, as did Spellman, Val, even White. Dan Fogel came as did his brother, Bobby, with both their wives. The mothers of the baby expat group came. Victoria, who had cared for Marcia and Max after the transplant, came. Pat Hirsch came and told Marcia she was available any time she needed, including on the weekend.

Marcia cried so much when Max died but, other than at the cemetery and then again when Lina Padilla—the liver doctor they had seen when Max was first sick—came to the house, she was mostly numb.

The night before she left to go back to New York, Barbara came into Marcia's bedroom and hugged and kissed her. She didn't say anything but just stood holding Marcia tightly for a little while before leaving the room. After, Marcia felt her eyes beginning to tear but she wiped them before any fell.

Michael and his mother flew back to New York together, two days after they stopped sitting *shiva*. Three days later, after Marcia took Barbara, Alan and Frank to the airport, she went to the cemetery to sit by Max's gravesite until the sun went down and the late November dampness and chill became too much for her. Afterward, she drove to Santa Monica and parked on Ocean Drive, where she watched the rising moonlight bathe the flat and waveless Pacific until it starting drizzling and she needed the windshield wipers in order to see.

Her street in Encino was silent except for the receding hum of a distant plane as she went up the rain-glistened driveway. When she fit the key in the front door the click of the deadbolt turning seemed very loud, shattering the silence. The living room and dining room, on either side of her, were in almost complete darkness except for the softly diffused moonlight seeping into the front windows, tinting the back walls a pale blue. Beyond the stairs, the flickering blue-green glow of the fluorescent light above the kitchen sink pulsed into the hallway. *I keep forgetting to get a new bulb.* She stepped to the wall behind the door and turned off the alarm system, immediately pushing the "2" and "set" buttons to reset the alarm for the night. *Or maybe it's not the bulb, perhaps it needs a new starter. I need to call Ramon. There are so many little things to do in this house. I better not let things get away from me.*

She put her purse on the hall table and pushed on the light switch, squinting as she walked into the kitchen to put the kettle on but then decided she didn't really want tea. The lit hall was much too bright for the way she felt so she switched that light off and just stood there, letting her eyes re-adjust to the darkness.

Marcia shrugged her shoulders a little to let her coat slide off and fall to the floor. She hesitated, wanting to pick it up and hang it in the hall closet, uncomfortable with just leaving it on the floor, but she didn't bend down. Instead, seeing well enough with only the moonlight to show her the way, she walked over to the Steinway. She let her hand come close to the smooth, solid side of the piano as she went by, not quite touching it but feeling its attraction, its pull. She eased out the bench, trying to not make a sound, almost succeeding, and then she sat down.

Her hands slowly passed over the keys, again not touching, just silently wandering back and forth.

Then, with that gentle first C, *allegro assai*, she was playing opus 57. As those first painful notes alternated with gentle and perfect trills, the sounds from the piano filled the room and then the house and then her head. Suffering, fountains of outrage, of pain, were all captured in the lines, caught in each bar by the notes, by the phrases of the F-minor sonata that she had studied for so long. She pushed and brushed and prodded and grazed and caressed the keys. She imagined the blur of her fingers as she glanced toward the hazy moon-glow outside that penetrated the rain. Tiny glints of light were on the lawn. *Blades of grass?* She thought about the performances she knew so well, the Berman and the Rubenstein, the Richter, and, of course, her mother's. But she had no doubt that the music she was making was hers alone, the sounds were hers, the notes were hers. They came from her head through her heart and into her fingers.

As she started the *allegro ma non troppo* at the end of the second movement, she wondered if she would ever play this sonata as well as she was playing it now. This deeply, this flawlessly. She also knew she would return to it many times in the months and years to come, that she would play it often and for the rest of her life and play it as well as it could be played. Others infused the piece with boldness and beauty and heart and, tonight, at this moment, she did also. It wasn't only the notes she was playing, it was the heart of it. She had taken a long and terrible voyage to get to this point and, at long last, she was playing the Beethoven of it.

She sensed each of her fingers, one-by-one, heard each of the notes, one-by-one, and then the surge, the sweep, the spill, the onrushing flow.

She had been thinking more and more about playing for others. No longer sure she could keep herself from playing concerts, realizing this was what she was supposed to do. What she needed to do. She wondered when Barbara would once again tell her she was ready. When Evelyn Kurtin would tell her she was ready. *I still have a lot to learn but perhaps I'm close.*

And then, near the end of the piece, the *sempre più allegro* and the *presto*, she felt herself flush with the prodigious power of Beethoven's passion, his courage and spirit and strength filling her, thrilling her, and his triumph, definitely his triumph—she always thought of him as triumphant—lifting her, protecting her.

And when she sounded the last note and slowly let the fading sound carry her unyielding arms and tingling fingers upward, her heart almost erupted with joy and sorrow. She let the tears fall noiselessly one after the other onto the keys and, her lips barely moving, her voice less than a whisper, she sighed, "Oh, my sweet baby . . ."

CPSIA information can be obtained at www.ICGtesting.com
Printed in the USA
BVOW02s0059300315

393710BV00002B/173/P